Marked to Die

By Sarah Hawkswood

Servant of Death
Ordeal by Fire
Marked to Die

Marked to Die

A Bradecote
and Catchpoll Mystery

SARAH HAWKSWOOD

Allison & Busby Limited
12 Fitzroy Mews
London W1T 6DW
allisonandbusby.com

First published in Great Britain by Allison & Busby in 2017.

A CIP catalogue record for this book is available from
the British Library.

First Edition

ISBN 978-0-7490-2240-2

Typeset in 11.5/16.5 pt Adobe Garamond Pro by
Allison & Busby Ltd.

The paper used for this Allison & Busby publication
has been produced from trees that have been legally sourced
from well-managed and credibly certified forests.

Printed and bound by
CPI Group (UK) Ltd, Croydon, CR0 4YY

For H. J. B.

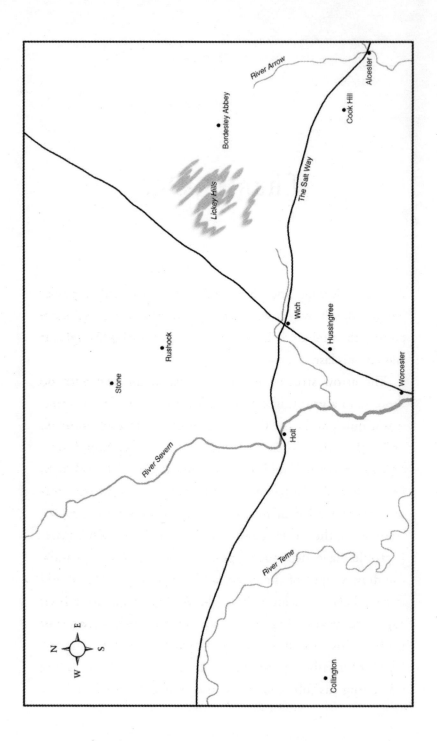

Chapter One

The man leading the short train of heavily laden ponies wondered, idly, why it was that his bunions always ached more around the time of St Luke's. It was an interesting thought. It was also his last.

The arrow struck true, and the packman died with no more than a grunting exhalation of breath. As deaths went, it was quick and easy, though unnecessary. In such troubled and violent times there were many such unnecessary deaths. Small comfort it would be to the widow, but it sat well with the Archer. Whilst technically a moving target, the pace was so slow that a lad of nine or ten, in the wavering stage of training at the butts, could have hit the man. Of course, it would have depended upon him being able to handle the draw weight of the bow, and he would not. Nor would it have been so clean a shot. The Archer would have been aggrieved at anything less. It was not so much a matter of pride as his own moral code, which he had learnt at the knee of his father, a hunter. The hunter stressed that killing was doing his job, and it was not wrong, but it had to be done right. An idle shot that wounded a beast was cruel, and also dangerous. The wounded animal was far more of a threat to the hunter. The Archer, plying his skill in the Holy Land for his lord, and after that man's death, for any with the money to pay for his services, held that if it was true of dumb beasts then all the more so for humankind. He had no compunction about killing, no thought for the victim, nor qualms about gender or age, excepting infants, and, for a reason unknown to any but himself, the blind. But he made sure it was quick and accurate.

The second arrow took the man at the end of the train even as he ran forward, striking where neck met torso. He fell with barely more than a gurgle. Then the three heftily built accomplices came lumbering out of the bushes to lead the ponies away and conceal the bodies in the undergrowth. The ponies were jibbing and sidling, and one bucked and lashed out at the first thief, who swore as hoof contacted thigh. The Archer was not interested; he was not a thief. He would even have refuted the idea, had anyone thought to put it to him, that he stole lives. Man's time was finite, and not guided by how he lived. Men died when their time was up. He was no more than an instrument of Fate.

He was turning away, about to unstring his bow, when he heard the hoof beats and the angry cry. A man, a man wielding a very serviceable sword in the manner of one trained in its use since youth, was bearing down upon the two men dragging away the corpse of the train leader. His blade sliced with an audible sound through the air, and one man crumpled with a curtailed scream. Without thinking, the Archer nocked an arrow and sent it to its mark. The mounted avenger toppled from his horse with a grunt, and the Archer turned away, unstrung his bow and disappeared among the foliage. He did not need to check whether the man was dead.

The lady in the solar was not initially concerned at the sound of a visitor, until a servant announced the Prior of Bordesley. Her lord was not due home before the morrow, for he had business in Wich and had then been due to visit the abbey of the White Monks, so she felt no stirring of alarm until one of that House was ushered before her. She rose, setting aside needle and linen with a polite, if watchful, smile of greeting that froze as she saw the man's face. Only a bearer of bad news would wear a look like that. It was then an invisible hand grasped her viscera, clutching where the first inklings of life lay quiet.

'Your visit is unexpected, Brother Prior.' Her voice was low, unnaturally calm. 'May I offer you hospitality?'

The Cistercian shook his head, and Christina FitzPayne noted the hands clenched together beneath the scapular of his habit.

'I have news, my lady, unwelcome news, I am afraid. My lord FitzPayne did not arrive at Bordesley as he had sent word to Father Abbot he would, and . . . there was an incident upon the Salt Road from Wich to Feckenham the day before yesterday.'

'An incident?'

Part of her wondered why this strange word dance was being performed. She already knew, with the inevitability of falling into an abyss, the end of it.

'My daughter, there is no easy path for this. He was found dead about a mile from Wich, and two other men also, each with a fatal wound. The men were taking a train of salt towards Alcester. It is thought your lord came across the theft of the salt in progress and . . .'

'My lord was cudgelled by some peasant thief? It is unbelievable.'

The denial was almost angry, as if she were trying to convince herself of it, and failing.

'No, all three had fallen to arrows. The bodies were discovered yesterday and taken to Wich, where one of our brothers had been sent upon business of our House. He recognised the body of course, such a benefactor as the lord Corbin FitzPayne has been, and with the lord's brother one of our fraternity. He requested that the body return with him to Bordesley, thinking he would be buried in our church, but, forgive him, he forgot you might wish him interred here.'

Christina's head was spinning with so many jumbled thoughts. How would she contact Robert, Corbin's other brother? Was he even still alive? All she knew was in whose train he rode towards the Holy Land to take service with the Templars. What must she do? She already carried Corbin's child, perhaps his heir. Was it right to call the brother home? How would she see her lord received justice? Her own feelings did not exist beyond this freezing numbness within her.

'My lady? Should you sit? You are most pale. It must be a shock indeed, but . . .'

'I am sorry. No, no I need not sit.' She tried to be logical. 'Yes, he would be glad to lie within the confines of Bordesley and arrangements shall be made to provide for Masses for his soul, of course. Might I return with you to be present for the funeral? I would see him again, once, if that is possible.'

She paused. 'Your journey has taken some hours; you should take a little food before we depart. Please, whilst I make preparations.'

She went to the door, calling for a servant, issuing instructions, working at practical things, avoiding the bottomless pit of darkness that threatened her. And then a thought occurred to her. She turned back to the brother.

'What of my lord's horse?'

'Horse, and sword also, were gone.'

The monk did not think it fair to mention that the body had been found half stripped. He saw the frown upon the young woman's face, the dark brows almost meeting.

'The horse is distinctive, a dark grey, dark as dulled mail, but with a white star and two white stockings. My lord is . . . was . . . very proud of him. Where the horse is found, and the sword too, will lie the trail to the man whose life is now forfeit.'

She spoke softly, more to herself than to the monk, but the tone was icy cold and hard as iron, and the prior crossed himself.

A little over an hour later, garbed for travel, she led the way down the steps from the upper chamber, and it was then, as the cold October air hit her, that her body let her down and she swayed, tried to steady herself and tumbled the last half-dozen steps. When she awoke, it was in pain and to the knowledge that there would be no posthumous heir to Corbin FitzPayne.

The Archer waited. He preferred to be in position early, and his honed senses told him of the arrival well before the man was in vision.

11

'Stand still, and throw the money into the bushes before you.'

The man did so, with great care.

'Now turn away.'

'There is further work for you.' The man spoke as he obeyed. 'Half of the sum is in the scrip, half to be delivered afterwards.'

'Fair enough. When and where?'

'Two days hence, on the road through the Lickey Hills, just where the King's land begins. There will be carts this time, two in number. Same plan as last time. Should be there a little after noontide for they are heading for Bordesley.'

'And I do not have a particular man as my mark? You want no survivors,' the Archer was matter of fact, 'just as before?'

'No survivors.'

'I will be there, and the payment two days later, by the dead oak on the track to Inkberrow, just off the Salt Road.'

'Yes, agreed.'

'And you will be there?' The Archer wanted that confirmed.

'Oh yes, be assured I will.'

'Then good day to you.'

The man would have echoed the farewell, but was suddenly aware that he was alone.

'I am sorry, my lord. I am merely delivering the message.'

The messenger shuffled his feet, and wished himself elsewhere. William de Beauchamp, Sheriff of Worcestershire, growled like a bear, and looked apoplectic.

'Upon the King's highway, and against the Brothers of Bordesley, you say?'

'And before that, my lord,' the messenger delivered the additional bad news in a rush to get it over with, 'there was the attack upon the pack train to the monks at Alcester, in which the lord Corbin FitzPayne of Cookhill was also struck down.'

'What?' If it were possible for the lord sheriff to turn an even darker hue, he did so now. 'You should have told me this first.'

'I . . . er . . .' The messenger quailed.

Watching on the sidelines, Serjeant Catchpoll grimaced. He did not waste any sympathy. William de Beauchamp was not a man to appreciate dithering, and more fool the man who could not see it.

The sheriff glanced to the right and caught Catchpoll's expression. The serjeant nodded. He knew where he would be heading.

'You say "and before that", worm.' De Beauchamp fixed the messenger with a steely eye. 'When was Corbin FitzPayne killed?'

'It would be,' the messenger shifted uncomfortably from one foot to the other, 'six days ago, my lord, though there was no news of the second attack until late yesterday afternoon.'

'You could come on foot from Wich to Worcester in under three hours, even if the place was suddenly lacking in horses!' bellowed de Beauchamp. 'Why was I not informed of FitzPayne's death immediately?'

'Earl Waleran's reeve did send a message to the earl's man, in his lord's absence abroad. Perhaps the reeve thought he might . . .' The messenger's voice trailed off.

William de Beauchamp ground his teeth, audibly. Robert de Bernay was away from Worcester, but would no doubt find out soon enough and be demanding to know what the sheriff had done about it all.

'And did not FitzPayne's lady think I might be interested?'

'I believe the lady was stricken, when she heard the news, and was unable to even attend the burial at Bordesley.'

'Heaven protect me from die-away women!' The sheriff halted, struck by a question. 'Why Bordesley?'

'His brother is a monk there, my lord, and he is . . . was, a benefactor. Indeed, I was told he was on his way to visit the abbot when he was murdered.'

It had a logic to it. The sheriff moved on.

'Are there indications as to the culprits?'

'None, my lord Sheriff.'

'Well, I shall straightaway . . .' de Beauchamp faltered as a clerk whispered nervously in his ear. The sheriff's frown became a black scowl. There was a perceptible pause, '. . . send for my deputy to investigate this, since I am called away upon the Empress's business. Catchpoll, go to Bradecote directly and take my undersheriff with you to Wich. And you can take that flame top with you.'

Catchpoll narrowly avoided grinning at the sheriff's description of young Walkelin, his protégé. He also wondered at the warmth of reception he might receive from Hugh Bradecote, the undersheriff. Not that it mattered much.

Hugh Bradecote had a measure of peace, though when his son's infant wailing seemed to fill his hall it was not of the auditory variety. At times, the crying was jarring upon the nerves, and yet he savoured it, giving thanks for the lusty cries that demanded attention. The womenfolk all greeted it with approbation so he knew he should not worry, and after the first heart-stopping panics, he learnt to smile at it. That was his son, Gilbert Bradecote. With a twinge he remembered the babe was Ela's son too, all that remained of her. It was odd, he thought, how fast she had faded from his thoughts, not his memory, but his everyday life. Even alone in their bed he did not think of her. He felt a mixture of relief and guilt, and, in the little church, prayed for her soul most devoutly.

The manor had settled remarkably quickly back into a rhythm, perhaps an easier one without a lady who tended to remember everything at the last minute and in a wild rush. Hugh Bradecote had returned from Worcester for the Michaelmas feast, if not happy, then at least not in the grey nothingness that had at first flooded him and left him barely functioning. He threw himself into the busy autumn tasks upon a manor in preparation for the winter to come, and wanted to achieve as much as possible before he had to return to Worcester upon his feudal duty at All Souls. The arrival in his bailey of Sergeant Catchpoll, with Walkelin at his side upon possibly the most moth-eaten horse he had ever beheld, more than a fortnight before he should depart, tossed that hope into the fire of lost aspirations. And yet he felt glad to see the pair of them.

Catchpoll's mount, as if able to mimic its rider's take-it-or-leave-it attitude, ambled in with head low and on a loose rein. Walkelin's horse arrived at a pace as mixed as its coat, which was in the midst of an early-winter growth, and in shaggy patches. Catchpoll nodded to the undersheriff, and dismounted, swinging his leg over the horse's neck with an ease at odds with his years, unless you heard the muttered oath beneath his breath. Hugh Bradecote did, and pretended not to notice the slight giving of the knees as the serjeant reached the ground.

'I take it you are not being social, Serjeant Catchpoll.' Bradecote smiled wryly and nodded an acknowledgement to Walkelin.

'Not as such, my lord. I leaves social calls to mendicant friars and gossipy women. Think of this as more a shrieval request you just can't refuse.'

The smile was met by the death's head grin that Bradecote had come to know well.

'That is how I think of all requests from my overlord.'

'Wise, my lord, very wise.'

Walkelin, understanding now that this must be by way of a near ritual re-establishment of the relationship, silently dismounted and gave his moth-eaten horse a look of loathing. It stared back at him, and he was convinced the feeling was mutual. He made a glancing assessment as he looked round the bailey. Serjeant Catchpoll had been training him to do this over the last weeks, and might well ask him where the pitchfork was leaning, or what he could deduce about the manor from the general environment. He would say, even if he did not know the undersheriff, that this was a manor run by an attentive steward whose lord liked everything orderly and no doubt had every barrel of apples and bushel of grain accounted for in the stores. The pitchfork was beside the small door to the right of the stable.

The heavens, which had been threatening to open for the full five miles of their journey, now gave up any attempt at restraint, and large, heavy drops spattered on the ground and seemed to go straight through the man-at-arms' cloak. Bradecote ushered his visitors up the steps and into his hall. The warm woodsmoke assailed the nostrils from the central hearth, and Catchpoll went to spread cold, and slightly stiff, hands before the heat, even though the smoke tendrils caught in his throat and made him cough.

From the solar came the sounds of an infant making its presence known.

'My son does not ask politely, he demands,' Hugh Bradecote grinned, and could not keep the pride out of his voice. Catchpoll would not begrudge it to him.

'I hope you intend to teach him to demand in good plain English, my lord.' Catchpoll's tone was respectful but with a teasing edge. 'He'll get further in life if he has the English too, like yourself.'

'Oh you can be sure he will, since wet nurse and nursemaid understand no other. Most likely it will be a trial teaching him anything else.'

The yelling reached a new pitch of intensity.

'He certainly sounds as if he is thriving, anyhow, and has learnt not to take no for an answer, in any tongue.' Catchpoll sounded approving.

'The nurse keeps telling me how big he is, and I am trusting her judgement.' Bradecote shook his head in mild wonderment. 'I never really studied infants before.'

'It's suddenly different when the mite's your own, my lord. I speak as one who had five and now,' Catchpoll paused for mental calculation, 'I have eight grandchildren dotted about. At least it was eight last time I looked.'

He omitted to say that the numbers did not always increase. Why rub in what every man knew: the early years of life were precarious. He had been fortunate to only lose one son in infancy and one daughter was gone now in childbed, but Catchpoll knew he was a blessed man, and gave heartfelt thanks for it.

Bradecote focussed his mind upon the matter to hand.

'So, what has the lord Sheriff of Worcestershire sent his law hounds trailing after this time, Catchpoll, just when I was settling back into my own life?' He wished the call had not come at this juncture.

Bradecote indicated a bench and Catchpoll sat upon it, leaning forward with his now warm hands between his knees. Walkelin was not sure the invitation extended to himself, and so tried to stand in an 'interested but not at attention' manner.

'Word came to my lord this morning from Wich. There have been two attacks on salt being taken from the town, in each case the packmen or drivers were killed by a single arrow. In the first case there was another death: Corbin FitzPayne, who owed fealty to de Beauchamp for at least one of his manors.'

'Corbin FitzPayne,' Bradecote frowned. 'Yes, I met him on several occasions, though I would not say I knew him well. He was a big man, not young but not in his dotage, as I recall.'

'Well, he won't reach his dotage now, for certain.'

'Would de Beauchamp not go himself for such a crime?' Bradecote frowned. The murder of a vassal lord was an important matter.

'He would but for a summons from Robert of Gloucester upon the Empress's business. It irks him not to go, I can tell you, and of course he wants justice for his vassal, as well as security for those upon the King's highway. This is one where we have to have someone to dance at the end of a rope, my lord, make no mistake.'

Bradecote did not voice his vague disquiet lest the 'dancer' turned out to be some ne'er-do-well who was guilty of some other crime but not this one. He had learnt that Catchpoll did have a deep-rooted sense of justice, but he also knew he was the ultimate pragmatist, and if a man was needed for the gallows to keep the sheriff from making their lives a misery, well, if the killer was long gone, it was just possible Catchpoll's gaze might alight on a miscreant thus far too slippery for the law to apprehend. The wily old bastard would not see the innocent hang, but might happily send a man 'guilty', by his judgement, of another capital offence. Bradecote's own conscience would not go to that extreme, but then, Catchpoll had been 'serjeanting' from the time when his lordly superior had still been too small to use his grandsire's sword. It warped a man's view of society in the end. He wondered idly if it would come to warp his own.

'He'll want us up to Wich as soon as may be, but that will mean tomorrow now the light has gone. You are welcome in my hall to eat and take your rest, though you might have interruptions if you are light sleepers.'

'I reckon as we can cope with that, my lord, and thank you for your hospitality.' Catchpoll nodded his head in thanks. 'As I reckon it, we will reach Wich before Mass if we set off betimes, and work from there, though the trail will be colder than I'd be wishing for. The reeve of Wich, pox on him, instead of sending to the lord Sheriff, sent to Robert de Bernay, as Earl Waleran's man, and my lord de Bernay is out of the shire. FitzPayne and the other victims are shrouded and buried, and the first attack the better part of a week past. We are digging in cold, hard ground,' the serjeant sighed, 'but we gets what we is given.'

Chapter Two

They set off in the first light of an October morning, with a lethargic sun crawling reluctantly between wispy veils of grey cloud. There was little wind to rustle the remaining leaves, brown and gold, crisp and curled of edge, clinging doggedly to grey-barked twigs. The hoof beats were muffled by the damp leaf carpet beneath them, and the horses' breath appeared as dragon smoke from their nostrils.

It was not far to Wich, especially since they cut across country to meet the north road from Worcester, and they arrived as many of the businesses were opening their shutters in the main thoroughfare. They asked after Earl Waleran's reeve, and an old woman pointed a bony finger in the direction of the reeve's house. Walter Reeve, a man of thinning pate and stocky build inclining to the corpulent, was keen to be of service, and gave details of the finding of the five bodies and their bringing before him.

'Two of the men were simple packmen, employed to take salt from the salt houses belonging to the Black Monks at Alcester, and two were carters taking salt to the House of the Cistercians at Bordesley. There are fatherless children and weeping widows, but the men themselves would not have attracted such a prompt response. The death of my lord FitzPayne is another matter entirely. I take it that is what has brought you so swiftly.'

'You see the death of Corbin FitzPayne as important and yet you did not send immediately to the lord Sheriff.' Bradecote's voice had an edge to it. The reeve looked uncomfortable.

'I sent straightaway to my lord the Earl's man in Worcester, my lord, knowing the Earl Waleran himself is away in his foreign holdings.'

'But this is law business, and the law should be informed,' declared the undersheriff, with an official tone which Catchpoll could not have bettered, 'at once. I would also say the murder of three men, of whatever rank, required swift action. Had we been told straightaway, perhaps the second attack could have been prevented and there would be fewer widows and orphans in Wich.' He did say it was only a possibility.

'My lord, I am sorry, but in the aftermath, what with the bereaved and every salt worker in the place demanding answers to questions I had not even thought of, and the general air of panic, well I sent to Earl Waleran's man, expecting him to set the law upon it.'

'For your information, Robert de Bernay has not been about Worcester for over a week. He does not spend his entire existence loitering in Worcester awaiting messages.'

'I did not think.' The reeve hung his head, showing the pink skull shining through the steel-grey hair. 'There was so much going on trying to placate the townsfolk. But when the second attack was reported, I did send straight to the sheriff.'

'Better late than never, eh,' grumbled Catchpoll, with an ostentatious sniff that showed his opinion.

'I can only say I am sorry, and that there was no intention of keeping the sheriff from—'

'Do you know who found the bodies?' Catchpoll set himself on the scent and was no longer interested in the reeve making long expressions of dutiful regret. 'We need to speak to him, or them.'

'Oh yes, they are local men. William Tanner and his son, Edric.'

Bradecote groaned inwardly. His last visit to a tanner's had left him with the stench in his nose far too long.

'I saw Edric but a few minutes ago. Here,' Walter Reeve grabbed a passing youth, 'find me Edric, son of Willam Tanner, and bring him to me straightaway.'

The lad went immediately upon the command, thus showing the reeve's importance to his visitors. He returned some five minutes later, breathless, and with an anxious-looking young man at his heels. The tannery stench clung as a memory of something revolting, although Edric had been at pains to conceal it, for he was trying, as the reeve had explained, to woo a glover's daughter in the town. Bradecote wondered if the courtship were advanced enough for her to be already no longer aware of its odour.

'You had need of me, Master Walter?'

'Edric, this is the lord Bradecote, the undersheriff, and Serjeant Catchpoll.' The reeve ignored Walkelin in the background. 'They need to know as much as possible about the finding of the bodies on the Feckenham road.'

The young man's pleasant, open face clouded, and he shook his head, crossing himself devoutly.

23

'A foul thing, my lord, foul indeed. I knew Thorold quite well, and him with a second on the way.'

'Could you show us exactly where you found them if we took you out upon the road, and describe to us everything you saw?' Bradecote thought they did not need details of the personalities and circumstances of the dead at this stage.

'Aye, my lord, for I am not like to forget such if I lives to be fifty years.'

'Walkelin, take him up behind you. Master Reeve, we will return when we have looked at the scene and will wish to speak again. Where can we find you by noon?'

Hugh Bradecote was showing that 'The Law' had arrived, and was active.

The tanner's son gave them directions, and they set off, with Walkelin's horse looking even less pleased than normal. The site of the attack turned out to be less than two miles from the town. Edric dismounted and led them to the north side of the road and into bushes. Catchpoll frowned.

'How come you found the bodies if they were concealed, Edric?'

Edric grimaced and said but one word. 'Crows.'

'Ah. And when you found the bodies, other than the crows, what state were they in?'

'They looked like sacks, all lumpen, except of course they were flesh – cold, stiff, greying flesh.' Edric crossed himself again.

'Had the bodies been stripped, then?' Bradecote had a feeling more flesh than mere hands and faces had been visible. 'Stripped bare?'

'Not quite bare, my lord, shoes and cottes and cloaks were gone, and the lord of Cookhill had no boots, nor outer raiment at all, indeed not even a linen undershirt, just his chausses.'

'Was there any sign of violence beyond the arrow wounds?'

'Oh no. No cudgel or stick marks, if that is what you mean.'

'What sort of men were they, in size?' Walkelin had been chewing his lip, ruminatively. 'Could you have moved them easily on your own?'

Edric suddenly panicked, fearing he was being implicated.

'I only moved them to our cart, and father helped with that. You can't say as I killed them, poor souls, you can't.'

Catchpoll gave Walkelin a look that both showed approval of his thought process and disbelief at his technique.

'Now then, nobody was accusing you, young Edric.' His voice was calming. 'We just wants to get some idea as to whether they were put out the way by a man on his own or several.'

Edric breathed an audible sigh of relief.

'I would have said it would have been much easier with two or more, unless he was very big. The lord, and Master Reeve knew who he was, was a big, strong man, for a start. I could not even have dragged him on my own, and the way they was all lying looked more as if they was tossed, I reckon, for Thorold was on his front underneath the others and the arrow shaft had snapped off.'

Bradecote and Catchpoll exchanged glances.

'Did you take up the broken shaft, Edric?'

'No, my lord. What use was it?'

Without being asked, Walkelin was already ferreting about in the undergrowth like a pig rooting for beechmast. A few oaths indicated that the bushes contained a fair number of briars.

'Oh aye, there's brambles that cut about something wicked.'

'Oh dear.' Catchpoll smiled wryly. 'Oh dear.'

This was followed by a cry, not of pain but of victory, and Walkelin emerged from the foliage with the broken end of an arrow, the flights bedraggled but still in place.

'Good lad. Did the other bodies have arrows in them with similar flights, Edric?'

Edric nodded.

'A man who is good with a bow would not hand his arrows around. Makes me think one man did the killing. And if he was good at his craft he might well make his own.' Catchpoll slid a finger and thumb along a barred feather, easing it back into shape. 'Can you tell us where the arrows had struck?'

'In the body.' Edric blinked at them.

'Yes, but where, Edric?' asked Bradecote, patiently.

'I . . . well, I do not remember exactly except for Thorold, because I knew him so well. I suppose I noticed more, and there was no shaft. The arrow stuck out of the base of his throat about an inch before it was broken off. The other two, well the lord was hit in the middle of his body and Edwin Pack over the heart.'

'Lucky shots,' murmured Bradecote, frowning.

'Not for them, my lord.' Edric sounded rather shocked.

'Or "good" ones,' Catchpoll muttered, and did one of his 'thinking faces', at which Edric stared quite openly. 'I would dearly like to know where the other victims were struck.'

'You mean there could be similar wound patterns from the second attack also.' Walkelin nodded, his mind, now set upon a course, ploughing a straight furrow.

The undersheriff was thinking on a different tack, wanting confirmation for this one.

'Your father, would he have seen anything more than you did, Edric?'

'I doubt it, my lord, for sure, since it was I who pulled the bodies out, but perhaps . . .' He faltered under the undersheriff's gaze. 'I do not know.'

'Then I will have Walkelin ride back with you to Wich and he will ask these questions of your father, just to be certain.' He looked to Walkelin. 'You are to go thereafter to the reeve's house, and meet us there or carry on to wherever the reeve may tell you we have gone.'

'As you wish, my lord.' His face betrayed just a twinge of regret in case he missed out upon some excitement. He was like a child sent to bed before the bear had danced. 'Immediately?'

'I think so. We will follow on and see the reeve.'

Catchpoll watched the retreating figures and smiled knowingly at his superior.

'Stomach couldn't take a tannery again, eh, my lord?'

'No, it could not, unless it was vital, and it is unlikely that the father will have seen much more than the son. Consider it part of Walkelin's training, Catchpoll.'

The death's head grin broadened.

'I will, indeed. And what are we going to do here, if anything other than give young Walkelin a head start?'

'At the risk of being snagged on the thorns, I think we also make a survey of the surrounding area. Pity that the weather has been damp. I do not suppose we will find clear marks of anything untoward.'

They tethered their mounts and tried to be thorough in their assessment. They had little or no hope of finding any tangible evidence, although Catchpoll did find where boot heels had scraped a slight furrow at the edge of the track.

'Just confirms what we, and indeed Edric, thought. This would have been FitzPayne's body being dragged to the undergrowth. So it looks like stealing his boots was almost an afterthought.'

'Or they stripped the corpses off the road in case anyone came along.'

'True, my lord, that is a possibility.'

'I suppose we might get confirmation about the other wounds from the reeve.' Bradecote did not sound particularly hopeful. 'He seemed efficient enough, but then Earl Waleran would not tolerate inefficiency. At the same time he did not look the sort to remember details.'

'Children are best for that, my lord. They look at the world differently from adults, and I do not just mean literally. You get a child of eight or nine, old enough to speak true, and they can "see" things we miss. I once investigated a killing where the only information I had on the man who did it was that he was of average height and dark-haired. That was from a woman who saw him briefly. The child at her skirts then piped up and said he was a bear, which nearly earned him a clip round the ear, but he was so adamant. When I got him to open up a bit it turned out he meant the man was very hairy. He had black hair quite thick upon the backs of his hands and tufts sticking out of his ears. Made the hunt a lot easier.'

'Then I suppose we hope a wide-eyed child saw the bodies. Let us go and see Walter the Reeve again.'

They returned to Wich at a gentle pace. The reeve had termed it a town, and it certainly deserved the title, but it was odd, being largely based upon a single product, the salt made from the brine in the earth. The eight salt pits, the salt springs, gave up the salinae, the shares of brine, which were reduced to salt in the many salt houses, damp places where shallow lead vats of brine were heated over stone wood-fired furnaces. The steam evaporating from the bubbling liquid condensed upon cold walls, and wicker baskets of the salty sludge dripped into trays as the salt dried and provided both the final product, the precious salt crystals, and the 'seeding' for the next vat of brine. Here was a centre of salt making that sent the vital commodity far beyond county borders, perhaps seventy miles. There were salt pits to the north in the Earl of Chester's palatinate, which were nearly as important, but no other places were so exclusively centred upon salt production from the earth. Toll was paid upon every load leaving the town, unless it was the property of a person or religious community owning one of the salt shares and houses. The Benedictines of Shrewsbury salted their fish with the product of their Wich salt house, as did monks in Gloucester. Everyone would always need salt, and Wich was comfortable, even a little smug, in the knowledge. It had a busy, industrious air and, on a cold October day, men without even a cotte to cover them laboured, skimming the impure froth, pouring, ladling, carrying, shovelling.

Walter the Reeve was not in his house when they arrived, and they were greeted by his wife, bobbing an embarrassed curtsey and offering bread and ale. Her husband, she explained, had gone out only briefly, and when he entered, still in the process of tying the fastenings of his breeches, and turning red of face, Catchpoll had to bite his lip not to laugh. The reeve's position was important, and Walter a self-important man who would not enjoy being discovered on return from a very basic act.

Hugh Bradecote caught his serjeant's expression from the corner of his eye and understood its cause. He accepted the hospitality with thanks, for, after all, they had not eaten since dawn. He turned then to Walter Reeve.

'We have seen the place of the attack, and Edric has told all he knows. We would like to know what happened when the bodies were bought here. Did they come straight to you?'

'Aye, my lord, and a fair to-do it caused and no mistake. There was one went to tell Thorold's wife he had been brought in dead, and she came half fainting and screaming fit to set her off in childbed, and the family of Edwin Pack came to take him for shrouding. My lord FitzPayne I recognised, of course, as did a brother from Bordesley Abbey. My lord was a patron, his youngest brother being one of the original brethren as came from away over at Garendon to build the place. The brother said he would arrange for the body to be given a respectable burial in the abbey church, and well, it seemed fitting, so he took the corpse.'

'Did you not send to the lady FitzPayne?'

'I . . . er . . . did afterwards. There was so much going on, with townsfolk all a-dither, and trying to prevent them setting out with a party of men with sticks and bows to find whoever did it, as if they would find them waiting . . .'

'You were glad to have one corpse and its attendant responsibilities taken from you.'

Bradecote was not totally unsympathetic, but felt that the reeve had a duty to inform the lord's widow, and it told in his tone.

'My lord, I am sorry for the omission, truly. I did send to the earl's representative in Worcester, as I said before, and when I did go to her, in person, she was unable to see me, being abed and ailing. I was told she lost the child she was carrying, though it is but what I heard from a wench.'

The undersheriff frowned.

'Did you take note of the injuries that killed these men?' Catchpoll wanted answers not explanations. 'And do not tell me they were arrow wounds, for we know that.'

'But they were.'

'Serjeant Catchpoll means what manner of arrow wound, Master Reeve.'

'Thorold must have died quick, for the wound was through his throat. Edwin, now I think there was the entry here,' he pointed to his chest, a little to the left of the breast bone, 'yes, right over the heart, and the lord was struck just below the ribs, here,' he moved his finger to his solar plexus.

'And the men killed on the way to Bordesley?'

'They were brought slung across a pair of ponies and the shafts removed, so I did not see really.'

'Not see a wound in bare skin?'

Bradecote sounded disbelieving.

'Oh they were not stripped, my lord.'

'Were they not? Was their garb tattered and not worth stealing?'

'Well, if I was a beggar yes, a burgess, no.' The reeve pondered. 'One had a shoe missing, that was all.'

'Either our thieves were warm enough or they thought they might be disturbed again.'

'Not sure that fits, my lord.' Catchpoll shook his head. 'If one of their number is so fine an archer, why not bring down any witness as they did with Corbin FitzPayne.'

'They thought they heard hoof beats?' Bradecote turned back to Walter Reeve. 'Were the bodies cold when they got here, and how many men accompanied them here?'

'I could not say as to warmth, my lord, I did not handle them. You could ask the brother of Oswin, who took his body for burial, or Father William who took charge of Ansketel, who had no kin living. And there were three men brought them here, travellers from the north. They were directed here from where they found the bodies, upon the Old Road up on the Lickey Hills.'

'Heading where?' Bradecote pressed further.

Catchpoll almost pounced on the words, like a cat by a mouse hole.

'I did not ask. What reason had I to ask?'

Catchpoll's look said enough.

'Direct us, then, to the priest and this brother, when we have finished eating.'

The reeve, thankful that he would be left in peace, almost chivvied his wife to refill the tankards of ale accompanying the food, and even pressed ale and a crust upon Walkelin when he appeared, shaking his head silently at Catchpoll in answer to a raised eyebrow. The crust was devoured swiftly.

As they left, Catchpoll wondered casually whether Walkelin's mother secretly starved her son. Walkelin grinned.

'So there was nothing to be learnt from William Tanner.'

'No, Serjeant, though I did as I have learnt. I asked him the same sort of questions, and he gave the same sort of answers, but not in such a way as I would think he and his son had planned their replies.'

32

'Good lad.' Catchpoll looked almost paternal, and patted Walkelin on the shoulder. 'We are now off to see the priest who took charge of one of the bodies returned from the Bordesley cart, to see if he recalls the wound, and then on the same task to the other victim's brother.'

'Well, at least a church won't smell foul. I could barely eat afterwards.'

'But you managed, somehow.' Catchpoll hid his grin.

The priest shook his head over the evils of man, and the mark of Cain, but frowned over the arrow wound.

'There was not much blood, I can say that, and what there was was upon his chest. I did not shroud him. Goodwyf Fletcher did that. She cleans the church, and is a godly soul. She knew Ansketel in her youth, I believe.' He saw Catchpoll's raised eyebrow and coloured. 'Not in the Biblical sense, no no. Her first husband and he worked together in the same salt house. Shall I call her, my lord?'

Bradecote nodded, and the priest trotted from his little dwelling to call the widow from her sweeping of the chancel. She returned in his wake, bobbing to the undersheriff and Catchpoll, and bestowing a motherly, if gap-toothed, smile upon Walkelin. The priest told her what the sheriff's officers needed to know, and her face grew solemn. She crossed herself.

'Wickedness, such wickedness. A comely man was Ansketel in his youth, before he took to too much ale, but that was after the flux took his wife, poor man, and her not nineteen. Never married again, he didn't. But what a way to end, I ask you.'

'Well, we are really asking you, Goodwyf Fletcher, about the manner of his end, and from your name you might have a better idea than most about arrows.'

Bradecote flashed her his best smile, and she simpered and blushed without thinking.

'Ah, but my Godric fletched 'em, my lord, not killed with 'em like this man did. The arrow was pulled out, but you could see it had not been a hunting arrow, no barbs. The archer used a bodkin, a man-killer, not for game. I mean both would do, of course, but the archer carried arrows best suited for taking down a man, not a deer or a pigeon. The wound was a clean hole and to the heart, as I reckon it.' She sighed. 'Leastways it was quick, poor soul.'

Bradecote thanked her, and the priest also, and they left to find the brother of Oswin, whose name was Azor. Bradecote thoughtfully conducted the interview outside, where mother and sisters were not therefore forced to hear the grim details over again, but it was a short and simple conversation, which corroborated everything they had heard about the skill and intent of the archer. The sheriff's men came away in no doubt that the same man killed all five who had been slain.

The obvious place to go next was the manor at Cookhill, and to see the lady FitzPayne. They set out along the same road that the ill-fated packmen had taken towards Alcester. It was a good road, an old road, straight as so many of those were that the Romans had made long, long ago. They paused again at the site.

'All the victims were shot from the front. Pity we could not see if there was an angle or we might know roughly where the archer concealed himself.'

'And you have to remember, my lord,' Catchpoll sniffed, almost as if the memory of the archer's scent might linger, 'that there were probably several accomplices to help with the bodies and also lead the ponies away.'

'Why,' mused Walkelin, half to himself, 'does a man who could earn a tidy sum with good archery skills, and who has presumably taken down men before, perhaps in battle, take up murder and robbery upon the King's roads?'

'A fair question, that,' noted Catchpoll approvingly. 'Might have committed some other crime and been outlawed for it, but I know of none close by Worcester who were archers by craft. Mind, he could be a stranger to the shire, taking advantage of not being known.'

Hugh Bradecote stared into the foliage of the bushes, imagining the man who had stood there.

'If Walkelin is right, and he has seen service, well a lordless man might turn to crime to eat, and from taking conies and roebuck might be content enough to kill men again if he fell in with thieves. But there,' he shook off contemplation, 'let us go and speak to FitzPayne's widow.'

Chapter Three

It was mid afternoon when the trio trotted into the bailey of Cookhill Manor, set on a windswept ridge, but in a good strategic position. There was a wooden palisade and outbuildings, and a hall raised above an undercroft and accessed via a flight of stone steps that abutted one end. A tired-looking man, directing the stowing of barrels, turned at their entry and greeted them politely, seeing that one was clearly some lord come to visit. When Hugh Bradecote explained who they were he showed no surprise.

'We would like to speak with the lady FitzPayne, if she is not still abed and—'

'My lady is confined within, my lord, but has risen from her bed. If you will wait briefly, I will tell her of your arrival.'

The steward bowed, and climbed the steps to the hall without haste. Catchpoll watched him and murmured to his superior.

'Old dog guarding his lady. Well, I suppose it is fitting.'

The man emerged within minutes and beckoned them up, escorting them into the hall itself where a woman, of almost ghostly pallor, sat upon the lord's seat, a seat too big for her delicate frame. The white wimple, framing her face, accentuated her bloodless cheeks, and her eyes were underscored with shadow. She nodded dismissal to the steward, who dithered and then obeyed, and half rose, slowly and with a flicker of discomfort crossing her features, to make the vestige of obeisance.

'My lord Undersheriff, I regret I am not in a . . . condition to greet you as you deserve, and I hope you will forgive me if I remain seated.'

'Indeed, my lady, I am sorry to disturb you in your loss,' Bradecote spoke carefully, formally, and thought his words well chosen, since they covered both spouse and child, 'but we are about the sheriff's business, and need to speak with you to see if you can assist us in taking whoever it was who killed your lord.'

'Yet you arrive nearly a week after the event. William de Beauchamp does not seem to account his vassal's life of any great worth.' Her tone was scathing.

'He was only made aware of it yesterday, my lady,' Serjeant Catchpoll was keen to exonerate the sheriff from blame, 'and was mightily aggrieved to find out so tardily. You did not send word yourself.'

'I would have done so had I not been so unwell. I have no doubt you have heard, I lost my lord's child, the son he wished for so long, the child for which I also prayed.'

Bradecote flashed Catchpoll a glance of annoyance, which was also a clear message to keep his mouth shut before he committed any more crass mistakes.

'Yes, we heard of it, and understand you were not able . . . My lady, we cannot undo what has happened, but we will make every effort to bring your husband's killer to justice.'

'Every effort, my lord?' Her voice was low, passion in every syllable, so strong it was almost tangible, and her eyes narrowed like those of an animal judging the distance to strike for the kill. 'You find who did this, and you had best find him quickly if you want a hanging, because if I find him first . . . I swear an oath that you won't want to string up what is left.'

He watched, almost mesmerised by the tensing muscle in her cheek, the incandescence in her eyes.

'You have a right—'

'I have a duty. We cannot know how our lives will end or when, but my child did not reach the chance to breathe God's air, and my lord was struck down upon the King's road, in broad daylight, by a man who did not even face him in combat, and his body was dishonoured . . . they stole his sword, not just his horse.'

Catchpoll wondered why the lady sounded so surprised. A good sword was worth a tidy price. Of course a thief would take it, and the boots from his feet too if he had sense. Thievery was not some honour-bound trade.

'. . . but I too have a duty, to see the law is followed. This is the law's domain, and in truth, there is no place for personal revenge here. If you find out anything of interest, send to us.' Bradecote spoke calmly.

'Where?'

This rather threw the undersheriff. He had not got as far as working out where they would base themselves. She looked at him, saw the confusion, and smiled, though it was calculating rather than welcoming.

'I make you an offer of hospitality, my lord, as my husband would do to the lord Sheriff or his officers.'

She made a half obeisance as she sat, knowing it would be

difficult for him to refuse. Catchpoll made a coughing, growling sound in his throat, which Bradecote chose to ignore, though he comprehended the problem.

'I . . . well, it is kind of you to do so, my lady, but . . .'

'You would not refuse the hospitality of Corbin FitzPayne, loyal vassal of William de Beauchamp? In his absence, I offer it as he would.'

Bradecote cast Catchpoll a look that said he could not escape this one. Catchpoll smiled in the manner of one being offered a poisoned chalice. The undersheriff replied with formal courtesy.

'Then I accept, my lady, in the spirit I would if Corbin FitzPayne had so offered. There is but myself, Serjeant Catchpoll and . . .' he wondered how to describe Walkelin, 'a man-at-arms.'

Catchpoll's approval was almost audible. No need to let the lady know Walkelin was more than a hanger-on. That way he could be used to ferret. Catchpoll permitted himself a small, secret smile; Walkelin the red ferret might be very useful.

'There will be accommodation for the man-at-arms with ours. I will make arrangements for you to have a palliasse within the hall and . . .' She looked a little uncertain as to the position of Serjeant Catchpoll.

'I would be happiest among my own sort, my lady. If your steward will find me somewheres.'

'Of course.' She nodded graciously.

'So we work from here.' Catchpoll did not sound delighted. 'Would have been as well to go back to Worcester tomorrow, since it is a mite closer to Wich.'

'Sorry, but she caught me on that one, and we have more work to the north of Wich this next day or two.' Bradecote shrugged.

Walkelin looked at his superiors and frowned in perplexity.

'But, surely, this is a good place to be? Did you smell the pottage in the kitchens? Nearly as good as Mother's.'

'If you thought with what brains God gave you and not your rumbling gut, you would see we are not well placed. We are, in effect, living with a suspect.'

'You think that she . . . no, she's real in her grief, surely?'

'Seems real, but how much is for the lost babe, eh, Walkelin?' Catchpoll's eyes glinted with cunning thought. 'And that same lost child, was it Corbin FitzPayne's? She is a second wife, I would guess, but the heir is his brother, not a son of his loins. So if Corbin's arrows could not strike the target, whose did? And if Corbin puts two and two together when his wife grows sickly and her belly starts to swell, he would not be a happy man. Seems a good motive for murder to me.'

'So why the second theft of the salt wagons, with the same kind of deaths?'

'That, young Walkelin, is called being clever, and throwing sand, or in this case, salt, in the eyes of your pursuer.'

'So she doesn't really want to catch the archer because he is her lover?'

Walkelin's thought processes were logical if not always swift.

Bradecote was pondering, almost to himself.

'I doubt the archer is her lover, just a minion. She might, even if she and some mystery lover employed him to kill her husband, prefer to find him first and silence him, and being the outraged widow,' he sighed, 'looks good.'

Catchpoll gave his superior a calculating look. Bradecote had shown a predilection for strong-minded women before, and this one was not barred to him by being a Bride of Christ, nor by him being married, and many men would have ignored the latter.

'Don't worry,' Bradecote caught the look and smiled, 'I am not going to be moonstruck over a pretty widow.' Yet in his head was the realisation that she was pretty, even pale and hag-ridden, more than pretty.

The evening meal was not marked by conviviality, but then Bradecote had hardly expected it. The lady herself ate so sparingly that he felt as if he were a glutton, even though he partook of less than normal, and little was said while the servants were in attendance. When the meal was over, Christina FitzPayne indicated she would leave him and retire, but he detained her. He wanted to know more about her husband, and in the course of that, about her.

'I am sorry if it is painful to think of this, my lady, but the more we know, the better our chances of finding the killer.'

'But my husband was murdered simply for coming to the aid of men being attacked. That was what I was told.'

'It is likely, yes, but we would wish to know if he was in dispute with any man, or had enemies. I met your lord on several occasions, but would not say I knew him. Describe him to me, as a person.'

She frowned, not in displeasure but concentration, and the thought struck him that Corbin FitzPayne was already fading in her memory. He understood that, the balm and guilt combined.

'He was a fair man, and I would say, by the standards of

men, a good one. He did not cheat anyone of his dues that I know of, he was a benefactor of Bordesley and genuine in his faith, he was courageous in combat . . . he was at Lincoln, on foot among the other lords, but was thankfully not taken, and after . . . well, since William de Beauchamp has turned to the Empress I think Corbin chose to be non-committal, though his heart was with the King. He was not a humorous man, rarely laughed, but was not foul-tempered, simply quiet. As a husband I could not fault him.'

'Forgive me, but you speak respectfully, but not with deep affection, not with . . .'

'Love?' She spoke the word sneeringly, as if it were a cheap trick. 'I was more than content to be quietly fond of him. What cause could I have to ever love a man, knowing them for what they are?'

Bradecote was confused, and it showed.

'Ah, I see your knowledge of me is limited. As you have no doubt guessed, having met him, I was not Corbin's first wife. There was nigh on twenty-five years between us. But then, nor was he my first husband. I, my lord Bradecote, had the misfortune to first be the wife of Arnulf de Malfleur.' She paused, noting the surprise upon his face, but also what she recognised as pity. Malfleur had had a nasty reputation in a time when strength was admired. He was not just strong but sadistic, with tales of cruel violence upon any who displeased him. She continued, her voice very quiet. 'He took me to wife when I was twelve, my lord, and I mean "took", though I was not then able to fulfil the duty of bringing forth his whelps and he knew it.'

The genuine disgust upon Hugh Bradeote's face touched

her. Most men would merely not approve. It was wasteful, unkind, and showed a lack of control to use a wife, in name but of child's years, for the bedchamber. There were women enough elsewhere until she was a woman grown at fourteen or fifteen and could bear heirs.

'I was not fourteen when the first came, but it came early, far too early, and never drew breath. He blamed me.' She laughed without any humour. 'So he beat me, lashed me like a cur, so the white scars linger on my back still as a remembrance of my failing, and dragged me from my sickbed to do so. In the end it felt a black sin to bring forth his sons. The daughter, ah she was different, and he ignored her even until the day I buried her, when she was four, but his sons . . .' She shook her head. 'Mother's love children, be they comely or ugly, wilful or sweet-tempered, but I had that driven from me. He did not want me involved with "his" sons; I carried them in my belly, nursed them at my breast, but thereafter they were his to mould, and he made them in his own image, without care of any creature, man nor beast, encouraged cruelty, taught them to despise me. But oh, he was proud of them. Have you sons, my lord?'

'I have one, a babe still.'

'And is your lady proud of him?'

'My wife died giving him to me,' Hugh Bradecote spoke softly, 'but I will raise him so she would be proud, yes.'

It was the acknowledgement of an unconscious thought. He knew he could tell Gilbert little of his mother, since in so many ways he had never understood her, but she had been gentle and dutiful and loving, and had been proud, even at the time of dying, that she had borne a son.

Christina FitzPayne bit her lip.

'I am sorry.'

'God's will.'

'Yes. Arnulf's sons died. I believe that was God's will also, but to protect this earth from Malfleur's evil blood. I should have mourned, but I was just relieved. One was killed in a fall, setting his poor pony at a ditch it could not cross, and urged on by his father; the other died of a sudden fever when in his first year as a squire to de Mandeville in the east. When Arnulf died of the flux before Lincoln, I was free.' Her eyes glittered. 'He suffered, so I heard, and I was glad. He did not even live to die with what men call "glory" in the battle, just in his own filth in some tent among the Empress's followers.' She saw Bradecote's eyes widen slightly. 'You are shocked, yes, that I can be so unforgiving, so unwomanly. Just know that whatever bad things you heard of Arnulf de Malfleur was only the part of it. The blood is tainted with evil. Baldwin, Arnulf's brother, has no child still, so, God willing,' she crossed herself, 'the world will be spared more of that line.'

'So you were married how long to Malfleur?'

'Nigh on fourteen years. Half my life and yet three lifetimes. Corbin, well, Corbin was safe and kind, in his way. His demands were not excessive and after a happy marriage, which was yet without a child, he was so delighted to find he had the chance at last. He was going to tell his youngest brother Eustace, who took the cowl years ago and is at Bordesley.' Her face clouded. 'And in the shock of his loss I slipped and failed him, robbing him of his posterity. Perhaps it was my penance for not loving the other sons I bore.'

Bradecote watched her, the pale hands, with their long, delicate fingers, entwined so tightly the knuckles showed white, the eyes dark with misery. This was not a woman who had betrayed her husband with a lover and arranged his death. Then he realised that she in turn was watching him, assessing him. Her eyes widened, not in horror but in anger as she read his thoughts. She caught her breath, stood swiftly, holding the edge of the table for support as she swayed with the blood rush, and swung her hand hard so that his cheek stung with the raised weal. It was totally unexpected, undefended.

'How dare you? You thought that I . . . that . . .' Words failed her.

The pale cheeks flew angry red patches, and she turned to go to the solar, but his hand went out and gripped her wrist. She looked down upon it as if on a defilement.

'Let me go, my lord. You are one with all the rest.'

Was there disappointment in her voice? His cheek throbbed. He was angry, but angry with himself.

'I am sorry. Really, I am. The thought had to be entertained. I did not know anything of you, of your past, of what manner of woman you are. I am sorry, lady, for I did you injustice.'

She did not look at him, but at the floor. All fight was suddenly gone from her, and her shoulders slumped.

'Let me go,' she repeated, but softly, and he freed her instantly. She walked slowly to the solar door, and then turned, raising her head high. There was a catch in her voice when she spoke, but she spoke firmly. 'Injustice, yes, but I will have justice for Corbin FitzPayne, and for the son I could have loved.'

Hugh Bradecote swore under his breath as the door

closed, and when he settled to rest for the night, his dreams were haunted by the keening of a woman for a lost child.

He woke with the dawn, not refreshed, nor in the best of tempers, and did not know whether to be cheered or not by the similar look of thwarted sleep upon Catchpoll's grizzled features, when he met him in the courtyard. Walkelin, however, appeared fresh and cheery, and full of news. His superiors gazed at him with undisguised revulsion.

'By the Rood, if you look that cheerful of a morning, I will have to throw you in the midden,' grumbled Catchpoll, morosely.

'It is a fine day, and the cook has a way with fresh bread that many a Worcester baker would envy.'

'You know,' remarked Catchpoll conversationally, 'most men are ruled by their bodies. It gives the law a lot of work. But if they were ruled by their belly, as Walkelin is, well the rate of killings would drop but the thefts of oatcakes would treble.'

Walkelin, unabashed, grinned, and permitted himself half a glance at a comely wench bending forward in an appealing manner as she sat down upon a stool and began to milk a goat.

'I agree with Serjeant Catchpoll, Walkelin.' Bradecote ran a hand through his tousled hair. 'The sight of your grinning visage is enough to turn a man's stomach before he breaks his fast.'

'But I have already broken my—' Walkelin halted at a warning look from Catchpoll, and attempted to school his open features into a more sober expression. 'Er, I got talking with a couple of men-at-arms over a cup of ale last night, my lord. I don't think the idea that the lady FitzPayne might have paid to have her lord done away with will work.'

Bradecote did not say that he was already convinced of that. 'And why is that, Walkelin?'

'He was married before and had no children, it is true, but his lady could not hold a babe it seems. She lost them early. So he had no reason to assume a child was not his. And besides, they were but married less than two years, and were said to be content, no shouting, no throwing of things.'

'Shouting and throwing things does not mean they were not happy,' Catchpoll scowled, thinking of some of the times ladles had been lobbed at his head when he arrived home late, to a dried-up pottage. 'Some couples do, some don't. Silence can be worse. Nonetheless, I have reached the same conclusion as Walkelin, my lord. She did not want him dead. The tirewoman says how she was anxious every month, hoping for a sign, and when she was sure she was delighted and told her lord straightaway. He could scarce contain himself, but was anxious for her health and would barely let her set foot out of doors for the last week or two.'

The undersheriff nodded, and agreed that everything pointed to the widow being innocent of any involvement in the deaths, without elaborating upon his own findings.

'Not that this is grounds for self-congratulation, of course,' he sighed. 'We have eliminated one person but have no idea how many others might be suspect. And although she was someone we had to ensure was not involved, she was not the likeliest. It would have meant her having an unknown lover and them being content to see four other men killed just to cover their tracks. It was not impossible but . . .'

'Trouble is,' Catchpoll sighed, scratching his stubbled chin, 'there is nothing so far to send us in the right direction. We need to find out why, if Corbin FitzPayne was simply in the wrong place at the wrong time, two loads of salt have been stolen and the carriers murdered. I have seen lots of thievery over the years, and most thieves are happy to hit the victim over the head and be away with the goods. Sometimes they live, and sometimes they die, and the thief cares neither one way or the other. In this case these men were clearly not meant to survive, and that worries me. It isn't normal crime, if you understand me.'

Walkelin, his flame-coloured eyebrows drawn now in a frown, sniffed and wiped his nose on his sleeve. 'What would you do with two loads of salt that were heading for those who owned it? I mean, is someone keeping it to sell? If they are trying to raise the price of salt, well, they would have to take a lot more packhorse loads, and they cannot turn up to the monks at Bordesley and Alcester in a week or two and offer to sell them salt at a higher price.'

'It might make our task easier.' Bradecote smiled. 'Is it some grudge against . . . I was going to say the Benedictines, but the abbey at Bordesley is a daughter house of the White Monks at Garendon. In that case, is it a grudge against religious houses in general?'

'If you wanted to do something, more like you would burn down their granges, put dead livestock upstream of their water courses, or poison their fishponds, my lord.' Catchpoll spoke meditatively.

'You have a nasty turn of mind, Catchpoll.'

'Thank you, my lord. It comes in handy.' The serjeant gave a modest smile, which was not a look he employed regularly.

'I think,' and the undersheriff sounded prepared to entertain any better ideas, 'we should go to the monks at

Alcester and then on to Bordesley anyway, just in case they have received threats or . . .'

'. . . kept the arrow from Corbin FitzPayne, my lord, since they would not bury him with it still sticking out of the corpse, and then we would have two.' Walkelin sounded quite excited at the prospect, but Bradecote winced at his loud exuberance, and Catchpoll gave him a hard stare.

'I think perhaps less joy in the dead man's own bailey might be in order, Walkelin.'

'Er, yes, my lord. Sorry, my lord.'

Thus chastened, Walkelin coloured, even more so at the sound of a small giggle from the goat-milker. He took a sidelong glance at her and caught a blushing smile, which darkened the shade of his cheek further.

'And keep your eyes off wenches,' murmured Catchpoll through the side of his thin mouth. 'Gives a young man ideas, a buxom maid like that, and you've not time for ideas that aren't to do with these killings.'

'No, Serjeant,' but the eyes did stray once more and got a wink.

Bradecote stood, with folded arms and a sardonic smile.

'So sorry to disrupt your love life, Walkelin, but perhaps you might just go and arrange for the horses to be prepared. I will make our temporary goodbyes to the lady and then we can be away.'

He turned, and was halfway up the steps when lady FitzPayne appeared at the top, her veil being plucked by the gusts of autumnal wind and a dark, heavy cloak wrapped around her. If anything it made her more wraithlike than the day before. The shadows beneath her eyes seemed deeper than ever, and her face was as emotionless as one laid out for shrouding. He stopped, looking up at her, and with a stab of regret that she could not face him with even the most formal of smiles.

'I was coming to tell you, my lady, that we are away to Alcester and then on to Bordesley. We may return here in a day or so, dependent upon what we discover.'

She looked at him coldly, and acknowledged his words with a regal inclination of the head.

'Then I wish you a safe journey, my lord.'

Her voice was flat, dead. She might as well have been ordering a goose for dinner. It should not matter to him, and yet it did. Last night she had been all passion, wounded passion but alive. Now she stood there like an empty husk of grain, and as likely to be blown away in the wind. He made her an awkward obeisance from his halfway position, and retraced his steps, aware the exchange was under scrutiny.

Catchpoll's eyes narrowed to slits. Body language alone told him much. So the lady had taken against his superior, had she? He wondered why, for the undersheriff was not generally a clumsy man in word or action. He also wondered when any mention of this falling-out might be passed on, if at all, but wisely kept his mouth shut.

Walkelin appeared, leading their horses, and the three men mounted up and trotted out of the courtyard, watched by several of those present. Bradecote did not glance back, and chided himself for a fool for having wanted to do so.

As soon as they had gone, the girl who had been milking the goat handed her pail to a child, wiped her palms on her skirts and, bobbing a curtsey at the base of the steps, approached her mistress.

'Well?'

'They seem to have no idea as to who did the killings, my lady, but they do not think the lord FitzPayne was the object of it, more that he was an accidental murder, if you see what I mean. But they do have an arrow, and hope they might find another.'

'They would take such a thing with them, but when they return it would be well if we relieved them of that burden. Good girl, tell Godwin to fetch you an apple from the storerooms.'

The maid thanked her, and the lady FitzPayne returned to the hall, one hand clamped against the echo of discomfort within her, the other twisting the end of the heavy, dark plait that coiled over her shoulder and peeped from beneath her headdress.

Chapter Four

The three riders chose to head north to the Salt Road and then turn east to Alcester rather than ride across country, for it was but some four miles and the Salt Road was quick and easy. They arrived at the abbey shortly after the brothers had finished Chapter. It was a comparatively new foundation, only a few years old, and the claustral buildings were still largely of wooden construction, although the abbey church now boasted a stone chancel and transepts, with signs that work would advance again come the spring.

Abbot Robert recognised Serjeant Catchpoll. He had been a monk and obedientiary at Worcester before the foundation of the abbey a few years previously, and Catchpoll's was a face that, once seen, was hard to forget. He greeted them graciously and bade them ask all the questions they wished in the modest abbot's lodging.

'I fear that we can assist you little, if at all, in the solving of this wicked crime, my lord. The salt was ours, from our salt house in Wich. All that we knew was that a rider came from there to tell us it had been stolen and two packmen murdered, and also my lord FitzPayne of Cookhill, a good man and generous also. We can tell you nothing but the results of the deed.'

'You did not know the date of the salt leaving Wich, then?' Serjeant Catchpoll was casting about like a hound for any useful scent.

'Oh no, Serjeant. We knew it would be coming shortly but the date of its arrival was not required, though,' Abbot Robert sighed, 'we might be short for the salting of our winter meats and fish. But our brothers in Worcester have said that they should be able to send some from their salt houses, for they have more. It is time that is our problem, not the quantity, in the longer term.'

'This must sound a strange question, Father, but has anyone cause for dispute with you?' Bradecote posed the obvious question.

'None, my lord, none that might lead them to such an act. The widow of Gerald the Cooper is in dispute with us over three tuns he willed to us, but you would surely not believe that . . .'

'No, we would not believe a cooper's widow would organise thefts of salt.' Bradecote permitted himself a small smile.

'Thefts? We lost but one pack train.'

'There was another attack, in the same manner, four, no, three days past, upon a cartload of salt bound for the Cistercians at Bordesley, and the two carters were killed.'

'God have mercy upon their souls.' The abbot crossed himself. 'We had not heard, my lord.'

'Is that not unusual, Father Abbot? There are not so many miles 'twixt Wich and here.' Catchpoll was frowning

53

still, on the verge of one of his 'thinking faces' again.

'You would think so, Serjeant, but all our visitors in the guest hall have been travelling towards Wich these last few days, and with so much to be done before the winter sets in, people are busy at home, not travelling. The news would have reached us in time, and all we can do is pray, for our brothers in Christ and those killed.'

Abbot Robert sighed. As one who was in the world but not 'of it', he despaired of the wickedness he saw around him. Hugh Bradecote, realising there was nothing more to be gained from him, made their farewells, and before noon the sheriff's men were heading north-east towards the Cistercian abbey at Bordesley.

The Archer rubbed chilled hands together and blew upon them silently. Waiting did not worry him. Waiting was part and parcel of his trade. He tore a hunk off the loaf that he had obtained from an old woman, with a heel of hard cheese, in exchange for the hind quarter of a hare he had caught the night before. His needs were simple, and the money that weighed in the scrip he carried meant little beyond the pence it was useful to have for things he could not barter in meat. That the meat was illicitly taken worried him not at all. His attitude to what he might catch in forest and hedgerow was not the same as towards a man's goose or sheep or pig. If he hunted an animal using his own cunning, if it was a wild beast, all was fair. Then if he took it, he had the right to it.

He had been told to wait beyond Bromsgrove, this time for the cart heading north, he neither knew nor cared where.

Only when he heard the slow turning of the wheels did he put his meal away, and string his bow, calmly, without any apparent excitement or concern. There were two men, taking their pace from the oxen, and they presented no challenge. The first had barely time to exclaim as his companion toppled, and followed with a grunting exhalation. The Archer turned away and was gone before the two thugs employed to take the cart had even taken up the first body. He would meet the thin-faced man who paid him on the road just beyond the eastern end of Alvechurch, at dusk. There was plenty of time, but he always liked to be the one waiting.

Hugh Bradecote trotted into the enclave at Bordesley, with Catchpoll and Walkelin in his wake, in the middle of the afternoon, a little after None. Brother Porter sent a novice to Abbot William, and directed a lay brother to show Walkelin to the stables. Bordesley, like Alcester, was a new foundation, yet to show the solidity of stone above ground, excepting for the green sandstone of the abbey church, still scaffolded and with its western end showing a wooden face. The White Monks, eschewing grandeur for imposing austerity, were already making money from their flocks and had worked hard upon the marshy Arrow Valley, draining land and diverting the river itself to their needs. There were lay brothers, but every member of the community had had to pull their weight, quite literally, to achieve what they had in so few years.

Abbot William met the undersheriff and serjeant with as much courtesy as Abbot Robert and with as little thought that he could be of assistance. At Bradecote's interest in Corbin

FitzPayne's interment he called for Brother Eustace, Corbin's brother, who had sought permission, which was granted, to prepare the body and shroud it. The monk did not look very much as Bradecote remembered the older FitzPayne, being lanky and with wisps of pale-gold hair about his tonsure.

'Brother Eustace, the lord Bradecote wishes to know about your brother's death.'

'But, Father, I know noth—'

'We are interested in what you saw when he was brought here, Brother. The position of the wound would help us.'

Bradecote already had a good idea of that but it was a starting point. The monk's face paled slightly, but his voice was steady.

'The wound was fatal of itself. He had not been beaten that I could see. The arrow projected from just below the breastbone.'

'You removed the arrow, Brother?'

'Of course.'

'What sort of arrow was it?'

'Oh, not one a man would choose to hunt game, but a long bodkin, a war arrow. It had struck deep, right into the backbone, without even mail to hinder it. I gave thanks that at least my brother did not suffer a long dying. He was a man with faith, and did not fear death, but which of us would want to die slowly?'

'Indeed. You removed the arrow, and then what?'

'I washed and shrouded the body, my lord.'

'He means what did you do with the arrow, Brother.' Catchpoll tried not to sound peremptory.

'Oh, the arrow! Er, I cannot recall. Laid it aside, I suppose.'

'Might it be where you left it, in the mortuary chapel?'

'Er, yes, unless it has been tidied away since.'

Catchpoll's eyes had lit up.

'Well, you take me and show me where, Brother.'

He took the brother by the elbow, and almost propelled him from the chamber. Abbot William permitted himself a half smile.

'Your serjeant is assiduous in his duties, my lord.'

'He is keen, yes, but that comes from long years in the work.'

The abbot's face became serious again.

'Do you think you will catch whoever did this?'

'I do not know, but I know we will make every effort.' A thought struck Bradecote. 'Father Abbot, might I also speak with your prior? I believe it was he who took the bad news to the widow, the lady FitzPayne.'

'Of course.'

A small bell was rung, and a novice sent to fetch the prior, who recounted his visit to Cookhill.

'The poor lady showed her grief in anger, as some do, promising vengeance upon whoever had killed her lord. She was most bloodthirsty.'

He sounded slightly shocked, but Bradecote had to repress a smile. Best not tell him she sounded equally bloodthirsty days later.

'And her fall?'

'Oh dear, that was terrible. From halfway down the steps she tumbled and was carried unconscious to her chamber. And then she lost the life she was carrying. I did not know, of course, when I told her the bad news, though it had to be faced, whatever her condition. However, I would not have entertained her returning here for the burial, which is what she had planned to do.'

At this point Catchpoll returned, wreathed in smiles as if he had found a scrip of gold, and with Brother Eustace trailing in his wake.

'We have it! One arrow, my lord, with the same fletchings as the other, of course.'

There was muted triumph in his voice. It was not a find that would change their ideas, but it was good corroboration, although Catchpoll would have merely described it as 'another piece of the pie'.

Bradecote nodded, and turned back to the abbot.

'I asked this question of Abbot Robert at Alcester, but I must ask it also of you, Father Abbot. Are there any in dispute with you at this time?'

The abbot shook his head.

'None but Herluin, whose pig drowned in the Arrow, and who blamed us because he said the water flowed the faster after our workings.'

Bradecote smiled and shook his head, then requested lodgings for the three of them for the night in the guest hall.

A barn owl flitted silently along the track, a pale ghost in the gloaming. Reginald, son of Robert, crossed himself. He would not choose to be out alone in the approaching darkness, but this was the assignation to which his lord had sent him, and he was not a man to disobey. The Archer was more ghost than living thing, not unlike the owl, and as silent a hunter. Reginald had not seen him since the first meeting in the tavern, and were it not for the fact that every commission were fulfilled and the silver taken, he would not now be certain he had a meeting with a real man at all. His horse, sensing his disquiet, began to fidget nervously. The last dwelling of Alvechurch was well behind him when he heard the disembodied voice call for him to halt. The horse jibbed, and then stood still, ears twitching for danger.

'You come with money. Do you come also with new tasks, Master Messenger?'

Reginald caught the disdain in the voice. This man, this 'Archer', thought himself so different, so superior, to a man who brought instructions. The other men, men he commanded, treated him with respect as one senior in their lord's service. The Archer did not understand, but it did not stop Reginald imagining, with pleasure, the day when the marksman's services would no longer be needed and he could show him how mistaken he had been.

'I come with both, Archer. There are to be no attacks for a few days. Meet me here three days before St Luke's and your next task will be given to you and half the payment.'

'Fair enough. Now for the silver. Throw it ahead of you and turn away.'

Reginald did as instructed. He heard the slight chink of coin as it was picked up from the ground.

'Why this mummery, Archer? I saw you when I hired you in the tavern.'

'You saw a man once, a man who is much as every other man. Your memory will play you false at every turn, and I will blend into the undergrowth, just as I do . . .'

The word was left hanging, for Reginald was alone.

* * *

The sheriff's men left Bordesley on the morrow, heading along the route the salt wagons should have taken to the abbey, back south along the ancient Icknield Street that the Romans had set on its straight course, climbing the King's hunting grounds of the Lickey Hills before dropping towards Bromsgrove. It was there that they came upon an altercation.

A horse trough stood in the street, and before it a free-for-all seemed to be taking place. At its edge, a dark-haired man with a close-cropped beard, swathing his jaw, sat upon an impressive bay horse, apparently watching the proceedings as if it was sport.

Serjeant Catchpoll muttered imprecations under his breath and set his heels to his horse's flanks, scattering many of the combatants by the simple expedient of riding among them at speed. Avoiding being ridden down was far more important than a brawl. Two or three resolutely remained trying to addle each other's brains, and Catchpoll, shaking his head at their foolishness, dismounted and approached. One man, facing away from him, did not notice, but the other let his eyes flicker to the death's head grin upon the grizzled face of Serjeant Catchpoll, and his opponent took full advantage of the moment, reaching for his knife at his belt. Whatever murderous intent he might have had was lost the moment a sinewy arm bore his own downward, and a booted foot crumpled him by kicking him in the back of the knees. Catchpoll pushed him aside.

'I don't think so, Toadbreath.'

The man he would have knifed seemed confused, so caught up in the adrenalin that he took a wayward swing at his rescuer. Catchpoll sidestepped, grabbed the unbalanced pugilist and 'helped' him into the trough.

'All finished, Serjeant?'

'Yes, my lord, just a minor falling-out of friends and high spirits, no doubt.'

Bradecote's attention turned to the man on horseback.

'Had you no thought to stop this?'

The man smiled lopsidedly.

'Not really. It was mildly entertaining, and these oafs would not give precedence to my men. You said "Serjeant". But you are not de Beauchamp so . . . ah you must be de Crespignac's replacement.'

'I am Hugh Bradecote, undersheriff of Worcestershire. And you, my lord?'

'Baldwin de Malfleur.'

Bradecote hoped his face did not betray his reaction. The words of Christina FitzPayne echoed in his head, that the family were evil to the core. What he saw before him did not give any indication that she was wildly wrong. He nodded acknowledgement.

'We have not met before, though I came across your brother.'

'Ah yes,' de Malfleur's smile was somewhat fixed. 'Once "come across", Arnulf was rarely forgotten. But I am not my brother. In fact, where I feel Arnulf would have rampaged around the county roaring, I am being remarkably . . . restrained.'

'With what cause?'

'Well, since you are the undersheriff of the shire I will tell you and not waste my efforts in going to de Beauchamp. Yesterday I had a salt wagon stolen and the drivers murdered by a man with a bow, a man whose accuracy would mark him as one skilled beyond normal work at the butts. This, I hear, is the third such attack. I want to know what the sheriff, or,' he smiled, 'the sheriff's subordinate, is doing about it.'

Catchpoll watched the pair of them, clearly vying with each other, jostling politely with words where common men would wrestle, though the words were in Foreign and he did not understand every one of them.

'We are doing whatever is possible, short of guarding every salt load that leaves Wich. There are simply not enough men to do that.'

'So you are wandering around hoping to find this archer ambling along your path?' There was insult in the tone.

'I did not say so. We are trying to work out who he is, how he manages to get about so stealthily. Then we have a good chance of catching him.'

De Malfleur was not fooled.

'Keeping things close to your chest, eh? Well, so would I in your boots. Now, you say there are not enough men to guard the salt. I happen to have a plentiful supply of men, those of my brother's and those also whom I took to the Holy Land as a virtuous knight. In fact, I had too many and had to turn some off. I shall protect any salt that I bring from Wich to replace my lost wagon, and, if they will but pay me a consideration to fund my men, I will protect any other load, be it abbey or lord's, that leaves the town. The law is fine as far as it goes, but Bradecote, I am not fettered as you are.'

'You must remain within the law, though, de Malfleur.'

'Of course, my lord Undersheriff. How else would I work?'

De Malfleur's eyes mocked. Bradecote gritted his teeth. He would dearly like to wipe the sneer from the weathered face. Without further word, de Malfleur wheeled his horse, and, calling his men as most would call their hounds, he trotted northward, back upon the way he had come.

Catchpoll hawked and spat into the dirt. Walkelin, who had kept very quiet throughout the interchange, looked from one superior to the other and wondered. Neither serjeant nor undersheriff looked at all happy. There was a pause.

'Where now, my lord?' asked Catchpoll.

'Well, we cannot indeed wander the shire in hope. Let us get back to Cookhill and look at things again. It is close enough to Wich and there is where I think we must find something to aid us. After all, the thieves know when and where to strike. The information can only come from the town.'

The trio watered their horses and headed south, not quite managing to feel optimistic. Little was said, although the silence was not unfriendly. The cloud had thickened by the time they passed through Wich, where they bought bread and ale, though Catchpoll was most uncomplimentary about the beverage, suggesting whoever made it had used brine instead of water.

The afternoon was cold and gloomy, and Bradecote drew his cloak about him as they neared Cookhill. He did not think his reception would be any warmer than the weather, and was again conscious of that feeling of regret. It had been his fault, his clumsiness, and he would have to face her over the evening meal in all her haughty coldness. They trotted into the courtyard and a lad came to take Bradecote's mount. The steward emerged and greeted them with the information that his lady was not yet returned. He sounded worried, in a paternal way.

'Not yet returned? But why did she go out at all? Surely she should not . . .'

The sudden relief upon the old man's face and the clatter of hooves told him the rising alarm was unnecessary. Bradecote turned, to see lady FitzPayne, accompanied by two men-at-arms, come through the gateway. Then he frowned, for her face was very white and pinched, ghostly in the fading afternoon light. She brought her horse to a halt, and as she began to dismount, a little unsteadily, he was there to lift her down. She would have remonstrated, but her knees buckled as he set her feet to the ground, and his light hold upon her waist tightened.

'My lord, I am perfectly able to . . .'

Her voice was thread-like, and Hugh Bradecote had no qualms about asserting his male authority.

'No, you are not, foolish woman. What possessed you to take to the saddle, I want to know?'

Before she could respond, he swung her into his arms and proceeded to carry her up the stone steps and through the hall to her solar, calling for a tirewoman. Her mind was full of outrage, but her body was just glad to be passive. In truth, for all that she would remonstrate at his high-handed behaviour, she knew she had undertaken too much too early, and for no result. Report had come of a horse that sounded like her lord's, being shod at the blacksmith's in Moreton, and she had set off on impulse, keen to be doing something positive, but the smith had shaken his head and told her it was a horse he had shod many times before. He could vouch for its ownership. Demoralised, and feeling distinctly unwell, she had come home. Her eyes were half closed, but she permitted herself a glance at Bradecote's unsmiling profile. He had a longish nose and a mouth that could look unforgiving, but if he smiled . . .

He drew back a curtain and set her upon the box bed in the corner of the chamber, then commanded the steward, who had followed him, to get candles and to light the brazier, for the lady was clearly cold, and sent a girl to fetch hot wine. Christina FitzPayne's face remained impassive but her eyes watched him.

'By what right do you take complete control of my hall, my lord?'

Her voice was still weak, but there was an edge to it nonetheless. His reply held anger, which surprised her.

'By right of still possessing my wits when yours are sadly lacking, lady. What possible cause led you to ride in your condition?'

'I do not have to explain my actions to you, my lord Undersheriff, since they do not break the King's laws, and as for "my condition", I—'

Without warning, and to her own intense annoyance, she choked and burst into tears. Hugh Bradecote stared at her in mute horror. He could do nothing, nothing within the bounds of decency. Part of him wanted to hold her, comfort her, and the other wanted her to pull herself together and cease embarrassing him. The arrival of the tirewoman, clucking like a mother hen and almost driving him from the bedside as though shooing pigeons from the pease field, was actually a relief.

In the yard, the horses had been taken to the stables, and Walkelin was overseeing them. Serjeant Catchpoll stood, arms folded, leaning against a wall, waiting. Bradecote's face was stormy.

'I asked one of the men-at-arms, my lord, about what was

going on. He said the lady suddenly called for her horse and had them follow her to the smithy at Moreton. She seemed quite agitated, and spoke to the smith for some minutes, but his answers did not please her, for she was silent upon the return journey.'

'To a smithy? But . . .'

Catchpoll watched the answer to his superior's own question hit him.

'Yes, my lord, we had not thought about the lord FitzPayne's horse. It seems it was quite a distinctive animal. A dark steel-grey with white stockings to its off hind and near fore. It seems the lady FitzPayne has had her men out hunting for information to find out if it has been seen.'

'And not thinking to help us by telling us of it.'

'It seems not, my lord.'

'Damn the woman.'

'Possibly, my lord. But at least we know now. A good animal must have found a home somewhere. Too good not to sell and make money.'

'But the thief would have to be careful. How many ordinary men would have a fine horse to sell?'

'Not many, to be sure, but there are those who would not question it if it was at the right price.' Catchpoll chewed his lip, ruminatively. 'I know a few less fussy sorts as would buy a horse on the sly.'

'You know a very disreputable collection of Worcestershire folk, Catchpoll.' The undersheriff's expression lightened.

'I do indeed, my lord.' Catchpoll grinned, clearly proud of this fact. 'Takes a time to er, cultivate, but comes in useful.'

'Well, see what else you can find out about that horse's

saddlery and yes, whether FitzPayne's sword had any marks to it we could recognise. I doubt the lady will be either in a condition or mood to play hostess, so I expect a very uninteresting evening.'

They parted, Catchpoll to ale and a pottage with dumplings, and Bradecote to a cheerless repast in a dead man's hall.

Chapter Five

Baldwin de Malfleur lounged with his booted feet upon a stool, and a cup of good wine in his hand. He stared into the flames of the brazier, and from a distance it might have been thought that he scowled, but closer scrutiny would have revealed a thin smile. He savoured the wine, and the smile broadened as a thought hit him.

'Ah, Arnulf, my oh-so-renowned brother, I may linger in your shadow now, but the day will come when you are just another forgotten harsh lord, and it will be my name that is remembered in this shire, for fate has provided me with an opportunity not to be missed.' He laughed. 'Just think, a Malfleur famed for his good works! And it will pay my men too. But the jest gets better, brother Arnulf, for by chance a victim of these crimes turns out to be the man who replaced you with the fair Christina, the Christina you described in such fulsome detail when you knew I could not have her, the Christina who told you of that one kiss I stole, so you packed me off to die, as you hoped, in some desert wadi. I wonder if she loved him? I hope she did, for it would make it so much the sweeter.'

A servant approached diffidently. You never quite knew where you were with Baldwin de Malfleur, especially if the wine had flowed, and it was not just with his tongue that he might lash out.

'My lord, the man you sent to Wich has returned. You said you wished to—'

'Yes, yes, bring him in. I want to know just what is going on among the salt houses.'

The man entered, bowing low.

'So, what have you discovered for me?'

'There is much nervousness, especially among the carters and packmen.'

'Fool!' de Malfleur snorted. 'I did not need to send you there to work that out. When will my salt house have enough to send me another cartload? And are others holding back their salt or risking the flight of an arrow?'

'A few are going out, my lord. The monks of Worcester have called upon their tenanted manors for "volunteers" to provide protection for their pack train, but they alone have enough holdings to do this quickly.'

'Then my offer of assistance must be made swiftly. Call my scribe. The religious houses can read of what I would do for the Church, at a modest price. I will send one of my men to the reeve in Wich to pass the information to the salt houses. That will filter quickly enough to those who own them. That will be all. You may go.'

'Yes, my lord.' The man backed out, relieved.

The Archer, having slept comfortably in a coppice, headed eastwards, crossing the shire border into Warwickshire. He was not so familiar with the country but had a good sense of direction, and knew roughly where he was heading. The empty days before the next meeting gave him plenty of time for what he wanted to do, what he needed to do. Few people saw him upon his journey, for he stepped aside long before they came into view, and those that did paid scant attention, except for the child who saw the darkly hooded man with the bow, and thereafter woke with nightmares.

It was perhaps twenty miles from Bromsgrove to the Priory of St Leonard's at Wroxall. The bells in the church tower, where the stonework was still new and unweathered, guided him the last mile as they rang for Vespers. He arrived as any other traveller, was greeted as such by the sister in charge of the small hall reserved for guests, and bidden eat and then attend Compline. At heart he would have liked to have done what was needed and left without fuss, but only by speech could he convey what must be known. He watched the prioress lead the sisters to their places in the Choir. It was not easy to tell much about the woman beneath the black habit, but her posture was erect and upright, and her step firm, so he judged her neither elderly nor infirm. Not that it gave him much to go upon; the elderly were sometimes far more needle-witted than those in their prime. He would sleep upon it and seek an audience after Chapter.

The Sister Hospitaller was surprised to be asked by the quiet man for an interview with the Mother Prioress, but saw nothing about him to concern her. He explained the bow, which never left his side. He was, he said, a man-at-arms returned from the Holy Land, and had a request to pass on. He was ushered into the little chamber in which Prioress Erneburga received guests.

She sat very upright, her face perfectly serene, and inclined her head at the Archer's respectful obeisance.

'Sister Felicia tells me you have a message? For this House?'

'A message, no, Reverend Mother, but the fulfilment of a wish, yes. This Priory of St Leonard's was founded by one Hugh of these parts, yes?'

The nun nodded.

'Does he live, still?' The Archer needed to know.

'Indeed, though not in the most robust of health these days.'

'Ah. Well, you see, I too was in the Holy Land, some years past, and my lord was a friend of this Hugh. He was grieved at his friend's capture and delighted at his freeing, though in such poor health, but did not see him again. He was killed, some four years back. My lord was a good man, a fair man. I respected him and, for my skill, he respected me. He said as there was no better archer in the Christian armies.' The Archer chuckled. 'Never said how I compared to the Saracen archers with their funny re-curved bows, though, God rest him.'

The nun frowned slightly, puzzled as to where this story was leading. The Archer shook his head and continued.

'My lord was a godly man, and I know as how his sins are forgiven him for his deeds upon Crusade, but he was never sure of it, I think. He trusted me to bring home certain moneys he had. His squire was dead and . . . he knew I would not steal another's coin. Being a lordless man, I took employment where I could, with whom I could, in the trade to which I was trained. I made my way home slowly, and over the course of time the coin was exchanged until what I have here is English silver, but it is for this House of Nuns as founded by his friend, and for the safety of his soul, for which he would have you pray. So I would have you remember in your prayers, my lord, Ivo of Clent, of the Knights Hospitaller. I added a little of my own, Reverend Mother, that you might also pray for the soul of Godwin the Hunter, my father.'

He took the scrip, weighed with silver, and set it upon the table between them. It made a hefty clunking noise as he let it go. The prioress blinked. She had certainly not been expecting such a gift. Her astonished expression pleased the Archer. It would put any awkward questions from her mind.

'Much good could be done with this, both for the fabric of this House and so that we can provide for those who come to us in direst need. God bless you for your diligence in fulfilling this task, and be assured that we will add both souls to our daily orisons.'

She did not say that it surprised her that a man of so humble origins as she judged would cross Europe and bring home a bag of silver at his lord's bequest, when none might have known, excepting God, for sure, if he used it for his own ends and comfort.

The Archer bowed his head, as much to hide his reddened cheeks as in acknowledgement of the blessing. Then he rose, made his obeisance, and withdrew. Before he left the enclave however, he went into the church and prayed for the forgiveness of a lie that he wished had been truth.

It was not far to the manor house, but the Archer took his time, uncertain as to how he would get to speak with the lord himself. He could claim to be bringing a message perhaps, but he thought the nuns had taken falsehood for truth very easily.

At the gates he hesitated, took a deep breath and entered to ask for the lord Hugh. The man-at-arms raised a sceptical brow but disappeared within the hall. When he emerged he was not followed by an ailing man of advancing years, but a young man in his twenties with all the arrogance of a cock on a dunghill, thought the Archer, smiling to himself. He schooled his features into respectful deference as the young man drew close.

'You wished for speech with me?'

The voice was proud, but the Archer had heard enough lordlings in his time to hear that this was a man trying hard to demand respect rather than earn it.

'My lord, I requested the chance to speak with the lord Hugh, who served in the Holy Land.'

'Well, my father is in poor health, and I run the manor in his stead. I am Richard Noyes. Any business may be discussed with me.'

'Forgive me, my lord, but it is not manor business. I wish to speak to him of the past. I served with your father, in the service of his friend Ivo of Clent, whose archer I was. I would speak of my lord, now dead.'

The young man's eyes narrowed. He assessed the man before him. He was certainly an archer from physique when one looked carefully. He was not a big man, but his upper body musculature was superior to any toiler of fields. He wondered, and then a slow smile spread across his face.

'Archer, you say. Perhaps you are "The Archer" of whom I have heard so much, the one my father rambles about, whose arrow strikes true without fail, who struck a Saracen lord upon a battlement when all that was visible was the swathed head, and from beyond the distance any other man could reach?'

'Aye, my lord. That was me.'

'A lucky shot?'

'No, my lord.'

Richard Noyes inclined his head in acknowledgement.

'Forgive me, of course not. Such a useful man to have in service. I believe my father was almost jealous of his friend. I fear you will find him much changed since you met him last. The imprisonment was hard upon him. We were blessed, of course, that he returned to us, and was able to resume the control of his lands, but his mind . . . soon began to wander.'

The Archer had the feeling that this 'wandering' was just what an ambitious youth who had tasted power might like, and that his regret was far from heartfelt. In fact, there was little of the sire's open honesty and goodwill, as he remembered it, that he could see in the son.

'Yet if it is possible, my lord, I would wish to try and talk with him.'

'Very well. My mother is in attendance upon my sister at her confinement, so you will find him alone. He may recall your lord. I do not know.'

The lordling led the Archer to the solar, where a man sat gazing into space. The Archer was shocked. The man he remembered was full of life and good humour. This was a husk of humanity, the skin weathered and lined but sallow, the eyes vague.

'Father, I bring you a visitor, a man who knew you in the Holy Land.'

Richard Noyes spoke slowly and loudly. Perhaps, thought the Archer, his father was also deaf. There was no sign of response, and the son came to kneel before his father's chair. It seemed a gesture of respect, until he reached out his arms and shook the older man, who blinked as if woken from slumber. The introduction was repeated and then the lordling got from his knees, brushed them, and turned to the Archer, as he left.

'Say what you are come to say, and then leave him to his nothings.'

There was no love in the tone, merely boredom.

The Archer went on his knee before the man who had been his lord's closest friend.

'My lord Hugh, I am Ivo of Clent's archer. Do you recall me? We were in the Holy Land together.'

The huddled man stared at him uncomprehendingly, and the Archer sighed, but then it was as if a candle had been lit within, and he smiled.

'Ivo's archer, yes. You took down El Misrah upon his own battlements. I saw it done.' The voice was dreamy.

'You did, my lord.'

'And Ivo?'

'Ivo of Clent died four years ago, my lord.'

'He is dead?'

'And buried. I saw it done.' The Archer's expression and tone grew hard.

The old lord frowned. 'He fell in battle, yes?'

'In battle, indeed, my lord, but the hand that slew him was not Saracen.'

The frown deepened.

'Trial by combat? It does not sound like the Ivo I knew.'

'Not trial by combat. The man who killed him was supposed to be fighting by his side, but slew him.'

'And lives still?'

'No, my lord. He died. I would have given my lord justice, but I was wounded and then fevered. When I had my senses, he was gone. Then I heard his ship was lost.'

'Justice is for the Lord. And justice was done, Archer.'

'Perhaps so, my lord. I have made my way home. I have brought coin to the nuns at Wroxall, for my lord heard you had returned and fulfilled a vow. They will pray for his soul. It is what he would wish.'

'I will pray for him also, and I think perhaps for you too, Archer.'

There was an understanding. The shell of a man that sat in his hall and did not know where he was, saw far too deep into the Archer for his comfort.

'I thank you for them, my lord. From us both.'

He took the pale hand, kissed it in submission and rose.

A few minutes later, Richard Noyes returned to the hall. His father sat as before, his hands upon his knees, staring at nothing.

'Were you glad to see him again, Father?'

The old lord turned. 'See whom?'

The son smiled. 'Oh nobody of import, Father, and of no use to you.'

Hugh Bradecote woke slowly, hearing the sounds of morning labour. A serving girl was carrying a pitcher to the solar in the half light. He lay still, mustering his thoughts, which were jumbled. He had been dreaming, he could not say for certain what, except that she had been in them, and the 'she' was not the serving wench. He wondered how she did today, and then the memory of her deception, or at best her determination not to aid his investigation, drove any soft thoughts from him. When she appeared, a short time later, he looked at her coolly. For her part she felt unsettled. They had parted yesterday at odds, which she regretted: she had been weak and tearful, which she despised; he had taken control without either right or permission, which angered her; and for all that, she too had dreamt. For the first time in her life there had been a man in her dreams without it being a nightmare. That of itself had stunned her. She could not say all that had happened, for dreams followed no logic, but he had been there and his presence had been protective, that much she remembered.

'I give you good morning, my lord.' She tried to sound cheerful.

'Do you, my lady? Is that something you think that you can give without revealing anything of use to the law?'

She winced at the cutting tone, and faltered, her cheeks growing pink.

'My lord?'

'Oh please, lady, do not come the innocent. I asked you to let me know anything that might assist me to find out who murdered your husband, and you kept from me that his horse was distinctive and likely to be important in our hunting down men who have killed a half-dozen thus far, and will probably kill again.'

'You are displeased, but—'

'Displeased?' Bradecote sounded incredulous. 'You think "displeasure" covers this?'

'My lord, I have a duty—'

'As have I, and I do not intend to allow you to get in the way. You seek justice for one death; I do so for many and within the law.'

She looked away.

'I am sorry.'

He thought she would dab at her eyes. It was a common female recourse.

'And do not think that tears will distract me.'

At that she spun round.

'Tears, my lord? For yesterday I apologise. I was shamed by my weakness.'

He registered surprise at her words, his eyebrows rising.

'I mean it, my lord.'

It was at this point that Serjeant Catchpoll entered, instantly aware that he had arrived in the middle of an argument. He wondered what made this pair strike sparks from each other. He nodded to the lady, his face inscrutable.

'Good morning, my lady, I was wishing to have speech with my lord Bradecote.'

'Oh, to be sure I shall not interrupt the law, Serjeant,' she threw at him, 'but will rather take refuge in my solar where my presence, in mine own home, might not offend.'

With which she flounced from the hall.

Bradecote exchanged looks with Catchpoll.

'Do not ask me what it is with women, Catchpoll; they are unfathomable.'

'Well, once you accept the fact, my lord, it is easier to bear. Mind you, that one seems especially unpredictable. Got spirit, if you see what I mean.'

'Spirit, yes, but as dangerous as an untamed horse.'

Catchpoll could not repress the lascivious grin and lewd reply.

'Well, a horse is always tamed once it is used to being mounted, my lord.'

Bradecote laughed, and rubbed his unshaven chin, thus concealing the faint colour to his cheek. Trust Catchpoll to have the earthy answer.

'I do not suppose you came to give me the benefit of that gem of advice, you old dog.'

'No, my lord. We have a little more on just how much effort the lady has been putting in to finding that horse, though. She has had men out to Worcester and east as far as Stratford, since before we came. And FitzPayne's sword – well, according to his men, it was "just a good, well-balanced weapon", with nothing fancy to it.'

'The scabbard?'

'Nothing was mentioned, which you would expect if it was very ornate, but then some men take things as said and asking about the sword, well, they might just think of the blade. I can ask again.'

'No, I will have the lady tell me.' Bradecote pondered, talking more to himself than his serjeant. 'I wonder if she would actually lie to my face?'

Christina FitzPayne, her ear to the crack in the door, clenched a fist.

The girl who came to the solar shortly afterwards gave her nothing to cheer her. Using the goat milker as bait to distract Walkelin, to his pleasure, and with the serjeant with the lord in the hall, she had gone through their meagre saddlebags. Neither had the arrow, or arrows.

'I am sorry, my lady. They must be with the lord Undersheriff.'

'Then if you see his bags left alone, you look there, at the first chance. He may leave them here if he is returning this evening, or for some minor matter in the manor. It is important. Now, away with you and keep alert.'

Bobbing a curtsey, the girl left, excited at the thought of her secret operation. It was unfortunate that she saw both Bradecote and Catchpoll in the yard, only to be then called away by nature. When she returned a couple of minutes later she saw Catchpoll with Walkelin, and went to the hall, which she found empty. Taking her chance, she rifled through the undersheriff's meagre baggage, and nearly whooped with success as her fingers closed upon a flight. What she did not know was that Bradecote was closeted with her mistress.

'So, my lady FitzPayne, now you are recovered, will you describe your husband's horse, and then both sword' – Bradecote paused – 'and scabbard to me?'

He sounded cold and formal. There was a gulf between them and it should matter to neither, but it did. She met his gaze but then looked away. The eyes accused her of duplicity, and she knew herself to be guilty.

'My lord's horse was grey.'

'Just "grey"? I said "describe". That is not a description, lady.'

She looked at him then, and for a second he thought he read apology in the blue-grey eyes.

'He was the grey of dulled mail, a dark grey, with a star upon his forehead, and two white stockings.'

'Thank you. And the sword?'

'It was a good sword but not remarkable to look upon. My lord said a sword was not an item of jewellery to flaunt for show. And he was right. It is a thing with which to kill, not to impress.'

'Indeed. So the sword would not have anything to mark it. What of the scabbard?'

'Unadorned, but there was an old "wound" to it, a slicing of the leather near the hanging, like a scar in the hide. That would be recognisable as very likely his, although another might just have such a mark.'

She had told him true. It rested more easily with her and since he probably knew about the horse already there was no advantage to a lie. As for the scabbard, well, she doubted staring at the sword of every man who wore one would discover it. Her hopes lay with the arrow and seeking the advice of the local fletchers.

The door opened. The maid entered, keen to impart her success. Bradecote had his back to the door but was sure to turn, and the girl had the fruits of her search in her hand. Christina panicked, and did the only thing she could think of to distract him; she suddenly threw her arms around his neck.

'I am sorry I was less than truthful to you.'

Her mouth touched his. It was a ploy, but as his arm tightened instinctively about her, it ceased to be so. She trembled, her mind flooded by conflicting thoughts. She had never offered herself in such a way, had always tolerated what she could not avoid as her duty, but this had an exhilaration to it, and for all its falsehood it had more honesty than any kiss she had ever experienced. It was a brazen, shameless thing, but she was not the passive 'victim', and it felt good.

Hugh Bradecote did not think at all for a moment. He was taken completely by surprise, and his response was totally natural. She was beautiful; she stirred his desire, desire which had had no outlet for so long. As Ela's pregnancy had progressed, relations had ceased, with her being nervous and he unwilling to upset her in her condition. Then she was no longer there, and he had not thought of a woman in months, until he had seen Corbin FitzPayne's widow. She was pressed to him, warm and soft and feminine. It was hardly surprising that all the repressed longing surfaced.

Then thought, cold and logical, filtered through to his brain. Had he considered her behaviour true he would have been shocked at its forwardness, but somehow he knew it was not. He swung her round, hearing the door close, but though he knew he should go immediately to see who had tried to enter, her fingers were at the nape of his neck, and she was so yielding it was impossible not to linger for a few precious seconds. He pulled away, reluctantly, and strode to the door, leaving her standing in the middle of the floor, breathing fast and with a look of surprise as great as his upon her face.

The hall was empty. Bradecote tried to muster his thoughts. He did not know for whom he was searching, but she had clearly had a reason for him not to turn to the door. Out of the corner of his eye he saw his bags, not quite as he left them. His mouth drew into a hard, thin line. He knew before he checked, what must have happened. He felt angry, cheated.

She was standing just as he had left her when he flung the door fully open, so hard the hinges rattled. His face was thunderous as he approached her.

'Very cunning, my lady, but I cannot see what stealing evidence will avail you. Or were you just lustful?'

His words cut. Her eyes widened.

'I wanted to see who fletched the arrows. I . . . but I didn't do this because . . . how could you think . . . ? For a moment I thought you better than . . .'

The words were disjointed, as angry as his. They stared at each other, fuelled by their mutual inner turmoil. She saw the muscle work in his cheek, the steel of his eyes, and in her confusion she reacted as she was used to do: she flung up an arm, expecting to be hit. He froze, then swallowed hard, revulsion sweeping over him. His eyes narrowed in disbelieving horror. His voice, when he spoke, was no more than a hoarse whisper.

'You thought me capable of striking a woman?' He swung on his heel, and at the door flung his parting words. 'You do not know me at all, my lady.'

She stared at the emptiness after he had gone, and her voice was choked as she whispered to herself, 'No, I do not. But I wish to heaven that I did.'

Chapter Six

Walkelin saw the undersheriff descending the steps, and cast his serjeant a warning look. Catchpoll had his back to the hall and was laughing with the steward in a 'we are much the same' conviviality that worked wonders for getting information. Bradecote was in no mood to be convivial in any shape or form.

'When you have quite finished your little joke, Serjeant, we are for Wich. Get a move on.'

He did not even stop, but continued straight on to the stables in the manner of one who did not care whether he was followed or not, his brows still drawn in an angry frown and his jaw working silently.

The journey to Wich was accomplished in near silence. Walkelin did not think asking Serjeant Catchpoll why the lord Bradecote was in such a temper, even in a whisper, was a good idea. The undersheriff was not, in general, an ill-humoured man, from what he had seen of him. This morning, however, he was in as foul a mood as Walkelin had seen even the lord de Beauchamp with toothache. Perhaps, thought Walkelin, charitably, and staring at his back, he did have toothache.

Catchpoll was not so charitable, but had a far better idea why his superior was snappish. Well, she was a pretty piece, and to a man deprived of a woman for a long time . . . He judged, correctly, that Hugh Bradecote was not a man to merely use women casually. Her antipathy was pretty obvious, and not, as he saw it, based upon grief for a beloved husband. From all that had been said, she had been a good and caring wife to Corbin FitzPayne, but not doting in her affections. Having said which, he was the lord Sheriff's serjeant, and did not enjoy being treated like some idle man-at-arms.

Wich was, on the surface, about its normal business. The salt houses were busy, the brine still being brought up from the springs and stored in the 'salt ships', the hollowed-out tree trunks that kept the brine for the next boiling. The workers toiled as they always toiled, but there were worried faces turned to the sheriff's men by those in the streets. A pall hung over Wich, and it was not the smell of sulphur, urine and woodsmoke that gave it odour, but death.

'You know, I think that the townsfolk are getting more worried very quickly. They were not so scared, even yesterday. I wonder why?'

'Someone has been stirring the fires, and not under the salt pans.' Catchpoll hawked, and spat into the mud.

Walkelin frowned and then contorted his features, as Catchpoll gazed at him in apparent consternation.

'You in pain, young Walkelin?'

'No, Serjeant.'

'Then watch how you wriggles your face. It ain't becoming in a sheriff's man.'

Walkelin blinked and looked at Bradecote, who in normal

circumstances would have smiled, but on this occasion showed no emotion. The serjeant's apprentice closed his mouth and kept his own counsel.

They saw Walter Reeve in discussion with a tired-looking individual, who effaced himself quickly as the sheriff's officers came towards them.

'Master Reeve, good day to you.'

'And to you, my lord.'

'The town seems . . . nervous this morning.'

'None so surprising, my lord, in the circumstances.'

'Yet it did not seem quite so disturbed yesterday as we passed through.'

'Ah, well, when you think upon how likely more attacks must be, my lord, it makes for nerves, and if Worcester Abbey and grand lords are going to protect their salt, what chance for those whose masters cannot afford protection? 'Tis they as will be the target for the Ghost Archer.'

'The what? Since when has this man attained supernatural status?'

'My lord?'

'Who started the idea he was a ghost?'

'I couldn't say, my lord. But word spreads.'

'Like muck on the fields,' murmured Catchpoll, sneering. 'And it grows the weeds as well as grain.'

The reeve scowled, not sure of his meaning, and not pleased by the analogy. He turned back to the undersheriff.

'You have questions for me, my lord?'

'Yes, Master Reeve. Does salt leave the town every day?'

'Pretty much, my lord.' The reeve could not keep the pride from his voice. 'Far more productive we are than the men of Cheshire.'

'And on all routes?'

'Ah, no, not necessarily, though sometimes that is what occurs.'

'Are the carters and packmen employed by the various manors and religious houses as needed, or are they attached to particular salt houses?' Walkelin's question was posed confidently, but he cast his superiors an apologetic look for not requesting permission to speak.

'It varies. Some lords send in to find out when their salt is ready and send a cart, like my lord de Malfleur, and likewise some of the abbeys who take regular deliveries and sell what is spare. They may retain men, but most hire the men of Wich.'

'So do you think these attacks were simply made by men who waited in hope that a cart might come along?' Bradecote pressed home the follow-up. The reeve thought hard, as did Walkelin, who opened his mouth to speak but only emitted a sharp yelp as Serjeant Catchpoll trod on his foot.

'Mayhap they did, my lord.' He sounded keen to give the answer that the sheriff's men wanted. Seeing their expression, he added, 'Or mayhap they didn't and were a-lying in wait.'

'Which means?' Bradecote encouraged.

'They didn't mind waiting, my lord?'

Walkelin suppressed a snigger with a thin disguise of coughing. Bradecote sighed.

'No, Master Reeve. It means somebody told them when the pack trains and carts were leaving.'

'But, my lord, nobody here would do that.' The reeve looked horrified. 'That would be selling your friends and neighbours to their deaths.'

'Then give me an alternative suggestion.'

'Er, we are being watched, my lord, by dark forces.'

The reeve crossed himself, and looked about him nervously. Catchpoll rolled his eyes in despair. Once one person introduced the idea of ghosts, it became a form of madness and good sense, if it was ever possessed, went out the window. Everyone saw death as they went through their lives, and Catchpoll's work meant that he saw a lot more than average folk, but he had never felt the corpse was going to sit up and tell him what exactly happened. Some places, admittedly, had a feel that made your hackles rise, mostly the Old Places, where man had lived before even the Romans came, where the elves, so his grandsire had told him, were wont to inhabit. The aelfshot, however, suffered pains; they did not bleed in the dirt. The dead were in God's hands, and there was an end to it. The evil he had seen was all perpetrated by living, breathing folk, and it was among them that he would look for culprits.

Bradecote could see the reeve was going to be of limited value if he reduced everything to superstition. His voice was firm.

'Let us be clear, Master Reeve, the men who took the salt and killed those escorting it used real arrows, and were real men. They are here, or come here, and they find out when and where loads are heading out. Has anyone new been seen only in the last few weeks? Ask around and report anything out of the ordinary to me, to us.'

'The horse, my lord,' murmured Catchpoll, without any perceptible moving of his lips.

'And I wish it to be made known we are looking for a dark-grey horse, dulled-steel grey, with two white stockings . . .' Bradecote looked to Catchpoll.

'Those being on the off hind and near fore.'

'The animal belonged to the lord Corbin FitzPayne. If any

88

have seen it, or perhaps even bought it in innocence, we must be told. You are the reeve, so it is your duty to see this is spread among the populace.'

'Yes, my lord, I will do so, of course.'

The reeve was eager to show that no ill report should make its way to the Earl Waleran, and he did not think the undersheriff was impressed, thus far, with his actions. He would have said more, but hearing his name shouted, he turned. A thin-faced man on a showy chestnut that looked underfed, overworked, or both, was walking towards them. He ignored everyone but the reeve.

'Well, wormling, is he caught yet?'

The reeve winced.

'No, my lord, but here is the lord Undersheriff who is looking into matters. He is best placed to tell you all that goes on.'

The note of relief, as he palmed responsibility upon someone else, was evident. The horseman looked at Bradecote.

'You are not Fulk de Crespignac.'

'No, I am not.' The man's tone irritated him, and Bradecote's reply was not designed to soothe.

The man frowned.

'Then who are you?'

'I am Hugh Bradecote, now the Undersheriff of Worcestershire.'

Catchpoll, comprehending, coughed, and provided elucidation.

'De Crespignac died of the flux this summer, my lord. I am surprised you have not heard.'

Bradecote looked at Catchpoll, his eyes questioning. The serjeant clearly knew who this man was.

'Well, I know now.' He looked the new undersheriff up and down, assessing the man before him. He sniffed. 'I hope you know your business, Bradecote, for de Crespignac had experience in his favour.'

Bradecote bit back a retort. As a morning, it had not been good, and he had no time for this lord on his badly kept beast, whoever he was.

'Salt is both valuable and vital. I do not expect my salt to be subject to attack; in fact, I forbid it,' the man continued. He was sounding more imperious by the minute, but his voice was getting higher in register at the same time. Bradecote gave in and laughed, though there was not a trace of humour in it.

'Your prohibition is interesting, but unless you are in direct communication with the thieves, or have access to a Higher Authority, it is meaningless.'

'You cannot speak to me in such a way.'

'I just did.'

Bradecote was making no pretence at politeness. The reeve looked scared. Walkelin was curious as to what would happen next. Catchpoll intervened, though he would clearly have liked to watch it continue.

'My lord, this is the lord Rannulf de Lasson, of Collington and Wolferlow in the shire of Hereford.'

Bradecote could not contain his look of disbelief. Everyone knew Rannulf de Lasson was one of the wealthiest barons in the Marches, thanks to the lands on the Welsh borders brought to the family through his mother. In his mind, such a man should be dressed, if not in finery, then, well, not in garb that looked as if it had once been good but had long since become faded and lacklustre. And as for the horse . . .

'You have come in person to check upon your salt house and its well-being, my lord? That is very . . . caring of you.'

Catchpoll gave his superior a look of admiration mixed with belief that he had taken leave of his senses. De Lasson might look a mean longshanks, but he had power, and the ear of Miles of Gloucester, Sheriff of Herefordshire and a strong supporter of the Empress Maud. If de Lasson moaned to his sheriff and Miles of Gloucester complained to William de Beauchamp, Bradecote could find himself languishing in his lord's severe displeasure.

The thought had occurred to Bradecote, but in his current mood he could not care less. De Lasson gave him a look of loathing, tinged with perplexity. He was not used to anyone treating him with less than fawning deference.

'I am come to make sure what is mine remains mine, and that those in my service work as they should. Any excuse to slack and they will. If they think no salt will be sent from here for a while, they will be idle. My salt is plentiful enough for me to sell the excess to the Welsh in Buellt at a tidy profit. The money buys more sheep, the sheep mean a bigger wool clip, and the wool sells at an even better profit.'

Bradecote was vaguely shocked. The man thought like a merchant. Of course, it was good to have spare silver to purchase things but this sounded like a man to whom 'profit' meant more than 'honour'.

'So do you know the culprits you seek?' Rannulf de Lasson spoke as if to a menial.

'As yet, my lord de Lasson, no.'

'Then,' de Lasson sneered, 'I suggest you get about your business, rather than linger doing nothing here.'

With which he yanked his horse's head around and trotted away.

There was silence. Walkelin studied the muddy earth, since lordly arguments were above him. Catchpoll scratched his ear and the reeve feigned deep interest in a woman arguing with a man over a chicken, which was dangling by its feet from her hand.

Bradecote did not look at the receding figure. He fought his anger, and when his pulse was steady, addressed the reeve.

'As I was saying, finding this horse is very important, Master Reeve. If any have seen it within Wich or upon the roads, we will hear of it or I will be asking why not, and of you personally. Now, direct us to the salt houses involved thus far, those of Alcester, Bordesley, and Baldwin de Malfleur.'

The reeve, glad to see a chance of escape, almost fell over himself in an effort to be of help leading them to the salt houses belonging to the monks at Bordesley. The workers, bare-armed and sweating though the world outside was chill, were suspicious of the undersheriff. Those in authority were bound to find fault and want a better rate of work. Walkelin and Catchpoll, however, slipped into conversation easily, Walkelin helping a comely if slightly overblown young woman move wicker baskets of warm, damp salt to drain. Seeing that his presence was less than helpful, Bradecote withdrew, after a murmured exchange with Catchpoll.

Out in the clear air, he took a deep breath. He was tying himself in knots, unsure where to head next, and at the back of his mind was the look of fear on Christina FitzPayne's face. It made him feel sick to think she thought him capable of violence upon her. At the same time he knew he should not be thinking of her at all. She was clouding his brain. There was a tavern opposite, out of the wind, and yet not, he hoped, smelling of brine, or indeed tasting of it, as Catchpoll had complained at an alternative alehouse.

On this occasion he was spared both. The host, almost grovelling in his obeisance at the presence of such a personage, brought him an ale worth the supping, and which drew an honest compliment. The man went quite pink with pride.

'Well, 'tis kind of my lord to say such, but I pride myself on the quality of my ale, and those who care what they drink, drink here. Master Reeve does, of course, in his position, but to be truthful, after the first jug, he could not care less about the taste.'

'I'll vouch for its quality, to any who might ask, but in truth I am not likely to be asked.'

He saw Walkelin and Catchpoll enter, and ordered ale for each. Walkelin looked a little green about the gills.

'I never knew they used blood as well as . . .' Walkelin swallowed hard.

'Thought it would not affect you after the visit to the tanner,' Catchpoll commented, grinning.

'We don't put the leather on our food.'

'True enough.'

'I'm not sure I can face Mother's salted pork she has hanging, after that.'

Walkelin shook his head, mournfully.

'Oh, you will lad, you will, when she serves it up on a cold winter evening with apples and onions.'

'Put that way, Sergeant,' Walkelin managed a grin, 'I might after all.'

'So did we learn anything useful other than how they make salt?' Bradecote sounded wry rather than irritated, and Catchpoll hoped the ale had eased his superior's mood. He pulled a face and tugged an earlobe.

'Not so as we could say so, my lord. I would doubt very much if the information came from the simple workers in the salt houses. They do not seem to know exactly when the salt departs. They just keep making it day after day.'

'So who decides when it goes? It cannot be upon whim.' Bradecote wished that something would be simple.

'It seems, my lord, that when there is enough for a load, which has to either pay toll or show exemption, the salt house sends to inform the reeve who collects the payment, and goes to the packmen or sends to the lord for him to send his own wagon. De Malfleur sent a wagon, but the religious houses used the Wich packmen.'

'So only the reeve has the knowledge of what is leaving?' The undersheriff was vaguely hopeful.

'Wish it were that simple, my lord.' Catchpoll was at his most lugubrious. 'Thing is, everyone in Wich knows everyone else. Many lords and abbeys have more than one salt house, so they work together. If a load was near ready, half the town would be in the know of it for days beforehand, and the packmen know their next run.'

Bradecote swore, softly but impressively, in English. Catchpoll smiled.

'There's nothing in Foreign can beat swearing in the native tongue, not for getting it out the system, so to speak.'

'But it does not make us any nearer an answer, Catchpoll,' Bradecote sighed.

'As we came in we did see the reeve flitting like a bee to flowers in summer, passing on the need to know about the horse, though, my lord.' Walkelin wanted to be positive.

'Somehow I do not think we will learn much more this afternoon.' Bradecote sighed. 'We might as well return to the manor, I suppose.'

Walkelin grinned. Bradecote could not be as cheerful. After all, Walkelin's return to Cookhill meant fresh baking and making eyes at the goat girl, whereas he faced a frosty reception from a woman who might well throw things at his head. What made it perhaps worse was that a little voice inside him was shouting that seeing her angry was better than not seeing her at all. He felt he was sliding down a slippery slope, losing control, and it was all at the wrong time and in the wrong place. He had to concentrate upon the investigation, not be distracted by a woman who seemed intent on driving him mad, with both anger and, if he was honest, deep-seated longing.

'The trouble is,' muttered the undersheriff gloomily, 'I fear we are merely waiting for another attack, not preventing one.'

They retrieved their horses and were on the point of departure when the clatter of hooves made them turn. Eight men-at-arms, mailed and clearly trying to impress, cantered into the middle of the main thoroughfare. They each wore the badge of de Malfleur, the black flower upon scarlet. They were, as they had intended, the centre of attention. Catchpoll sneered, but conceded that however obvious, it was just the show of force de Malfleur would wish.

'Come to show off the advantages of their lord's protection. If you was a packman, you would be hoping they would escort you. Bully boys, mind, just look at 'em.'

'They cannot stop an arrow, Serjeant.' Walkelin sounded pious.

'Oh, many a man-at-arms has stopped an arrow, young Walkelin.' Catchpoll grinned at his own sally.

'But I meant . . .'

'I know what you meant, and you are correct, but even a good archer will not choose to take on trained soldiers, when there are easier options. No, those who pay will be safe enough.'

They trotted off upon the Salt Road, with hardly anyone watching them, though one who did smiled.

Chapter Seven

The sun was making sporadic attempts to pierce the cloud, but its sallow rays did not offset the chill of the wind, which still tugged at the remaining leaves, beggar's tatters upon beech, ash and oak. The occasional rising swirl of rattling leaves would spook one of the horses, but not so as to unseat the rider. They arrived at Cookhill with several hours of labour still left in the day, and found it busy. Walkelin took the horses to the stables to attend to them, and Bradecote and Catchpoll mounted the steps to the hall. It was only at this point that Bradecote realised that he had not informed the serjeant of the theft of the arrows from his bags. He was not sure how he wished to impart this information, and was still pondering it when they entered the hall and found lady FitzPayne entertaining a visitor, whose back was towards them. Bradecote felt uncomfortable, recognising that he had entered as one with a right to do so, not as a guest. The look she gave him told him what she thought of it, but her voice, which he had expected to be most unfriendly, was distinctly warm, and had an edge of relief to it.

'My lord Bradecote, you are returned.'

He frowned at her statement of the blindingly obvious. The man who had been sitting with her, engaged in some earnest conversation, turned. He was not known to Bradecote.

'My lord Jocelyn, this is the lord Undersheriff of the shire, who currently enjoys my hospitality,' she invested the term with deeper meaning, and lowered her gaze bashfully for a moment, 'whilst he hunts my husband's murderer, and, er, Serjeant Catchpoll, his . . . serjeant.'

Again, Bradecote wondered at her manner of speech, and his dark brows drew together.

'This, my lord Undersheriff, is my lord's cousin, Jocelyn of Shelsley, come to offer condolences upon my loss, and assistance, since I am but "a tragic, weak woman".'

Even Catchpoll looked astounded at her description of herself, though Bradecote could hear the dripping sarcasm and was almost tempted to laugh. He looked at the man. He was about a dozen years Bradecote's senior, with white hairs in his beard and greying locks, and with a look of sincere concern that Bradecote found quite sickly. The lady's change of attitude was now explained. Failing to catch the undertone, Jocelyn of Shelsley leant forward and patted the widow's hand. Christina looked at Bradecote. It was a warning, which said if there was so much as a hint of a laugh he would pay dearly. She smiled at her husband's kinsman, and he was apparently quite impervious to its forced sweetness. Bradecote was quite bemused. The man was either an almighty fool, or supremely confident of his own importance. No, in fact, he was probably both.

'My lord, I am sure the lady FitzPayne is grateful for your

kindness in visiting her in her grief. She has,' Bradecote paused for a moment, 'managed, managed well, but to know that you are . . . on hand, must be very . . . reassuring.'

'Indeed. She will be able to rely upon me to guide her, until Corbin's brother returns, if indeed he is able to do so.'

So that was the underlying reason for his concern. The good Jocelyn had hopes of controlling the manor, if Corbin's heir was dead in the East, and with the youngest brother choosing the cowl over the secular world.' Bradecote thought he would find the lady had her own ideas on that.

'The lord of Shelsley is remaining here for the night.' Christina FitzPayne spoke through nearly gritted teeth.

'Or longer, dear lady, if needed.'

Catchpoll noted the lady's knuckles showing white as her fists clenched. She ignored the comment.

'So there will be three of us to eat tonight, my lord Bradecote.' She stared at him. He had not looked forward to a meal with glowering looks that would poison his meat, but this might be worse. He murmured a lie of pleasure.

Catchpoll was enjoying this. In a plainer world he did not have to bother with a fear of treading on social eggshells. But then Catchpoll had a reputation to keep up, a reputation for blunt speaking and sheer bloody-mindedness that had taken years to cultivate. Bradecote was excusing himself upon some pretext, ignoring the lady's eyes pleading for him to remain. With a nod to Jocelyn of Shelsley, Bradecote extricated the three sheriff's men from the hall.

Out in the courtyard he quizzed the serjeant upon the visitor.

'Not a man as has come to the attention of the law, my lord, though he holds of de Beauchamp and so has been around on service. Surprised you have not come across him.'

Bradecote shook his head.

'No. But then, I have not met all the sheriff's vassals. Is he as dim as he looks? Surely he cannot be?'

'Well, if he truly did not see the lady's lack of, er, enthusiasm, he must be.' Catchpoll sniffed. 'But, you know, I think he is well aware, but putting a brave face on. As another vassal, and a kinsman, if the brother does not return, well he might be the one to inherit a tidy manor or two. He might think playing stupid has its advantages.'

Bradecote sighed.

'And I have the joys of his conversation at dinner.'

Reginald, son of Robert, savoured the ale. He sat quietly, avoiding drawing any unnecessary attention to himself, sitting half in shadow. He appeared absorbed only in his cup, but he listened, and listened attentively. What was causing much discussion was the instruction to be on the lookout for the steel-grey horse with the white stockings. It was a fine animal, but clearly a liability. The reeve ambled in. He was in loquacious mood even before his jug of ale. Having had a nerve-wracking day, he was glad to unburden himself to a more appreciative audience than his wife. He found the pressure from the undersheriff a worry, and the intervention of de Lasson had been a welcome relief. Retelling what then went on between the two elevated his position, since he had grasped the gist of it, and made him feel that someone else might end up in worse trouble than himself.

'My lord de Lasson will send his own men to guard his salt next time it is ready, you can be assured. He cannot afford to lose it if he has trade with the Welsh. They will look elsewhere soon enough if he fails them. And the de Malfleur men will be about their duties by Thursday to the priory at Leominster. Lucky the men with that cartload, and pity is for the poor souls, undefended upon the Worcester road.'

He rambled on about the Welsh in a way that would have angered any man of that lineage had one been present. The reeve was spared a beating, however. Reginald emptied his cup, wiped a hand across his mouth, and left, very content, and with a smile playing about the corners of his mouth.

Hugh Bradecote half filled his cup with wine. He needed a clear head for the morrow, and keeping up with the other man was out of the question. Jocelyn had drained three cups already and there was still meat upon the table. The conversation, if it could be called such, veered from slightly slurred monologues designed to show the lady how competent and great a lord Jocelyn of Shelsley was, in his own eyes at least, to effusive compliments upon his hostess's person, which she obviously found embarrassing. Bradecote's own efforts to keep the talk more general were ignored. He was desperately trying to find something to catch the man's interest, and thus it was he let loose the information that Baldwin de Malfleur had lost a salt cart and was now offering to provide guards for others, at a price. The lady Christina froze, one hand halfway to her mouth with a morsel of bread. Bradecote instantly regretted his thoughtlessness. She paled, and the bread was crushed between her fingers into a shapeless, doughy lump.

'If Baldwin de Malfleur has a hand in this, then you need look no further for your culprit, my lord.' Her voice was a husky whisper. 'Wickedness follows them, those of that name, like flies behind a dung cart.'

The slightly befuddled Shelsley looked owlishly at her.

'But, my lady, this cannot be. De Malfleur lost a cart.' He frowned, trying to concentrate upon his words. 'A man does not steal . . . his own cart. You are letting your own female intu . . . intu . . . thinking, take control. After all, none knew Corbin would be upon that road, and there was no reason for de Malfleur to want him dead.'

Bradecote said nothing. For all the wine he had taken, Jocelyn's words held true upon the latter points, though he would not wish to voice them out loud to the lady. She glowered at Jocelyn.

'You know nothing, nothing, I tell you. You think because a man is a lord, because he went to the Holy Places, that he is some paragon? And he had no reason to want my lord dead? Well, the fact that he was married to me would be enough.'

'I hardly think—'

'Correct. You hardly think.' She turned to Bradecote. 'Baldwin would want to hurt me, twist the knife, aye, and heat it red-hot first. Arnulf taunted him with me, for spite, when Baldwin was young and more hot-headed. My husband was happy to have his brother lust after me, as long as he thought Baldwin would not dare to do anything. Well, he drove him too far, but I would not be caught between the two. I told Arnulf when his little brother stole foul kisses, and Arnulf offered him Outremer or oblivion. So you see . . .'

'What you say may be true, but . . .'

'You doubt me?'

'No, I did not mean that. But, my lady, there is absolutely no way in which your lord could have been killed because of who he was. It was simply *where* he was.'

'If it was known from here? My lord had the journey planned some days beforehand.'

'There have been two other attacks since, one upon de Malfleur's wagon itself. No, truly, it cannot be that, though you never thought to tell me of the connection, did you?'

'I . . . no. But it does not mean that what I say now is less valid.'

'Not less valid, but there is no logical reason—'

'So you think me just a weak-headed woman too?'

Bradecote sighed. This was so difficult to explain.

'No, please believe me . . .'

'Believe you, whilst you do not believe me?'

She was flushed, and her voice had an edge, a tinge of panic.

'There, there, do not be distressed.' Jocelyn smiled and his voice was patronising. 'I shall protect you from this nasty Baldwin man if you are afraid of him.'

'Afraid?' Her lip curled in a sneer. 'If he came here I would kill him.'

She took her eating knife and stabbed it into the tabletop. Her kinsman blinked.

'But you are a woman. You need looking after.' He leered and belched. There was nothing protective in his tone.

Christina's complexion paled and the fire went from her. She looked suddenly vulnerable and distinctly uncomfortable. Bradecote frowned in surprise and then cursed himself for a fool. Of course she was worried. Her experience of men, intemperate men, would make her fearful of having the drunken Jocelyn in her hall while she slept. The mangled bread was discarded, and she picked listlessly at the remains of her meal. Jocelyn of Shelsley grew more voluble, giving his opinions upon a variety of subjects, driving Hugh Bradecote to the point where he could happily strangle the man with his bare hands just to get some peace. The hostess, by contrast, became monosyllabic. At the earliest opportunity, she rose to excuse herself, and Bradecote rose also, upon the pretence of going to open the door to the solar. As she passed him, he inclined his head and spoke quietly.

'Be easy, my lady. However drunk, he will not disturb your rest, I swear it.'

She did not look at him, but he heard her whispered thanks, and a stuttering intake of breath, as if she would succumb to tears in private.

In fact, the undersheriff did not have to waken to prevent any assault upon the lady's privacy, for two reasons. The first was that he barely slept, and that was entirely owing to the second; Jocelyn of Shelsley snored long and loudly in his wine-aided slumber. Bradecote lay wondering, in a detached way, whether the man might even dislodge rafters with his rumbling. At one point he got off his palliasse and went and shook him, hard. This produced a grumbling moan and a brief cessation of noise, but it resumed within minutes. Only shortly before dawn did Bradecote achieve a measure of rest, but he was a light sleeper and was awakened in the pale daylight by the sound of his erstwhile noisy tormentor moving around. He opened one eye. Jocelyn was nowhere near the door to the solar, but was pacing up and down, clearly lost in thought. Bradecote lay still, and wondered at it.

Serjeant Catchpoll, who had spent an enjoyable evening in the manor kitchen and had woken in a good mood, strode into the hall, evincing all the signs of a man ready for anything that life might throw at him. Bradecote groaned, and rubbed his tired eyes and stubbled chin.

Catchpoll watched his superior, who looked decidedly rough in comparison to the lord of Shelsley, and approached with the vestige of an obeisance.

'You shouldn't take so much wine, my lord.' He whispered in a fatherly way. 'Makes for a thick head on the morrow.'

The undersheriff grunted. 'For your information, Catchpoll, I was most abstemious. It was him,' he cast the other occupant of the hall a look of loathing, 'who drank till rambling and then kept me awake all night with his snoring, pox on him. I swear I was awake till nigh upon cock crow.'

'Ah.' Catchpoll's lips twitched a fraction, but his face remained otherwise blank, then his eyes narrowed as he surveyed the erstwhile snorer. 'You would have to say, my lord, that he does not look like a man with an ale-head. In fact, he looks remarkably fresh. Did he say anything of interest last night?'

'Well, it is clear he hopes FitzPayne's brother may be dead in the East and that he will get the estates. He cannot claim the widow, the Church would forbid it through consanguinity, should he not be married already, but that doesn't stop him hoping for some less formal relations, judging by his tasteless compliments.'

'Doubt she'd be amenable.'

'Of course she wouldn't be,' Bradecote snapped, running his

hand through his hair and wishing his brain would clear. 'But this is not our problem, the law's problem. We are for Wich, to see if Walter Reeve has news for us. Besides, our presence may steady nerves.'

'Only until the next attack, my lord, and I doubt very much they will cease.'

'Agreed, but there is little else to go upon, as yet. I will have speech with the lady, and then we will be away. Have the horses made ready, and drag Walkelin from the kitchen if you can.'

'You will not break your fast, my lord?'

'I have not the stomach for it as yet, but see if you can find bread, and perhaps cheese, that I can take with me.'

He nodded dismissal and, as Catchpoll departed, turned to find Jocelyn making his wishes known to the steward, who looked most uncomfortable.

'I am sorry, my lord, but I am my lady's man. I takes my instruction from her.'

Bradecote, in passing, murmured, 'If you have sense, my lord, you will not treat what is not yet yours as your own,' and headed for the yard, to force himself to full wakefulness with a pail of icy water from the well. It was not pleasant, but it certainly worked, and as he shook the water from his ears and eyes, he saw Jocelyn traverse the yard to the kitchen. He went back up into the hall, which was empty, and on to the solar. Out of politeness, he knocked before entering.

Christina FitzPayne sat with steepled fingers, her expression thoughtful, though it lightened a little with the undersheriff's entrance.

'I hope you slept well, my lady.'

'If my sleep was disturbed, my lord, at least it was not by him.' She jerked her head in indication of the unwelcome guest in her hall. 'And for that I thank you, truly.'

'We must be in Wich today, but you should not have cause to worry about him, other than he is already trying to run your manor.' He raised a hand as she started to get up. 'Oh no, do not disturb yourself. I think it has been made clear by your retainers that you are mistress here and it is your word they obey. You are well served.'

'I am, but the man is an insufferable, grasping fool.'

She spat the words derisively.

'Less a fool than appearances may indicate, my lady, so keep your wits about you. But I am here to ask that if you intend to use those arrows you stole, that you will do me the favour of letting me know what results from your questions.'

She reddened at the term 'stole', as the memory of that incident flooded back, but nodded.

'Be sure I will send round every fletcher in the area, my lord, though of course it may be that the man fletches his own arrows.'

'At least we will have tried, and if you are well enough to go in person you will be spared Jocelyn of Shelsley.'

She grimaced.

'He is so thick-skinned he would probably think I wanted him with me, as "protection". Ugh, horrible. If you find him dead, my lord, you will not need to look for who did the deed, but I will claim it as self-defence, for my sanity if not my flesh.'

'And no rushing about madly, mind.'

'You are a physician also, my lord?'

She spoke lightly, without venom.

'No, lady, but I am, I hope, a man of sense. Take a care to yourself, and I do not command but entreat.'

She smiled, and curtseyed, upon which, and for once in amity, they parted.

Chapter Eight

Waltheof the Fletcher sat in the best light outside his cottage, a neat pile of ash shafts at this elbow. He worked without rush, but with the ease of years in the craft. He looked up at the sound of hoof beats, and saw a gentleman astride a good bay horse, accompanied by a lady, and two men upon less favoured beasts.

'You there, fletcher! I would have speech with you.'

The man sounded imperious. The lady winced. Poor dame, he thought, wed to such a man, but then memory stirred and he recognised her. Ignoring the loud man, he stood and addressed her.

'My lady, it's sorry I am at your loss. The lord of Cookhill was a good man, God rest him, and will be sorely missed.'

'Thank you, Master Fletcher,' she was especially polite to highlight her disapproval of Jocelyn's manner. 'It was a great blow, and the sheriff's men are trying to find out who did the evil deed. I have here the arrow that killed my lord.' She withdrew the arrow, wrapped in cloth, from a quiver, which she had slung upon her saddle. 'I wondered if you recognised the fletching?'

Leaning forward, she placed it, carefully, in his outstretched hand. He bowed, and then studied the arrow as if it were some precious relic, turning it one way then the other.

'I did not make it, that is for certain, my lady, but it is well crafted. The binding to the flights is distinctive, I would say. Here, Father, can you make ought of this?'

He turned and placed the arrow in the hands of a gnarled old man whose hands shook perceptibly and who had to peer within inches to see the flights.

'What use can he be?' murmured Jocelyn, derisively. 'The old man is best part blind, and addled of wit, no doubt.'

Waltheof threw him an affronted look.

'My father learnt fletching from his own father, and first made arrows before even those that flew into the enemy at Tinchebrai, my lord. If his sight stops him working, his mind is as sharp as a bodkin head, even now.'

Christina's eyes were upon the old man. He closed one eye, looked down the alignment of the flights upon the shaft, pressed feather between finger and thumb caressingly, and studied the binding.

'There was a fletcher to the north of the shire made arrows just like this, but he has been dead, ooh, more 'n fifteen year, by my reck'ning.'

'The arrow is old?'

'No, no, my lady,' the old man chuckled, 'but I would not be surprised to hear that whoever made this arrow watched Tostig, and learnt from him.'

'How can you be so sure?' Jocelyn's disbelief was patent. 'You might know your own arrows, I will grant you that, but to know those from so long past . . .' He snorted, and pulled a face, which the old man did not see, though his son growled at him, lord or no lord.

Christina held up her hand to silence her unwanted companion, but the old man just laughed, a laugh like dry twigs cracking.

'A fletcher is not just some labourer, my lord, to follow the plough. He is a craftsman. We know the arrows of men who fletch in the shire, course we do. We repair damaged flights, for who would waste a good hunting arrow for the sake of one damaged feather, and so we learn, and we remember. Each fletcher is an individual. No, I would be pretty certain the arrow was made by a man from near Stone or perhaps over the Shropshire border.'

'We hunt a fletcher?' Jocelyn was sceptical.

'Hunt, my lord? If fletching is his trade I doubt he is the killer, especially since that has a bodkin head. If it was a blunt and you were looking for a man taking partridge, now . . . mind, there's archers, the finest archers, who likes to fletch their own. I would guess that is the sort of man you seek.' The old man was respectful in tone but refuted the idea.

'Thank you, I am indebted, Master Fletcher, and I am sure the lord Undersheriff will be also.' Christina smiled, although the old man could not see it. The son took the arrow, wrapped it and returned it. As she took it from him, she dropped coin in his hand.

'No, no, my lady, there is no need . . .' Waltheof would have returned the money to her, but she closed his fingers over it.

'Ah, but there is. We have kept you from your work, and you may have something important enough to find justice for my lord. There is no price upon that to me, Waltheof Fletcher.'

They left the fletcher and his father to their business, though as they rode away Jocelyn upbraided Christina for foolish generosity.

'What need had you to pay for the information? They must have made it all up, seeing you as soft-hearted and simple enough to believe any tale. It is not worth embarrassing yourself with the undersheriff by telling him this weaving of fiction.'

'You think it false, my lord?'

'Of course. You were taken for a fool, my dear.'

She grimaced at the affectionate epithet. This man made her flesh crawl, as it had crawled in the past. She knew men like Jocelyn far too well.

'So why did you accompany me today, my lord, upon this pointless enterprise?'

'Because you were so set upon it, and it might take your mind from . . .'

'Baldwin de Malfleur?'

'Well, yes. Distraction is best, to let your little mind settle.'

He smiled as he might at a child, but the look in his eyes was not paternal. She was angry, she was disgusted, and deep down not a little afraid. Her hands tensed, and her horse jibbed and sidled at the pressure on the bit. 'Thank you for your kind concern my lord, and your oh-so-generous estimation of my character. I am "simple", I am "soft-hearted" and have a "little mind", have I? I wonder that I have the strength to organise the provision of food in my hall.'

Her eyes flashed, and she set her heels to her horse's flanks and was away, her veil streaming behind her, leaving the men to follow in her wake.

*　*　*

The sheriff's men took the now familiar road into Wich without any great enthusiasm, and in no expectation of receiving any information of note. However, Walter Reeve proudly divulged that he had had Widow Herdman knocking at his door and reporting a strange man in her yard the night before, and the loss of two ducks. He made this sound as if their hunt was thereby at an end. The undersheriff and serjeant did not look as impressed as he had hoped.

'You said as I should pass on any information, my lord. Surely this—'

'Yes, I did, Master Reeve, but is it likely an archer who can drop a man at will would stoop to stealing ducks when he can keep concealed and hunt his meat in the forests?' Bradecote did not sound cheering.

'Well, it is all that is new for you, my lord.'

'And I thank you for it. Catchpoll, go and find out if this duck thief might be more than just . . . a thief of ducks.'

Catchpoll took directions to find Widow Herdman, and departed with an even greater degree of scepticism than his superior, and wondered why Walkelin had not been set upon the task. When he confronted her he scratched his chin. The old dame was vociferous in her claims. Most likely it was a common theft, but it had to be investigated since she claimed the thief was the 'Ghost Archer' and if they ignored her, who else would come forward with information?

'I knows what I knows and saw what I saw, and my ducks was stole by that "Ghosty Archer" everyone is talking about. My ducks was good 'uns, being fattened for Christmas. The likes of him would not want thin scraggy ducks, like her up the street has.'

The serjeant groaned inwardly. This was going to be a waste of time.

'So what happened, mistress?'

'I am trying to tell you. I came back from the house of Alys Plint, who is a-dying slow, poor woman, just after dark. I came in and went to strike a light when I heard the ducks quacking, all flippy-flappy and fearful, and my first thought was a fox had got among 'em. Well, I got me broom, and opened the door into the yard out back, and there he was, large as life, climbing over the wall with my two best ducks.'

'What did he look like?'

'It was dark.'

'Then how do you know he was the man we seek?'

'Well,' she paused, 'because he had good strong thighs.'

Serjeant Catchpoll was totally bemused, and could not resist asking why this indicated the master archer. The dame gave him a look of withering scorn.

'Why, because an archer has mighty strong muscles. I heard Martin Turner saying so, and he was a good shot at the butts in his youth.'

'Mistress, an archer has strong muscles in his arms and shoulders and chest.'

'No reason he can't have 'em in his thighs too, though. Besides, he admitted it.'

'What?'

'I called after him, cried thief and scoundrel, then I realised who he must be and shouted "Are you the Ghosty Archer?" and he waved as he disappeared. What more proof could you want?'

Catchpoll muttered under his breath about old crones with the wits of village idiots. He sighed, and obeyed his 'serjeant's hunch'.

'The woman with the "scraggy ducks" up the street, does she have a husband, or a son, or sort of lad who is swift?'

'Aye, my nephew, Baldric.'

'Your what? Are you saying this woman you call "her up the street" is your sister?'

'By marriage. My brother, long dead he is, and probably from her cookin', was fool enough to marry a Tillman wench, and them all idle cold-hearths.'

'Right. Whereabouts up the street?'

She told him.

'Now you stay here, and I will do some investigating and see what I can turn up. Thank you, mistress.'

The serjeant rapped upon a door up the street two minutes later. The woman who opened the door had a haggard look, and wisps of hair trailed from under her coif. She wiped her hands on her skirts, and asked his business in a wary way. Catchpoll had met her sort many a time, and it was a simple matter to overawe her with his importance and gain access to her home. It was dark and, he had to admit, very uncared for and dirty. He asked to see her son, but she said he was out back feeding the ducks.

'Well, let us go and see him there, shall we?'

Catchpoll sounded very reasonable. The woman looked suspicious, but did not try to prevent him. In the yard was a well-set-up youth, sat upon a stump of elm, stroking a very decently sized duck. The lad looked at Catchpoll, and the serjeant's heart sank. He had seen more wit in a sheep.

'You Baldric, lad?'

The youth nodded, and kept nodding as if stopping was a problem.

'Your aunt needs her ducks back, you know that, don't you?'

The youth looked very miserable, hugged the duck tightly and shook his head.

'You cannot take her ducks, son. Your mother should tell you that.'

'She has plenty,' the woman grumbled.

'Mistress, the lad is not to blame, but you, you have your wits. If you don't tell him he cannot take things he'll end in the noose, can't you see?'

She blenched.

'But he's not all there.'

'Aye, but there are those who want their vengeance more than true justice. Now you stay here, and let me take young Baldric to return the ducks where they belong. And since he cannot be trusted to tell right from wrong it is up to you as his mother, understand?'

She nodded dumbly.

'Come along, Baldric, those ducks are sad, missing their friends.' He held out a hand. 'Bring them home with me to your aunt.'

The lad got up. He did indeed have good strong thighs. Pity it was his head was so weak.

His aunt was aghast, at first angry, then, when she saw how he looked at the birds, shook her head.

'Poor daft soul he is.'

'Well, I take it you don't want to make anything of this, mistress, him being simple, and kin?'

'No, Serjeant.'

She hung her head in the face of his stare.

'Good. Well, if you take a care to your brother's son, as well

116

as his mother, who is, as you said, a poor house-wyf, he has a better chance in life. Good day to you.'

Catchpoll returned to find Walkelin and the undersheriff trying to persuade a bellicose-looking individual that the undersheriff's own horse was not the grey for which everyone was meant to be on the lookout. Bradecote glanced at Catchpoll, who shook his head.

'Wild duck chase, my lord.'

'That's far enough.'

Reginald had thought to arrive early at the meeting place, but the Archer was earlier. The voice sounded lighter, less serious than before. He halted.

'You are here in good time, Archer.'

'Ah, I find it safer so, Master Messenger.'

There was something in the tone that told Reginald that the Archer was smiling. It irked him.

'I have your next task.'

'And the payment?'

'Of course. Tomorrow, you strike upon the Worcester road, before Hussingtree. They are setting off about the usual time in the forenoon. Here is the payment, as promised, half in advance. I will meet you by the stricken ash the far side of Ombersley an hour before dusk in the evening, the day after the feast of St Luke.'

He threw the purse of coin and turned away, just so that the Archer did not give him orders.

'And I would have you—' he stopped. A blackbird pinked its alarm call, and then there was silence, the silence of standing alone upon the road.

* * *

The sheriff's men trotted into Cookhill quite early in the afternoon. Their morning in Wich had shown their presence, but beyond that had achieved nothing. They had no useful line of investigation and feared they were fighting a losing battle. Christina FitzPayne had asked the steward to direct the undersheriff immediately to her solar, where she had withdrawn upon her return, making no effort to entertain Jocelyn of Shelsley. He had merely shrugged and commented that she must be exhausted and should take to her bed . . . alone. This last comment had nearly driven her to throw a pitcher at him. She stomped away in high dudgeon, and did not see his slow smile.

Bradecote took the hall steps with a speed that Catchpoll interpreted correctly. Jocelyn sat in the hall, in the lord's seat upon the dais, his booted feet upon the table as if he owned it, and smiled over his cup at Bradecote, though the smile became fixed as the law officer passed him by and went directly to the solar.

Christina sat with some stitchery, though she had not set a single stitch. She looked up, and the eagerness in her face made Hugh Bradecote's heart lurch. He had seen her sad, tired, amazingly angry, and smiling as a cover, but this was a genuine look that said she was glad to see him. Her lips parted in a smile, and she stood up, letting linen and needle fall to the floor.

'You asked to see me, my lady?'

'I think I have information, my lord, perhaps not much, but something. I hope it pleases you.'

Bradecote was guilty of a thought worthy of Serjeant Catchpoll, and coloured.

'I . . . er . . . am sure it must, my lady.'

'I went to four fletchers in the area.' She pulled a wry face. 'And guess who decided he had to come too?'

'Ah.'

'Yes. He would have made any poor man shake his head and deny his own trade. But at the last, the fletcher's old father, when he inspected the arrow, said the fletching and binding were like those of one Tostig, at Stone up near Kidderminster.'

'Tostig in Stone. Right.'

'No, no, my lord, I fear it is not as simple. Tostig died years ago. The old fletcher says, though, that he would swear that whoever fletched the arrow that killed Corbin had learnt to do so with this Tostig. If the Archer fletches his own, then he must originate from Stone or thereabouts. Does this help?'

He smiled at her enthusiasm. Even if it did not solve their problems it was something for them to chase, and might just set them after the right hare. He tried to deny to himself that if it gave her cause to smile at him like that it was a huge help, even if not in the investigation of crimes.

'Well, it is more than we have thus far, my lady. Today I had to persuade a man I was not riding the grey horse we seek. If we know where our man originated it might be possible to work out his identity. After all, he must have shown promise with the bow in his youth.'

'I fear you say this merely to make me feel less useless, my lord Bradecote.'

'No, it is true enough, but I will not lie and say our path lies clear before us. My lady, I cannot promise you success, only that we will do the best possible. If the attacks ended now, well, I do not rate our chances highly. The more often they take place, the more likely for them to leave a clue, make a simple

119

mistake, and then we will have our archer and the gang.'

'That means more poor men will die.' Her face grew solemn.

'It does, and I am sorry for it.'

'The world is full of such wickedness, sometimes it seems black.'

Her voice was sorrowful, and the eyes she raised to his were moist. He was filled with a desire to protect her, comfort her, shield her from the blackness that had haunted her past. There was a foot or so between them. They did not touch, not even by so much as a fingertip, and yet, in that moment, they felt as close as if they had kissed. She blushed; he looked at his feet, and cleared his throat.

'I should . . . um . . . that is . . .'

His tongue tied itself in knots. Christina found release in the simplest manner; she laughed. It was a soft, pleasant sound tinged by neither bitterness nor sarcasm. He grinned, boyishly, and in that moment she knew, more certainly than she had ever known anything, that here was a man who would never hurt her, a man to whom she could give, and she wanted him. It was a revelation that made her tremble. He frowned slightly, unsure what would happen next. She opened her mouth to speak, and at that moment the door opened, and Jocelyn of Shelsley ambled in, announcing loudly that his poor cousin's widow was not fulfilling her duties as a hostess.

'I mean, you may be closeted with my lord Bradecote here upon shrieval business, but, by the Rood, I am left loitering, and with not so much as a jug of good ale for company. Look,' he belched loudly, and held up an empty pitcher. 'It is not fair, I tell you. I am kindred. I have rights. I demand—'

'No right, my lord, kinsman or no, to demand in my solar. I shall be with you directly, and will provide you with more

120

ale to slake your no doubt prodigious thirst. In the meantime you will leave us.'

He gaped like a landed fish, blustered and withdrew, muttering. Hugh Bradecote watched her. She was regal, magnificent, but the moment of unexpected intimacy was gone, though not forgotten. He smiled wryly.

'I fear he is jealous, my lady, that I am welcome where he is not.'

As the words hung in the air for a fraction of a breath, he realised their depth of meaning. His eyes widened, and, stammering an excuse, he made to leave.

'My lord,' her words halted him and he turned. 'You,' she paused, and her voice dropped to a whisper, 'are.'

Her cheeks suffused; she dashed past him into the hall, calling in an unnaturally casual voice for a maidservant.

Jocelyn of Shelsley saw the flushed cheeks and pursed his lips, for he held his drink far better than he let show. He had initially assumed the undersheriff was just entertaining himself, as he was, in the presence of a pretty female. He now sensed something more, and had found out that Bradecote was wifeless. It galled him, and he railed against the laws of affinity that barred him from taking his cousin's comely widow to wife. If Robert FitzPayne did not return to claim his inheritance, and crusade was a dangerous enterprise, he could make claim to this, the caput of Corbin's honours. But there was also the outlying land to the south, near Evesham, which would go as the widow's portion. Realistically, he had hoped Christina would ask to take the veil and give that and her inheritance from de Malfleur to a house of nuns. It seemed less of an insult than another man getting them. Then a worse thought occurred to him. Bradecote was the sheriff's vassal, just as he was. What if the undersheriff solved the salt thefts and was basking in de Beauchamp's favour? Might a grateful lord not reward him with both the woman and the manors? It was a horrible thought, one which Jocelyn tried to dismiss, but which lingered like a foul taste in the mouth. Thankfully, he saw his way clear to preventing the situation. His face relaxed into a sly smile. It would even be enjoyable.

Bradecote emerged a minute or so later, his features schooled into nonchalance even as his mind raced. He ignored Jocelyn and strode through the hall and out to find Catchpoll.

The serjeant was already ingratiating himself with the cook in a manner that Walkelin would have been wise to learn. The serjeant's apprentice relied upon boyish eagerness to gain titbits and second helpings. There was not even the memory of boyishness to Catchpoll, and yet he could be most efficient when he set his mind to it. There were apple dumplings being prepared, which happened to be one of Catchpoll's favourite sweet dishes, and he was angling to make sure he received a generous portion.

Bradecote leant against the doorway and watched a master in action. Catchpoll could be brusque, intimidating, downright offensive when he chose, which was most of the time. Yet he had the ability to be one of the crowd among his fellows. Here he was, making much of his missing Mistress Catchpoll's cooking, and implying that his life was not his own at the hands of the oppressive nobility. Well, the sheriff certainly ordered him about at will, but he had the same power over the undersheriff. Bradecote hid a smile and decided to play along with the image.

'Serjeant, I want words with you, now.'

The tone was tetchy. Catchpoll turned in genuine surprise.

'My lord, I—'

'Now, not when you choose to stop talking about puddings.'

At first nonplussed, Catchpoll had caught the glint in his superior's eye, and had to fight the urge to grin. Instead, he adopted a long-suffering demeanour, threw the cook a look which said 'see how I am treated', and followed Bradecote into the yard.

'You are clearly a difficult man to work for, my lord.'

'Yes, I thought I gave that impression rather well.' Bradecote smirked. 'But if you do as well out of that charade as you hope, remember to have Cook put away some dumplings for us to take with us tomorrow.'

'Seems a reasonable request, my lord, since you worked for them.'

'Mmmm, and by the by, remember this time it was you who dragged me from my manor.'

'At the lord de Beauchamp's command, mind.'

'True.' Bradecote's expression became more serious. 'And I think we might have the glimmer of a clue about our archer, thanks to the lady FitzPayne.' He realised he would now have to reveal the arrows were no longer in his possession. Well, Catchpoll did not need to know precisely how the lady obtained them. 'Yes, I let her have the arrow that killed Corbin FitzPayne so that she might visit the local fletchers and see if any recognised it. She is known to some and they would not hold back from assisting the widow.'

'Is that so, my lord?'

Catchpoll's scepticism was clear.

'Er, yes. And it has proved a potentially useful exercise.

She found a fletcher whose father recognised the manner of fletching and binding as one used years back by a fletcher up in the north of the shire, close by the Shropshire border. His view was that the man who made the arrow learnt the craft from the fletcher Tostig, alas now dead.'

'Hmmmm,' Catchpoll pulled his ear ruminatively. 'Well, it helps and doesn't. If we go to where the fletcher worked there may be others who recall a young archer who learnt from him. I am assuming we are not thinking a fletcher by trade is doing this.'

'I agree, though knowing the name of our man is only a start. It is more than we have so far so I want us to set off at dawn tomorrow. Warn Walkelin he will miss his breaking of fast.'

'Yes, my lord.' The death's head grin appeared. 'Hope he won't just fade away through starvation.' Catchpoll decided it was better not to ask what had occasioned this thawing between the undersheriff and their hostess, but since it had clearly put the lord Bradecote in a far better temper, it was a good thing.

Jocelyn of Shelsley seemed in ebullient mood over the evening meal, his earlier faux pas a thing of the past. It was noticeable that he gave little scope for Bradecote to engage the lady of the manor in conversation, but it did spare her his condescension. She was, however, the subject of effusive compliments, which made her squirm and blush, and cast Bradecote fleeting looks of embarrassed anguish. The lord of Shelsley was a bore, but if listening to him protected the lady, Bradecote was happy to stand bluff.

'I was wondering if I might accompany you to Wich in the

morning? I do not possess a salt house, but the salt I purchase comes from there, of course. I was wondering if production is curtailed whether the price of salt might rise. I would be interested to see how they fare in Wich, and travelling the Salt Roads is best done in numbers at present.'

Bradecote looked less than enthused by this, but saw the relief upon Christina FitzPayne's face.

'To be sure, you may do so, but I do not think you will find much to detain you and we are heading north for the day.'

'To where Tostig the Fletcher worked?' Christina FitzPayne made no attempt to conceal the excitement in her voice.

'To Stone, my lady, yes. There is a chance someone may recall a lad who learnt the craft from Tostig, and was an able archer.'

'So then you will know the name of the man who is killing so many.' Jocelyn paused, his manner suddenly far less friendly. 'That will be such a comfort.'

Bradecote flashed him a look of irritation.

'No comfort, but from such beginnings are endings found.'

'And how many lives have been ended thus far, my lord Undersheriff?' That stung, as he knew it would. 'Must be nigh on a dozen by now.'

Christina FitzPayne stood abruptly.

'That, my lord, is in poor taste when you sup in the hall of one of the victims. And nor would it show my hospitality to let you insult a man who is here, not by kinship, but at my invitation. You will withdraw those words, or you will leave my hall.'

'You would not cast me out into the darkness, now, would you?'

'Find out, my lord, if your courage permits.'

'You are overwrought. I humbly apologise, of course, both to you and to the estimable lord Bradecote. I spoke unthinkingly.'

Bradecote considered the last comment far from the mark, but nodded an acceptance. Christina could not but do the same, though it rankled. At least he would be away for the following day. The atmosphere remained cool, however, and shortly afterwards Christina withdrew to the solar. Jocelyn watched Bradecote's eyes follow her to the door, and considered it an evening well spent.

Chapter Nine

Jocelyn was less pleased at being shaken when the dawn was only just breaking as a thread of pale light upon the eastern horizon. In truth, Bradecote could have waited a little longer but rousing the snorer early seemed justifiable revenge, and gave him at least a moment's pleasure.

'Time to rise, my lord, for we have a long day before us and depart upon full light.'

Jocelyn of Shelsley made a groaning noise indicative of how much he regretted that statement, and Bradecote grinned in the semi-darkness and listened to the low grumbling that ensued with a depth of pleasure out of all proportion to the deed.

It was only as they were about to depart that Christina came to the top of the steps, her shoulders wrapped in a fur to keep out the chill, for the morning was distinctly cold. Their breaths hung upon the air as if the ghosts of words, and if Bradecote and Christina exchanged but formal phrases, he knew she was watching as he led the party out of the gate.

Catchpoll watched Jocelyn of Shelsley's back, and was

grateful that he could do so. Listening to him would have driven him to some very impolite language. There were, he thought, certain advantages to not being of the lordly class, and not having to seem to listen to such a windbag was one of them. That Bradecote had not turned upon the man and threatened to ram his teeth down his throat if he did not use them to bite his tongue showed remarkable restraint, in his considered opinion. He was fairly sure the man meant to goad by prattling on in such a way, and wondered whether the lack of animosity between the undersheriff and the widow had anything to do with it. The lord of Shelsley was the sort of dog-in-a-manger type who would resent another man having what he could not, and if he sensed Bradecote forming a tenderness, then he would be keen to make things difficult.

'Of course, this day to Stone is a wild goose chase, though it will pander to the lady's wish to seem to be doing something. And you have no better use for the day, I assume?'

Bradecote did not reply, which was taken as confirmation, but his jaw was set, and the older man smiled to himself.

'Then perhaps you might as well lay claim to be doing something. I would be very surprised if the old fletcher could tell arrowhead from goose quill, so poor were his eyes. Did the lady not tell you he had to peer within inches of the thing to see it? Oh well. The horses will enjoy the exercise.'

Catchpoll could see his superior's back stiffen, and was conscious of a feeling akin to sympathy, which was most irregular in him. The undersheriff urged his horse into a canter, the quicker to reach the 'haven' of Wich where this incubus could be abandoned.

* * *

Walter Reeve was a worried man. Several lords had beaten a path to his door over the last few days, eager to blame him personally for something over which he saw he had absolutely no control. There were mutterings about collusion, hints of sending baleful reports to the Earl Waleran. He was beset by the law and the landed, all telling him he was not doing enough, when there was nothing he could do.

He watched the packmen load their beasts to head south to Worcester. They had the look of the condemned about them, in contrast to the carter and his ox leader, basking in the security of Baldwin de Malfleur's men-at-arms. In normal circumstances such bully boys as they appeared to be, all swagger and arrogance, would be avoided by peaceable men such as the carters and packmen, but these were not normal circumstances. Already one had caused trouble by taking liberties with a wench in front of her swain, and drawn steel to ensure his inactivity. It did not bode well.

A small crowd gathered. Women wept. He had seen more jollity at a hanging. The carters departed toward Leominster, with their ostentatious guard. The packmen left with every sign of reluctance, and the salt workers returned to their labours heavy-hearted.

The sheriff's officers and Jocelyn of Shelsley arrived almost as the packmen departed. A few resentful glances met them, but they could not escort every salt load out of the town, or pick out certain ones, seeming to show favouritism. Walter Reeve began his self-exculpation before they had even halted their horses.

'I have no news, my lord, but unless it is brought to me, what can I achieve? I am at a loss. I do everything within my power, but in this I am helpless.' He spread his hands.

'Hopeless, more like,' muttered Walkelin, under his breath.

'But I shall expect you to send word to me if you do hear anything, anything at all, Master Reeve. We are heading north to Stone, but will pass through Wich this afternoon. In the meantime, we leave my lord Jocelyn here, who wishes to . . . pass the day in Wich.'

Before the reeve could say anything, Bradecote had wheeled his horse, and the much relieved trio were cantering out of the town on the northern road. Jocelyn of Shelsley looked down at the worried reeve and smiled, which somehow worried the man even more.

'How you kept from cutting out his tongue, I do not know, my lord,' chortled Catchpoll, now riding abreast with Bradecote. 'About as welcome as a dose of pox, he is. If that is what he is like of an evening . . .'

'Oh, he varies between garrulous ale-sot, which, as you first noticed, Serjeant, is more act than reality, and seemingly solicitous guest who has the tongue of a snake and the poisoned fang to match. The lady FitzPayne finds him disturbing, and if I were a woman, I think I would be of her mind also. He has more faces than a pair of dice, and they keep changing to keep you from the man beneath.'

'Your natural schemer, my lord, and not usually one who risks his own neck if he can send others to do so for him.'

'Very true, very true. Let us dismiss him from our minds for a few hours at least, and concentrate on the identity of our archer.'

The Archer's fingers were cold. He blew upon them and rubbed them together. A roebuck, grazing by the side of the track, was alerted to the slight sound. It raised its head, ears twitching, and prepared for flight. The Archer smiled.

'You are fortunate, my friend, for today I have other targets,' he whispered, with a smile.

The soft words were enough to send the animal darting into the nearest thicket. The Archer sighed. Venison stew would have been good in this autumnal weather. He settled back into silence, and waited. The men who were to steal the salt arrived with as little stealth as rampaging boar, and halted at his whistle. They concealed themselves in the undergrowth, after a fashion, but the Archer grimaced. True concealment was as he used, so that a man might pass within two handspans and not know anyone was there.

The packmen were nervous. It was a woodland road and they knew they were vulnerable. They were trying to get the laden ponies to trot, as if the slight increase in speed would give them protection. The Archer took his first arrow, caressed the flights with a loving finger, and nocked it. He took aim, calmly, focussed entirely upon the path of its flight to the target. He loosed, and heard the arrow singing in its freedom before thudding home. Only as he reached for the second arrow did he become aware of the traveller coming from the opposite direction, a stout staff in his hand. The Archer took down the second packman and nocked a third arrow, but as he took aim he eased the tension. The stick was being swept before the man's path, ensuring he did not trip over root or stone. The man had halted, and now cried out.

'Who is there? God's Grace be upon any who take pity on a blind man.'

The thieves leapt out of the bushes, one brandishing a

staff and clearly intent upon striking the sightless man.

'Hold there.' The Archer's words flew as urgently as his arrows. 'If you so much as aim a blow, I'll drop you where you stand. Be about your business and go.'

'But . . .'

'Where you stand.'

The blind man, confused and frightened, stood stock-still.

The cudgel-bearer drew back, and turned upon the calling of his name by one of his companions, to help cast the bodies into cover. With much noise, they led the ponies away. The blind man still stood, listening, unsure. A robin sang upon a bough as if what had just passed was unimportant. The Archer stepped from his cover.

'Be at ease, friend, I mean you no harm.'

The man turned to the sound.

'What has happened?'

'Nothing that need concern you. Be on your way, and pray for the souls of the dear departed.' He reached out and took the man's hand, pressing silver coins into the palm. 'God go with you.'

The man's fingers closed upon the largesse, and he smiled bemusedly.

'And with you also, friend.'

Unlike Reginald, he heard the Archer depart.

The sheriff's men reached Stone before noontide. It was a small village, and they made their way to the manor hall out of courtesy. Giles le Gris was absent, but his lady, nervous but attentive, offered them hospitality and any assistance they might require. She looked too young to have known the old

132

fletcher, and this indeed proved to be the case, but the manor steward was an old retainer, and he both recalled the man and could name those others who had had dealings with him and still lived.

'We are trying to find out if any recall a lad who learnt the fletching craft from old Tostig.' Catchpoll spoke with a degree of nonchalance.

'His apprentices?'

'No, probably not.' Bradecote did not want to be taken down that path too early. 'More like a young man who was good with a bow and wanted to fletch his own arrows.'

The steward frowned, his thick grey brows forming a solid bar across his forehead.

'Well, that would be more difficult, my lord, if they wasn't with him all the time. There are always the young men who go after pigeon with their blunts, and some are quite able. Young Edwin, now he is a very good shot.'

'You need to think back,' Catchpoll saw the steward drifting from the point, 'perhaps even twenty years.'

'Let me see, now.' The old man pursed his lips. 'There was Turold, he was good . . . but he died three years back, coughing blood. And Aelward, though he was not from here. Good lad, came to live with an aunt after his father . . . died. But he went away years back, off to the Holy Land with the lord of Clent, and I would wager man, like master, died there. He has not been in the village these seventeen, maybe eighteen years, and his aunt is long dead now, poor woman. Dunstan is still here mind, though he is a wheelwright nowadays, with little time to nock an arrow. Would you like to speak to him about Tostig?'

Bradecote assented, in no small measure just to avoid further rambles. The steward went off purposefully, if slowly, and returned some ten minutes later with a broad, well-muscled man with a deep bass voice. He made a stiff obeisance to the lady and, upon introduction, to Bradecote.

'You wished to speak to me about Tostig Fletcher, my lord?'

'Yes. Does this look like one of his arrows?' Bradecote nodded to Walkelin, who withdrew the arrow from its wrapping. 'We know it is newer, but is it his style?'

'Bless me, yes. Uncanny that, to see one fresh after all these years. As if he were here this moment.'

The big man crossed himself, and looked unnerved.

'Tell me, Dunstan,' Catchpoll did not want another diversion into the supernatural, 'did you know young Aelward, who learnt fletching from Tostig?'

'Aelward from over Rushock?'

Catchpoll looked to the steward, who nodded.

'Quiet, he was. Used to go off on his own a lot, tracking the animals. Mind you, he learnt that from his father, of course. Came here when he was twelve after the business was over.'

'What business?'

'With his lord, Arnulf de Malfleur. Aelward's father was a hunter, helped his lord whenever he went out to hunt, and a man like the lord of Rushock, well he needed help hunting. Aelward said he scared the game. One day he found his hunter had brought down a buck that was ailing, the eye was damaged and poisoned or some such. The hunter would have brought it for his lord, but de Malfleur found him carrying it, and decided it was theft. He put the man's eyes out himself, then and there, and laughed as he did it. The poor man lived, but only a few months. The forest was

134

his life and it was torn from him with his sight.' Dunstan shook his head. 'Cruel, and unfair.'

The wheelwright had everyone's attention. Catchpoll already felt that this Aelward was their man, if he wasn't bleached bones in the desert.

'Go on, tell us about Aelward and Tostig.'

Bradecote sounded eager.

'Not that much to tell, my lord. He was a good archer, I will say that, even when a stripling, but he was . . . odd. I never saw him kill for sport, if you see what I mean. As lads we would have a try at all sorts – fox, pigeon to eat, even fish in the stream. But Aelward only ever wanted the true shot, and to eat. He said shooting fish was a shame on the archer's skill, beneath him. He was, well, like the difference between the average man who goes to Mass and the man who takes the cowl.'

'And he would make an arrow like this?' Bradecote had to be sure.

'Oh yes, my lord, as I would, as any man would who learnt from Tostig.'

'And he went away?' Walkelin wanted the end of the tale.

'Yes, for his skill was seen by the lord Ivo, Ivo of Clent, a mite west of here. He took him as his own hunter, and then when he went on to the Holy Land, Aelward went too. S'pose he must be dead now. Ivo of Clent was killed, oh, was it three years back?'

'It was four years, my lord,' murmured the lady le Gris, softly. 'Killed his poor mother, did the news.'

'And nobody has seen Aelward here since? You are sure of that?'

'If he came, my lord, I reckon as I was nearest he had to

135

a friend, so he would have found me out. I would swear an oath on that.'

'Then tell us what manner of man was Aelward to look at, when you saw him last.'

'Oh, Aelward was your average sort of fellow, would have been the skinny sort if he had not the build from his archery. He was proud of the fact he could manage a man's draw weight long before the rest of us.' Dunstan grinned. 'Not that I would have much problem matching him now.'

The wheelwright flexed impressive biceps, and strong forearms, but then coloured. Walkelin, at least, showed admiration.

'Sorry, my lord. Yes, well, as I said, he was the sort of lad who blended in, be it in the forest or in a crowd. You could lose him in an instant. He was of a common height, straight, rat-brown hair, good teeth, I will say that, very even. When he smiled, which wasn't often, he had a smile that maids would, well, not stay maids long for.'

'Did he use that?' Catchpoll wondered if the archer might be in 'comfortable' lodgings with some woman. 'Was he popular with the wenches?'

'Aelward!' Dunstan laughed. 'Bless me, no. Very shy he was with anything in a skirt. Lost his mother very young and never really learnt anything about them, how they think, you know, until he came to his aunt. Took some getting used to on both sides, but she was genuinely fond of him. If Aelward found himself a woman,' he shook his head, 'it would be a thoughtful one who could understand his need to be alone a lot.'

There was a silence. Dunstan considered a man he had

known half a lifetime ago, and the sheriff's men tried to envisage the man for whom they were hunting.

'That would be about all I could say, my lord.'

Dunstan, having said all that he could do upon the matter, wanted to get back to the secure peace of his wheelwright's workshop, where the only unknown was whether he should have left his apprentice to fit the felloes on the new wheel for the Widow Thorn's barrow. He was glad to be dismissed, with thanks from the undersheriff.

Lady le Gris provided them with ale and meat, clearly keen to be able to report to her lord that she had been the model of hospitality to the sheriff's representatives, and heaved a sigh of relief at their departure.

There would be no moon, so the three men took part of the way at an easy canter, giving themselves more chance to reach Cookhill before total darkness. Walkelin's ungainly mount was leaving him sore in places he would rather not discuss, and he was glad when they slowed for a space. In between considering his aching body, Walkelin had been considering the advance they had made.

'What I cannot see, my lord, is how much use this is to our catching the salt thieves.' He spoke confidently. 'We know, or at least have a good guess at, the name of the archer, but we cannot trot up and down the Salt Ways calling his name and telling him to give himself up to the noose.'

'You mind your ways and words, young Walkelin,' Catchpoll growled. 'That sounds too much like you setting yourself up on a par with your betters.'

Walkelin coloured to the roots of his ginger-red locks.

'I am sorry, Serjeant, my lord. It was not my intent, I . . .'

'No matter, Walkelin. What you say is true.' Bradecote sighed.

'In a way, my lord, it does tell us that hunting for him is a waste of time.' Catchpoll had clearly been thinking without recourse to his facial contortions. 'I had wondered if we should follow a few salt wagons at a small distance, close enough to hear anything untoward, but I doubt not our archer would melt away.'

'It would save life, just as paying de Malfleur does,' sighed the undersheriff.

'Yes, my lord, for a while. But we cannot do this without end. If they did not die now, they would die in a week's time. Only by catching these men do we halt this.'

'The archer, Aelward, is a lone hunter, not a pack wolf, yes?' Walkelin stuck to his line of thought.

'That is what the wheelwright said, yes, Walkelin.' Catchpoll looked suspiciously at the man-at-arms, as if he might say something dangerous. 'So that leads you to what?'

'It leads me to wonder why he associates with the others.'

'He could not take the ponies or the carts alone, wiltbrain.'

'Ah, but why take them at all, Serjeant?' Walkelin ignored the insult. 'I said it earlier and say it again. This man has a skill for which lords pay. Why take to this life if he is not already outside the law? And even if that is the case, why not kill wealthy travellers encountered upon the road, rob them of coin and possessions? He only attacks the salt trade. So where is all this salt going? And why?'

Catchpoll smiled slowly. It was the sort of smile that could mean many things. On this occasion it meant that Walkelin basked in the glow of Catchpoll's approval.

'I knew I was right picking you for the craft, despite the hair.' He watched his protégé grow pink, the hair clashing with the colour of his cheeks. 'You think clear, not in a rush, but clear. Now you just learn to think mean, meaner than the people you are after, and you will do well,' he paused, 'in a few years.'

Bradecote was only listening with half an ear. What Walkelin had said was true. There seemed no sense to stealing the salt. Indeed, where were they putting it? They had stolen from the bodies, but with the exception of Corbin FitzPayne they were men not worth stealing from, so why them? He voiced his thoughts.

'Why does it seem such a tangle?'

'My lord?'

'None of it makes any sense. We know the man who is probably responsible for the deaths, but he has no motive. We have the salt, which is important because only the salt trade is attacked, but there is no gain in stealing it. The attacks are premeditated, but the only people who know when the salt leaves are the people most vulnerable, and now the most scared. Everything we know counters what we know, and none of it fits together.'

'That can be the way of it, my lord, sometimes. We have to look at it from another way, and also hope our culprits make a mistake,' Catchpoll said, sagely.

'Preferably before the death toll depopulates Wich.' Bradecote bit his lip at Catchpoll's words. 'So, if we look at it from a different point, what do the thefts and killings achieve? Fear.'

'And perhaps wealth,' Walkelin added, 'if the salt is sold elsewhere.'

'But most of the people who use the Wich salt would not need more and the supply has not ceased, lad.' Catchpoll was sceptical.

'Ah, but what if the salt was going where it did not usually go, Serjeant, where we would not follow it?' Walkelin's eyes grew bright. 'Wales. Remember the lord de Lasson sells salt in Wales.'

'And word has not reached us of a sudden salt shortage there so . . .' Catchpoll did not like the idea.

'Ah, but if he offered it more cheaply, there are places that would buy from him. After all, he would not be thought a criminal.'

'Walkelin has a point, Catchpoll. Yes, I know you do not like it, and nor do I, for without good reason we would have to go and hand this over to the Sheriff of Hereford, who is on good terms with the man, and will call down curses upon our heads for a start. But, there is a possible motive. He could use his own men and employ the archer. He could even increase the price because he is having to "protect" his salt. By that token, though, de Malfleur has a motive.'

'But his own salt was stolen, my lord.' Walkelin kept to his preferred line of thought.

'Not if he "stole" it himself; he still has it.' This time Catchpoll did one of his thinking faces. 'He has many men-at-arms to pay and keep occupied. He also has a family reputation to keep up.'

'But he has not shown himself to be like his brother since he inherited, Catchpoll, to be fair.' Bradecote felt he had to be, however reluctantly.

'Being fair has nothing to do with Baldwin de Malfleur, my lord. You could see what sort of bastard he was in Bromsgrove, and that was a particularly nasty one. He may not have come to the notice of the lord Sheriff as his brother did – and I can tell you Arnulf de Malfleur was nearly taken for capital offences several times – but the younger brother is true to his blood, for sure.'

'You sound like the lady FitzPayne.'

'My lord?'

'The moment she heard Baldwin de Malfleur's name, she said he must be behind all this. She also said Arnulf sent his brother off to the Holy Land because he taunted him with her and then objected strongly when Baldwin stole a kiss. She says he would harm her out of spite and that is why Corbin FitzPayne died, though that vessel holds no water. The salt thieves could not have known he would be coming along the road at that moment. Not that I can convince her of that.'

'That means,' muttered Walkelin, almost to himself, 'that the lord de Lasson's motive is greed and the lord de Malfleur's is . . . simply that he is an evil bastard. Neither thing is against the law, of itself. And,' he added miserably, 'there is also the possibility that there is another lord, or man of wealth, with the same motives, but who we do not know about yet.'

'The voice of cheer,' grumbled Catchpoll, and urged his horse into a canter, 'and there is the lord of Shelsley to brighten our final miles to Cookhill too. Praise the Lord!'

Chapter Ten

Jocelyn of Shelsley had spent a surprisingly pleasant day sowing the seeds of panic among the folk of Wich. It was almost too easy. He watched the effect, and smiled to himself. People gathered in nervous huddles like sheep when they caught the scent of wolf. By the next day he imagined the reeve would be inundated with complaints and also with sightings and hearsay. Let the undersheriff chase after those moonbeams and get nowhere. It would keep him out of the way at Cookhill and make him look a fool. William de Beauchamp might reward success, but he would make Bradecote pay for failure.

He had paid a child a *fourding* to keep an eye open for the return of the sheriff's men, and this enabled him to spend a cosy hour with mulled ale to keep out the cold, and when the half-frozen boy came to tell him of their arrival he reckoned it a halfpenny well spent. He left the tavern, drawing the fur around the neck of his cloak tight about his throat. They did not appear delighted to see him, but then, he had no intention that they should. He smiled up at Bradecote when the undersheriff drew up before him, and belched ostentatiously.

'Ah, the industrious undersheriff of the shire and his doughty henchmen. I do hope you have had a good day galloping about.'

Serjeant Catchpoll ground his teeth, audibly, and Walkelin looked surly, his naturally open and cheery face set. Whatever was being said it was not a compliment. Bradecote looked down his long nose at Jocelyn of Shelsley.

'There was no need to gallop, and our journey was far from wasted, my lord. Indeed, it has made certain things the clearer.' He did not say how few. 'Yours seems to have been only as far as the nearest alehouse.' His look was disdainful.

Walkelin, catching 'alehouse' and the tone, could not quite conceal his snigger, and a flash of anger crossed Jocelyn's slightly chubby cheeks.

'I have not been idle, my lord, I assure you. I have ascertained that the salt workers are not sure whether these deaths are caused by man or the embodiment of the Devil, and that the packmen are threatening to send word to earl and sheriff over the conduct of the reeve and your noble self.'

He did not mention that this had sprung from his own suggestion, secreted in an attentive ear, nor that he had a fine game for them based upon a horse he had seen being led out of the stable where he had left his bay for the day. A few choice words in the ears of women, who would not only give credence to his tale but embellish it, might yet get the sheriff's trio hunting some innocent individual who happened to own a chestnut horse with a white blaze. It would be most enjoyable. The undersheriff gave him a look of intense dislike, informed him that, if he did not wish to ride alone to Cookhill, they were leaving immediately, and swung his horse's head away without a backward glance.

* * *

Christina FitzPayne told herself she was not eager for the sounds of her visitors' return, but knew it was a lie. Whilst the absence of the vile Jocelyn had been a boon, she was keen to hear if the visit to Stone had been successful. It mattered to her that what she had found out should assist Hugh Bradecote, and that filled her with guilt, for her duty, which she had so loudly and fiercely proclaimed less than a week before, was to get justice for her dead husband. Gaining justice was, however, not at the forefront of her thoughts. What she wanted was the undersheriff's approbation. No, that was another lie. She wanted him to give her his smile, and warmth in his eyes. That one so recently bereaved should feel as she did was wrong, and yet . . . She had been quietly fond of Corbin FitzPayne, conscious of his consideration and care. She had been a good wife to him, but he knew he never inspired passion within her, had never attempted to do so. He had happily been a safe haven for her, and had been content with that. She smiled, a sad smile. She thought perhaps Corbin would not be displeased if she found the things she had never expected to discover, attraction, longing, even that mysterious thing, 'love'. She gave herself a mental shake. This was foolishness. She was making assumptions based upon what? There had been a few moments, a few words, looks, that she felt had import, moments when she had felt bonded to this tall, dark-haired man, with the furrowing brows and the rare, luminous smile. Yet for every one of those there had been the arguments, misunderstandings, the desire to throw things at him. How could that be a sign of love? And why should he feel as she did? Could it not just be loneliness for a woman's 'comfort'?

She frowned. She knew all about a man's 'needs', and it was

an ugly side of them; at least it had been so in the past. But she had kissed this man, admittedly not from any desire, for she had never felt that. It had been merely to distract him, but his response, the mixture of uncertainty, tenderness and the stirrings of desire, which should have repelled her and yet did not, had touched something deep within her, unfathomed until that moment. It had taken her totally by surprise, and left her shaken. She had felt herself not divorcing herself from her body as she had learnt to do, but following its dictates, willingly, excitedly. She had actually wanted the embrace to continue, had dreamt of what it would be like to lie in those arms, not captive, but protected. Her world was upside down, the known had become the unknown, and the feared, the anticipated.

It was Jocelyn's voice she heard first, and she shuddered, the warm feeling dispelled by the mere thought of him. She sighed, and rose to play the hostess. He entered the hall, clearly in good spirits, followed by Hugh Bradecote, who looked at the end of his tether. Her heart sank. Had his day been wasted? Then their eyes met and her doubts were set aside. There was a smile in the blue-grey eyes and hovering about his mouth, and an easing of the weary frown. She did not register the words of her husband's kinsman; they were merely sounds eddying about her.

'Did you find anyone who knew Tostig the Fletcher, my lord?'

'We did.' He wanted to say more but in the presence of Jocelyn he felt inhibited. 'Perhaps I might tell you in private, my lady.'

'I am not sure that would be seemly,' Jocelyn commented, in a voice that blended mock outrage with proprietorial prohibition.

The look he got from both parties would have frozen

the Severn, and he laughed as if to pass it off as a joke.

'Since the lord Bradecote is seeking the man who murdered my husband, I hardly think it unseemly he should discuss progress with me, my lord. You are but a kinsman, and not close.'

Christina's words bit deep, and Bradecote noticed Jocelyn tense.

'I shall go, therefore, and ensure my horse has been taken care of to my satisfaction, my lady,' announced Jocelyn, trying to keep the tatters of his pride about him, and, with a stiff bow, he left.

She turned a face filled with triumph to Bradecote. He smiled, but his voice was serious.

'For all his oafishness, my lady, I think you were right to be afra—concerned about your husband's cousin. The more I see, the less I like, or trust. I would advise you to be cautious and alone with him as little as possible.'

She tried to look arch, but her trepidation shone through.

'And this from the man who stands boldly alone before me?'

'You have nothing to fear from me, my lady.'

She dropped her gaze and coloured.

'That I know, my lord Bradecote.' She looked up, shyly. 'I . . . I am safe with you.' Her face clouded. 'I am sorry.'

'Sorry that you trust me?'

'Sorry that I seemed not to at first. I was angry, am angry still, at what has befallen, and I have not had cause to "trust" . . .' Her voice faded to nothing, and unconsciously he reached out a hand and touched hers. She jumped and half pulled back, but looked apologetic.

'I am sorry,' he whispered, mortified.

'No, it is I who am sorry, my lord. I am . . . confused. Please, sit and tell me about Tostig, as we are meant to be discussing that, not my failings.'

She gestured to the lord's seat, but he shook his head, requested that she took it, and sat instead upon a bench.

'Your failings?' He frowned. 'No, not failings, my lady. I understand it cannot be easy for you.'

'Easy?' She laughed, but it was bitter. 'No, never easy, my lord.'

He wanted to say that he wanted to make things easier for her, but even in his head it sounded trite. Part of him wondered if, with such a past, she would ever be able to lay the spectres of her life and be happy, and then he imagined her cradling Gilbert in her arms, his little baby fingers plucking at her veil, his eyes focussed upon her face. She would be smiling and without care, and would love Gilbert not just because the motherless infant would draw out her maternal feelings, but because he was his son. It was but a figment of his imagination, but it made his throat tighten.

'Tostig. My lord?' She noted the faraway look in his eyes. 'We were to speak of Tostig.'

'Yes. Yes, indeed, of Tostig.' He cleared his throat, his mind making calculations. Aelward's father would have died before ever Christina came to Rushock. He would rather not bring any mention of Arnulf into the conversation and see the shadow cast upon her again. 'I think we have a name to our archer, thanks to you.'

'You do?' She looked childishly pleased.

'Yes. Another man, the village wheelwright, had been a keen archer in his youth and remembered a lad called Aelward, who came to the village when about twelve, to live with his aunt. His parents had died. He was a loner, and a good bowman even before manhood. He went away in the employ of a neighbouring lord, and thence to the Holy Land with him. He has not been seen since in Stone, and might indeed be dead, but the wheelwright recognised the arrow as of Tostig's style so I, and Serjeant Catchpoll also, think we seek Aelward the Archer.'

She pondered, her fine, dark brows furrowed.

'You have a name, and yet . . . does this advance you much, my lord?'

He smiled ruefully.

'That, my lady is what we have discussed most of the way back from Stone, at least until Wich, when the lord of Shelsley took over all conversation. I have to admit that in a direct way it does not, but the more one knows about the man you hunt, the more likely you are to find him.'

'Do you think the lord he went to is the man behind the thefts?'

'No, for he died in the Holy Land some four years past. But a lordless man with archery skill might be used by others. He would have a reputation if he is as good as his shots have been thus far.' He suddenly realised that 'good' might offend. 'I meant not "good" but "accurate".'

'I understood it that way, my lord, never fear.' She sighed. 'So it was but a small step forward for so many miles on horseback.'

'Every step forward is important, my lady, even a small one, and especially when we have otherwise been travelling in circles.'

He passed a hand, wearily, over his face, and she stood and went to the door of the buttery, where she turned.

'I am indeed a poor hostess. You have had a long day's riding in cold weather, and I have not so much as offered you refreshment.'

She called a servant to prepare mulled ale. Bradecote dared not say what he felt: that her very presence refreshed him and made him forget cold limbs and tired brain. He remembered returning home after such days to Ela, who would fuss about him like a hen with one chick. That had not been restful – had irritated him, even. She had attended his every physical comfort but never eased his heart and soul. Poor Ela, she had tried so hard, too hard, to be the perfect wife. It occurred to him that Christina would not try to be perfect. She would berate him for not having worn a thicker undershirt, or letting his favourite hound come, muddy pawed and wet, into the solar. But she would be able to listen, and unlike Ela, comprehend, if he told her his problems. He let himself drift into a reverie, imagining her curled in his lap, her head upon his shoulder, talking over some problem, a cup of spiced wine in his hand, the brazier warming the chilled feet he extended to it.

'My lord? Mulled ale?'

He blinked. Christina stood before him, presenting a cup.

'Er . . . I am sorry, I think I must have . . . er . . .'

'Fallen into a doze? Yes, my lord. It is no matter, except that we are about to be joined by Corbin's so unwelcome cousin.'

Jocelyn, whose nose for ale was clearly exceptional, ambled in, smiled in a reptilian way, and said how grateful he was that Christina had remembered her duties. The lady stiffened, and the look she cast Bradecote told him she would love to fling the pitcher of hot ale at the man's head, but she turned and spoke in as false a tone as her guest, requesting that he take a seat and let her serve him. The smile became a lascivious grin, and her flesh crawled.

The atmosphere had chilled as if the east wind blew through

the hall, and drove the warm tendrils of half sleep from Hugh Bradecote. He sighed, and gave himself up to acting as a buffer for the rest of the evening.

Jocelyn of Shelsley had no doubt he was a most unwelcome third at dinner. His hostess and the undersheriff were trying so hard not to gaze at each other it was almost droll, as long as his plan to keep Bradecote from de Beauchamp's favour worked. The atmosphere had a tension as taut as the bowstring of the murderous archer, he thought, and smiled to himself. The previous evening he had been keen to keep them from talking, but this time he attempted to raise personal topics to embarrass them. Mocking the sheriff's man's lack of success angered the lady, and discommoded Bradecote, especially when phrased in such a way as could be taken as a veiled derision of his manhood. He also delighted in making fulsome compliments about his hostess, and asking Bradecote to agree with him, since to do so made both blush and to deny them would seem rude and churlish.

Hugh Bradecote squirmed like a worm on a fish hook. His Adam's apple bobbed up and down and he appeared acutely uncomfortable. Three times he ran a finger round the neck of his undershirt as if it strangled him.

'Our undersheriff appears to find his garments ill-fitting. Perhaps he lacks thread for his needle, and a dame to thread . . . it. She could make him comfortable again. Or is the needle no longer sharp enough for pricking?'

Bradecote's grasp about his wine cup became rigid. Christina had reddened cheeks and a bosom, which, since he ogled it quite openly, Jocelyn could watch rise and fall far more than normal. He let the vulpine smile lengthen. Bradecote was the honourable type who would wait to be invited, but he had no such scruples. He had plans for that bosom, and even if the undersheriff eventually got to wed and bed the pretty widow, well the Church might prevent the wedding part but he had every intention of having bedded her first. Admittedly, Bradecote would not know, for the lady would not tell him in her shame, but he foresaw untold pleasure in revealing subtle hints should they ever meet again.

In the warmer and more convivial atmosphere of the manor kitchen, Catchpoll put up his aching feet upon a stool, savoured the smells of a good barley stew, and appeared to be asleep. In reality, he was moving all the small pieces of knowledge about in his brain, trying to make connections, connections that must exist, but which eluded him. If he had but one piece more, he was sure things would begin to fall into place.

Walkelin entered, a bit pink and failing to contain a grin of satisfaction. Half an hour spent in the company of the goat-milking maid in a warm stable had done much to improve his mood. He was far from being a ladies' man, and was in fact rather shy, but whispering sweet nothings and a little fumbling dalliance with a comely girl who was only too willing to oblige as long as he did not go too far, and had actually gone further than he would have dared, left him with a sense of contentment.

'Serjeant, I've been thinking.'

Catchpoll did not so much as open an eye, but the grin that spread across his face was so lecherous that the dame slicing onions blushed as if he had caught her bending and goosed her.

'Not sure what you've been thinking is suitable for company, lad, if you've been where I'll vouch you have.'

'Serjeant!' Walkelin turned beetroot. 'I never . . .'

Catchpoll opened one eye, slowly.

'Been furtherin' your edificatin', has she? Country girls are a bit more forward, or so I found at your age.' He winked at the onion slicer, who looked affronted but then giggled, rather girlishly. Walkelin did not know where to look, so studied the floor.

'Come on, then, out with it.'

'What!' Walkelin's mind was still in the stable, and he blushed fierily.

'Your thought, woolbrain. What thought was it brought you to disturb my deep study of the evidence?'

'I thought you were in deep study of the back of your eyelids, actually, Serjeant.'

Walkelin grinned and ducked as, with lightning speed, Catchpoll reached for an onion and lobbed it at his head. The onion slicer gave them a look that suggested men never grew up.

'Grab a stool and tell me proper, young Walkelin.'

Walkelin did as ordered, and drew a deep breath.

'Well, if the Archer is working for a lord, I don't see this lord wandering the countryside to meet with him. He could go to the lord's manor, but if he should be caught, well, the lord would be pointed out straightaway.'

'True, though he might think his word would count for far more than a mere archer, and he could find oath swearers easily enough to "prove" him innocent. But go on.'

'So if the Archer does not go to the lord, and the lord is too grand to go to the Archer, then there must be . . .'

'A go-between, yes. I had worked that one out also, Walkelin.'

'Oh.' Walkelin's face fell. 'I just thought . . .'

'You thought you might be first with it. Well, it was a sound idea, but just remember, lad, you have to get up mighty early to be before Serjeant Catchpoll. It deserves a cup of ale, though. Mistress, would you be so kind as to provide my serjeanting apprentice with a drop of your home brew.'

With which the conversation moved on to food and drink, but Serjeant Catchpoll's brain still worked upon the knotty problem.

Chapter Eleven

It was a subject that exercised the minds of the sheriff's men next morning as they rode to Wich. Bradecote was glad to have something to drag his mind, however reluctantly, from the lady who had come out, well wrapped against the wind, to wish them a successful day. It was the flimsiest of reasons, and Walkelin stared quite openly, wondering at her surprising change of attitude. Catchpoll, wise in the ways of women, at least in comparison with the inexperienced Walkelin, ostentatiously adjusted his stirrups, and showed no obvious interest as the lady FitzPayne stood looking up at the undersheriff, so close she was almost touching his knee. It might have been the bending down to catch her words that made Hugh Bradecote flustered of cheek, but Catchpoll would swear there was another cause.

The Go-Between was an interesting advance.

'We therefore have someone else who could provide the key to the whole investigation, and since, logically, he must have either a contact in Wich, or be there to gather information secretly, we have a comparatively small area over which we need keep a lookout. Perhaps we should have considered this before,' remarked Bradecote.

'Perhaps, my lord, but identifying the archer made it much more definite. Before, well, we was just casting about like hounds without a scent to follow.'

'And now we have Aelward the Archer, a man who tells him where to strike and a lord who has reasons for this that remain unknown.'

'Unless it is greed, and the lord de Lasson,' Walkelin reminded them.

'He is your chief suspect, eh, Walkelin? Any reason other than he is a miserly-looking misery with a high opinion of himself?'

'Well, my lord, I would say, as Serjeant Catchpoll would be like to do, "it seems a good enough reason to be getting on with".'

The three men laughed, and were still in a hopeful mood as they entered Wich and headed for the reeve's house. It was clear that Walter had been looking out for them, however, since he came out of his door whilst they were still a couple of hundred yards away.

'My lord Undersheriff,' Walter cried, hurrying towards them – 'Like a charging goose', mumbled Walkelin from the side of his mouth – 'there is so much to tell you. We may have solved our crime! There is salt and a strange occurrence and a man with a bow and . . .'

Catchpoll noted that it was now 'our' crime, when before the reeve had wanted as much distance as possible between himself and the problem.

'Stop, wait, and take a breath!' Bradecote held up a hand. 'Master Reeve, do not simply throw everything at us in a jumble, like a basket of eels. Let us go into your house and sit calmly, and you can tell us everything, just as calmly.'

The reeve nodded, and appeared to 'shoo' them towards his house.

'Now he thinks we are the geese,' whispered Walkelin to Serjeant Catchpoll.

Once inside, he bade them sit upon the bench at his board, and called for his wife to bring refreshment, though Bradecote brushed the offer aside, with suitable thanks.

'Tell us piece by piece, and slowly now,' he recommended, though his words seemed to fall upon deaf ears.

'Mistress Agar vows she saw a stranger in a hooded cloak, trotting north the day before yesterday. She lives at the edge of town by the northern road.'

'What was so suspicious about a man on the northern road? It is well used.'

Catchpoll was frowning. He remembered the last woman's sighting that he had to investigate, and did not want another waste of his time.

'But she said he looked "odd".'

'Hmmmm. In what way?'

'Strange. He did not acknowledge her when she told him to be careful upon the road.'

'Ah, so a lack of courtesy makes a man a killer, does it?' Catchpoll was scathing, and the reeve pouted.

'If you do not wish to hear—'

'No, go on, Master Reeve.' Bradecote threw his serjeant an admonishing glance. 'We do have to sift what comes our way, though, to decide which line we should, er, follow first.'

'And she said she has heard from someone, she thinks it was the Widow Carpenter, that the Ghost Archer rode a chestnut horse with a lightning flash blaze down its nose, and this man's horse had just such. She said it made her shiver, and she was almost glad he did not turn his face to her in case the hood contained no face at all.'

Catchpoll groaned. It was just as he had feared. Once you added the seasoning of the spectral, imaginations ran wild.

'My lord, might I suggest we first send Walkelin here to speak to the Widow . . . Carpenter, and find out just where she got the information on the horse, and then see Mistress Agar.'

'Good idea, Sergeant Catchpoll. Walkelin, get directions to this dame and nip off to see her. I have no doubt you can be back here before we head out upon a more "vital" trail. Be swift.'

Walkelin nodded and, after a few words from the reeve, left in suitable haste.

'Now, what next, Master Reeve?'

'The bowman, my lord.'

'A man with a bow or The Bowman, Master Reeve? There is a huge difference.'

'Er, I cannot say for sure, my lord, for I did not see him myself, now. But three children saw him at the edge of the town.'

Catchpoll's eyes narrowed.

'Of what sort of age?'

'They could not say that, Serjeant, they were too far away.'

'No,' Catchpoll kept his patience under control, 'I meant the age of the witnesses.'

'Ah, I am sorry, I thought you meant—'

'Yes, Master Reeve, we understand what you thought.' Bradecote was as impatient as Catchpoll, and hid it less well. 'Now just tell us.'

'The lad was about twelve, yes, for he is old enough for the tithing come next Whitsuntide. The other two, his brothers, are younger. They must be, as I reckon it, eight and six, for there was a sister in between, though she died last Lammastide of a fever.'

'What exactly did they see, these lads?'

'As they told me, they saw a man, right at the edge of town, sort of creeping about, furtive-like, and he had what looked like an unstrung bow in his hand. They saw him bend it to string, look about him, and then he saw them. He turned and raised the bow as if to fire at them, and . . . they ran.'

'We need to speak to these boys.'

'I thought you would, my lord, and they live barely a stone's throw, or should that be an arrow's flight' – he suddenly sounded quite jocular – 'from this house. I sent the wife to fetch them after you needed no sustenance.' As if on cue, Mistress Reeve returned, a little flustered, fearing she was tardy, but having had to wait whilst the boys' mother 'made 'em respectable' to go in front of the embodiment of the law.

'Here they are. Right, boys, you tell the lord Undersheriff here what you saw, and no lies, or he'll have your tongues out,' the reeve declared, with relish.

The youngest child's eyes widened in horror. The eldest tried to look brave, but failed. Bradecote pursed his lips and shook his head at the reeve. He then looked at the three boys, and smiled, he hoped, encouragingly.

'You sit upon that bench and perhaps Mistress Reeve might find you a honey cake.' He looked to Mistress Reeve, who bridled, but in the face of Hugh Bradecote's most charming smile, became as sweet as the honey itself, and nodded.

The eldest lad looked suspicious, but the younger two relaxed. After all, why should a man who offered honey cakes then want to cut out your tongue?

'So, now, you tell us what you told Master Reeve, about the man you saw yesterday.'

'We was at the south edge of town, by the brook, my lord, just sort of messing. I am in charge of the swine that were rooting at the edge of the wood,' and here the oldest boy's chest swelled with pride at having a proper occupation, 'though there are far fewer since the culling for the winter. I hate that.' He sighed. 'So there were not many to oversee, and, well, I could join in the games.'

'Playing soldiers,' piped up the smallest, helpfully.

Catchpoll smiled at him, which made him look imploringly at Mistress Reeve for motherly protection when she returned with a honey cake for each of the trio.

'What did you see? Tell us in detail.'

'There was a man, not as tall as yourself, my lord, just where the trees thin out. He had a long staff as I thought at first, but then he set his foot to the bottom and flexed the top, so it must have been a bow he was stringing. He reached up, the way you do to loop over the top to tension it. Then he looked to either side, as if he did not want to be seen, but he caught sight of us, and then—'

'He would have put arrows through our hearts,' interjected

the middle brother, with just a touch of ghoulish relish, since the dreaded deed had not taken place.

Catchpoll and Bradecote exchanged looks. Something was not quite right, though the boys clearly spoke the truth.

'He raised the bow, aiming straight at us, so we ran, my lord. I feared he would have taken a pig but when I went back they was all there.'

'He was old, for an archer.' The youngest, fortified by a honey cake and Mistress Reeve's presence, spoke up.

'You couldn't tell,' chided his eldest brother, and looked to Bradecote. 'He was cloaked and hooded, my lord.'

'But I saw the beard, I'm sure of it,' complained the little boy, in the whine of one who is frequently ignored, 'and it was greyed, so he was old.'

The eldest brother would have spoken again, but Bradecote held up a finger to silence him.

'Describe him as you saw him; I am listening.'

There was a moment's hesitation, and the little boy screwed his face up in concentration and shut his eyes. It was a face worthy of Catchpoll.

'He was old. Not young and thin. His cloak did not hang down straight from his shoulders but went out,' the little hands illustrated a ball shape. 'And I saw a whitish beard. I did, honest.' His confidence suddenly drained. 'Don't cut my tongue out!'

'No, more like I shall give you a silver halfpenny, if you just tell me what sort of whitish beard. Was it long? Is that how you saw it?'

The child shook his head.

'I could just see under his hood. I am littlest.'

There was a logic to it, Bradecote admitted.

'Thank you,' he said, 'you have been more use to us than soldiers, you know.'

The boys were obviously impressed by this statement, and even more by the silver halfpenny that was given to them upon dismissal. Once they had gone, however, the sheriff's men shook their heads.

'I'd swear that was not our man,' murmured Catchpoll. 'Those boys spoke true enough, what they saw, but it is all wrong.'

'We cannot even be sure they saw a bow. None mentioned a quiver and arrows and what would the Archer be doing, stringing his bow there? In fact,' Bradecote paused as an idea formed in his brain, and then continued slowly, 'you know it all seems a bit of mummery. A hooded and cloaked man creeping about at a distance where he might just be seen, and our man apparently a stickler for a good shot, and a hunter's son, brought up to stealth; they do not go together. But a man keen to lay a false scent and watch us chase our tails, that is another thing entirely. This "bowman" was portly rather than lithe, and bearded. Remember how the lord of Shelsley was so smug and mocking yesterday?'

'Aye, he was. And that would fit. No doubt he thought up the chestnut horse, too. Why else come to spend the day in Wich, when he would rather be sniffing about the lady FitzPayne and think of Cookhill as his?'

Bradecote did not like the thought of Jocelyn 'sniffing about' Christina FitzPayne, but did not let it show upon his face.

Walter Reeve was only just catching up.

'You mean this is of no use to you, my lord?'

'No, Master Reeve, it just shows us there are those who would rather see us fail than succeed.'

'Might Jocelyn of Shelsley even be . . . No, it does not hang together.' Catchpoll was thinking out loud. 'The death of Corbin FitzPayne could not be covered up so elaborately, not with all these attacks, and besides, who would have known he would be upon that road at that hour?'

'Could it be coincidence?' Bradecote was alongside Catchpoll, in thought. 'Could he have planned the attacks and then Corbin been a bonus?'

'What motive, my lord? He has one now, but . . .'

Bradecote's brow furrowed.

'I do not see why he should want mischief, Catchpoll.'

Catchpoll pulled a face. This was neither time nor place to explain, and it was a delicate matter. Catchpoll disliked delicate matters. He skirted round as best he could, with half the truth.

'My lord, Cookhill is held of the lord Sheriff. If FitzPayne's brother is dead and dust, then instead of handing it to the uninspiring lord of Shelsley, a sheriff grateful for the successful end to this might be of a mind to hand it to the man who proved his worth.'

'You mean Jocelyn of Shelsley thinks that I . . .'

'It is logical, my lord.'

Catchpoll left it at that. Bradecote would work out that the lady was also involved, but at least the reeve would remain in the dark. The undersheriff assimilated this new information and was silent some minutes. The reeve, still more concerned that his information had not inspired plaudits, coughed and asked whether he should continue.

'Also, my lord, there came in a man from along the Leominster road, who reported villagers at Holt frightened by strange happenings. It would seem unlikely his information was set there by the lord of Shelsley. When there was a sharp frost yesterday there was a field with a patch where no frost took upon the ground, and the buck from the woods came out and sniffed it, they did.'

Catchpoll was about to speak when a thought hit him, and he could see by the look upon the undersheriff's face that it had hit him also.

'Is that man still in Wich, Master Reeve?'

'Er, I do not know. He brought a damaged wheel to our wheelwright, their own one having taken and died last month. I would suppose he is still there.'

'Send for him, please.'

While the reeve hurried away, Bradecote and Catchpoll took the opportunity to talk.

'Salt would do that, my lord, if dumped, but why they did not think of that, I do not know. Must be fools, the lot of 'em.'

'Possibly, but more like they simply do not think ahead much. They just accept what they see and do not try to connect things. What is important is the position. Perhaps it means we should look to the west for whoever sets the Archer on his path.'

'Might do, my lord, but might also mean the opposite.'

Bradecote ran a hand through his hair.

'That is true enough.' He sighed. 'We had best wait for the man.'

It was Walkelin who arrived first however, his face set and not at all happy.

'So was it another wild duck chase, young Walkelin?'

'Oh yes, Serjeant. The widow who saw a hooded man upon a chestnut horse was all talk of ghosts and evil deeds but had nothing more than her "feelings" as evidence, as you might imagine, but what rankles is where she got the gossip that sent her running to the reeve. Widow Carpenter, the one who told her the Ghost Archer definitely rode a chestnut with a lightning blaze, had the word of it from "a very grand man, a lordly-looking man with grey hair and white-flecked beard". Sound familiar?'

'We should have guessed. Jocelyn of Shelsley, again, the crafty bastard!'

'Couldn't have put it better myself, Catchpoll.'

'Again?' Walkelin looked from one to the other, but received no direct answer.

'Thing is, has he sown the seeds of everything we are going to hear today?' Catchpoll sucked his teeth.

'We will not know until we have delved further, but well done, Walkelin, that saved us going after some innocuous man on a chestnut horse. We could have wasted the day upon that alone, and had half of Wich running after us about every chestnut they saw, if we asked around. I will want words with the lord of Shelsley, strong words, and, by the Rood, he will not enjoy them.'

Walter Reeve arrived back, somewhat out of breath, with a worried individual in tow. The man, by name Edwin, was obviously very much in awe of the law. He was also encumbered with a stutter, which his nerves made worse. Bradecote winced when upon being asked about salt the poor man repeated the word, or tried to do so.

'Yes, we wondered if anyone had seen ponies, or a cart perhaps, containing salt, shortly before the "strange happening".'

'Er . . . often w . . . w . . . wagons, h . . . h . . . heading . . .' he pointed west to avoid a stuttered 'west'.

'Any that day or even the day before?'

Edwin shook his head. Then he frowned.

'Wh . . . wh . . . wh . . . wheels at n . . . n . . . n . . . night.'

The man rolled his eyes, fearful that his brusque responses might land him in trouble, but the undersheriff looked delighted.

'Really. Night before?'

There was another nod.

'Then what we want you to do is take us to the field where the frost did not lie.'

The frown deepened.

'Wh . . . wh . . . wheel.'

'Yes, we under—oh, the wheel to be mended! Master Reeve, you are to send the wheel back upon repair. Edwin, you come with us.'

'Must it be on my beast?' grumbled Walkelin, remembering how uncomfortable it had been with Edric up behind him.

'Yes, it must,' averred Serjeant Catchpoll, without any trace of sympathy.

They rode west from Wich, through Ombersley, crossing the Severn with the punt ferrymen to the cluster of cottages that made Holt. There was a village reeve, thankfully enabling the stuttering Edwin to stand down from answering questions. The relief was mutual. Wilfrid was a sensible man, who, when

165

the consternation of his fellows was revealed to him, shook his head, and tut-tutted.

'I never understands why so many folk cannot see the real when there is the chance for unreal. I could have spared you the journey to see this "miracle" since it was none. I tried telling 'em, but who would listen to sense when there is talk of elves and evil spirits?'

'Oh, we know what caused it, never you fear,' declared Catchpoll, 'but we would be mighty interested in seeing where it happened, and hearing from anyone who heard or saw a cart the other night, when carts should not be abroad.'

'Now there's a thing, for I did hear a cart, but right about then our William burnt his hand and there was such a to-do as took my mind from it. Mind you, if anyone was being crafty and illegal, they were not quiet about it, since others seem to have heard. Odd, most odd. Now, you come along with me and I will show you the place where someone must have spilt salt.'

He led them just off the road on a cart track beside which was an area where the tired grass now looked decidedly died away. There were deep wheel marks within a few feet.

'Why here?' mused Catchpoll.

'Well, I suppose they were bringing salt to my lord de Lasson's barn up yonder. Perhaps a beast had gone lame and they were delayed. Looks like it nearly toppled here, in the dark. Must have hit uneven ground. Better to lie up in his barn than carry on. Then they could continue on their way to his manors in the morning.'

Walkelin made an excited, choking noise and Catchpoll gave him a severe glance.

'But this manor is held by the lord de Beauchamp, surely?'
Bradecote was confused.

'Indeed, my lord, but my lord de Lasson holds one virgate and his barn.'

'Then I think we should go and look inside this barn.'

'My lord, I have no right, and—'

'On behalf of the lord Sheriff and the King's Grace, we do. Come.'

Wilfrid the Reeve looked uncomfortable, but it was out of his hands so he made no further demur, and followed the three men, now leading their horses, to the well-kept barn. They lifted the heavy timber latch and entered the darkness that smelt of winnowings. They blinked, trying to get used to the low light. There, in the middle of the barn, was a cart, a cart with bags of salt piled upon it, though some had fallen over and others were split.

'Well, bless me, why did they not take the cart onward, since they took the beasts that pulled it?'

Wilfrid sounded genuinely perplexed.

'Tell me, has the lord de Lasson ever left his salt here before, when taking it to his manors or on to Wales?'

'No, my lord. And come to think of it, I had heard he was not moving any salt for a week or so.'

The sheriff's men exchanged looks. Walkelin had 'I told you so' written in his expression.

'Thank you. We require no more of you, except that you see none come and take this cart away in the next few days.'

'As you decree, my lord.'

The man withdrew, and hoped that the lord de Lasson would not hear of his assistance to the undersheriff, for he was an unforgiving man.

'That seems to seal it, my lord.' Walkelin could no longer contain his delight.

'Before you turn cartwheels, young Walkelin,' remarked Catchpoll, drily, 'should we ask ourselves why the salt was not indeed taken further?'

'Simple, because if the lord's manor was under suspicion for any reason and searched, there would be nothing inc . . . incrinim . . . to make him look guilty. We had no idea he held land here, did we?'

'He has a point, Catchpoll. Admit it,' Bradecote murmured.

'A point, yes, my lord, but . . . it is not writ in stone in my opinion, and I do so wish it was, if we are going to ride in on de Lasson and make accusations.'

'Cannot be helped, Serjeant. There is enough here to make "riding in on him" perfectly justifiable, and indeed, unjustifiable if we did not. How do we explain if this cart is identified, as I am sure it will be, as either de Malfleur's or even the one heading for Bordesley? We cannot say, "Ah but it meant speaking to the lord de Lasson, and we did not like to upset him."'

'Forgive me, my lord, but from your last meeting I would say that upsetting him would be high on your list of things that would please you no end.'

'Ah yes, but I am keeping an unbiased view here, Catchpoll.' Bradecote kept a straight face.

'Very commendable, my lord. Shall we go and see the penny-pinching bastard now, then?'

'Oh, I think we should. I really do.' The grin could not be contained any longer.

* * *

It was a little after noon when the sheriff's men cantered into the manor of Collington, chief honour of Rannulf de Lasson. They were greeted by a wary steward, who was used to handling nobility with caution. He was respectful but unforthcoming. His lord, he said, had ridden out, and had not informed him when he might return. Bradecote groaned. The steward was about to suggest he return at another time, when a clatter of hooves in the gateway announced the lord's return. They turned, and Walkelin's jaw actually dropped. Rannulf de Lasson, with a rather tired-looking, fur-edged cloak about him, was astride not the sad specimen they had seen in Wich, but a very tidy grey, a grey the colour of dulled mail and with two white stockings and a star upon its forehead. Even Catchpoll was stunned.

'Bradecote, and the full panoply of the law, well, well. What brings you to Herefordshire and out of your remit, my lord?'

Rannulf de Lasson's tone was haughty, and showed no sign that his discovery upon a murdered man's horse discommoded him in any way. Hugh Bradecote was momentarily nonplussed, and sounded it.

'We, er, we found a cart of salt, almost certainly stolen salt, in your barn at Holt, my lord, and wished for explanation.'

'Salt? In Holt? There was no indication that my salt house had produced enough to send by cart as yet, and besides, I left firm instructions for them to retain it until I said otherwise. I will have whoever gave the order to move it flogged.'

'No, my lord,' Catchpoll spoke slowly, but with a veneer of deference, 'this was not your salt. It is most likely to be that of the lord de Malfleur.'

He thought this a crafty move, for telling de Lasson it might belong to the Cistercians of Bordesley would not worry him. Telling him it might be de Malfleur's would. It did. The lord of the manor blinked and grew pale.

'De Malfleur's? But . . . how?'

Bradecote had recovered his composure, and only wished he had thought of throwing Baldwin de Malfleur into the mix. The effect was worth seeing, though if it was an act it was a good one. If he had ordered the stealing of the salt, he must have known whose it was. No, that did not quite hold true, for if he had but instructed his intermediary to discover departures of salt from Wich and arrange their theft, he might not have known about de Malfleur's loss until after the event, when it was too late to undo what was done. Thereafter he could only bluff his way through. It might certainly have sent him to Wich to find out how much was known and to play the outraged lord to side with de Malfleur.

'That, my lord de Lasson,' Bradecote smiled innocently enough, though de Lasson was not fooled, 'is what we were hoping you could explain to us.'

'I do not know. How could I know?'

'You could know if your men hid it there, though why they waited until last night to do so is a little odd. Was there a problem with the cart, perhaps?'

'You are accusing me – *me* – of these crimes? How dare you? I shall make report to Miles of Gloucester, the sheriff of this shire. And you cannot come here. It should be him if anyone need speak with me.'

It was a moot point, but Bradecote felt that since at this stage the evidence was so good and immediate, this visit, at least, did not require the Sheriff of Herefordshire.

'Accusing you, no, not yet, but you must admit it does look dubious, when a cartload of evidence is found in one of your outlying barns, all tucked up quiet, and,' here Bradecote paused for a moment, before delivering the coup de grâce, 'when you are mounted upon the horse Corbin FitzPayne was riding when he was struck down by an arrow.'

Rannulf de Lasson stared at Bradecote as if he had taken leave of his senses.

'What?' It came out as a hissing whisper.

'Oh yes, that very nice grey, which you clearly have not possessed long enough to ruin, is exactly the animal described to us by FitzPayne's widow. It is a very distinctive horse.'

'But I bought this beast but the day before yesterday, my servants will vouch for it, from a man coming from the Welsh border. He was some poor knight down upon his luck. There had been Welsh brigands crossing the border and he had lost wife and manor to sword and flame. He was a broken man, and had all he had rescued, his best horse and the one he had been riding when he returned to find his manor under attack. He was heading east to the Benedictines at Alcester, he said, and would take the cowl. The grey, well, I offered him a fair price for it, since he needed but one horse to ride upon, and it would give him coin as well as a ruined manor prone to Welsh attack, to offer the monks for his admission.'

'Fair?' murmured Walkelin, so low only Catchpoll heard it. 'On the cheap, I would swear oath.'

'He accepted at once,' continued de Lasson, 'and departed upon the lesser beast.'

'This mythical unfortunate, describe him to me, my lord.'

Rannulf de Lasson grew purple in the face.

'You think I lie? You dare to—'

'Describe him.' Bradecote's face was impassive, but the command was firm and at such a volume that heads turned, even those pretending not to listen to what was going on. De Lasson complied.

'What manner of man? Ordinary, not badly dressed but not in his finest. He was tall, and thin-faced, and in his forties, I should have guessed, with receding hair. You could see him as a monk. The chestnut was an average animal with a jagged blaze down its face, and he wore his sword like one who had used it; the scabbard had old "scars" upon it.'

The tower of hope within Bradecote and his companions, crumbled to dust. There was little that de Lasson could have said to exonerate himself, but this did so, unless he was so clever he had considered that they would be hunting sword and scabbard as well as the horse, and decided to make up a horseman who carried them. But the chestnut with the lightning blaze was real. It was the animal that Jocelyn had almost certainly seen in Wich and used as a false trail, not knowing it was a true one. Bradecote heard Catchpoll's slight hiss. It was now a case of extricating themselves without appearing defensive.

'Where were these scars, my lord?'

He carefully chose to sound as yet unconvinced.

'Er . . . there was a deep cut into the leather near the top, and some scuffing also.'

'Hmmm, and you thought this tale of Welsh brigandage sounded likely?'

'What reason had I to doubt it?'

Bradecote saw his opportunity.

'It did not perhaps occur to you that a man who turns up, unannounced, with a tale of woe and a good horse he is willing to sell cheaply – and do not tell me it was not cheap, my lord – might not be honest?'

'No,' lied de Lasson.

'Well, we will return the horse to lady FitzPayne, of course, and request everyone to be on the lookout for this thin man on the chestnut.'

'But I paid for it,' de Lasson blustered.

'My lord, it is a lesson well learnt, that some things are too good to be true. You will be more careful in the future from whom you buy, I am sure. And the cart of salt will be returned to Baldwin de Malfleur, should it be his, with your compliments, since you say you knew nothing of its presence in your barn, and we, of course, accept the word of so important a lord.'

Bradecote inclined his head. De Lasson was confused now. Surely the undersheriff had not believed a word before, but now? The loss of the horse was an embarrassment and good money wasted, but he had wondered at the story he was given and chosen to play along. Better to be rid of the whole problem, though he would complain of his treatment to Miles of Gloucester. He dismounted, ordered a groom to remove his saddlery from the grey, halter it, and hand it to the undersheriff. He made no attempt to offer hospitality, but 'thanked' Bradecote, for the sake of the onlookers, for drawing these matters to his attention, and wished them a safe journey, whilst secretly wishing Bradecote would break his neck.

As the trio, with Walkelin leading FitzPayne's grey, left the courtyard, Serjeant Catchpoll cast his superior a look of undisguised admiration.

'That, my lord, was masterly. Considering the depth of the hole in which we found ourselves, and a hole deepening as we stood there, it was almost miraculous. He will complain to his sheriff, of course, but will most likely sound a fool. Miles of Gloucester is no idiot.'

'Thank you, Serjeant. From one so versed in the art of wiliness, that is indeed a compliment. Trouble is, it leaves Walkelin's theory dead in the dust, and . . . Sweet Jesu, the hooded rider the widow woman saw might well have been the "poor knight" from whom de Lasson bought the horse and also the Go-Between. We were so dismissive because of Jocelyn's meddling, and the foolishness of "Ghost Archers" that we linked what the Widow Agar saw to him, but the fact was she saw a hooded rider the day before Jocelyn came to Wich, and so was not part of the deceit. It was pure chance that the real horse was chestnut as well as the one Jocelyn invented to distract us.' He swore, volubly.

'No point in regrets, my lord,' declared Catchpoll, reasonably. 'Even if the man was the link between Aelward the Archer and whoever is directing him, what could we have done? Chestnut horses are common enough, even with a blaze, and all we know is that the man was heading north. It helps us, but only a little, and prevents nothing.'

'Sorry, my lord. It is my fault for being so keen on the lord de Lasson being behind it all.' Walkelin shook his head, sadly.

'Don't apologise, lad. It's a sign of weakness.' Catchpoll gave a small, grim smile. 'We all would have liked to see de Lasson at the centre of it all. The thing is, he was the best motive we had. Greed is a powerful thing.'

'So is being an evil bastard, and de Malfleur was next on

our list. We may even have to look carefully at the miserable Jocelyn, who seemed so unlikely.' Bradecote sighed. 'The man on the chestnut could have been heading to de Malfleur at Rushock, but might have been off to meet Aelward, though I hope not. And Shelsley is in this direction, so leaving the salt at Holt for a while might have been a good idea, before taking it on to there when quieter.'

'But if it is him, my lord, there has been no opportunity for the Go-Between to see him.' Walkelin paused. 'At least we have some vague idea of what the man looks like now, which is a start. We can warn about one such in Wich.'

'We have not watched him, the lord of Shelsley, and the lady FitzPayne is probably so glad when he is not underfoot, she would not ask where he had been if he slipped away for an hour.' Bradecote considered the matter. 'He would certainly know everything we discover by being on hand. He may even have given the Go-Between orders just to keep arranging attacks until he calls a halt.'

'All well and good, my lord, but his motive is almost non-existent.' Catchpoll sighed. 'It gets no easier.'

It actually got more difficult when they reached Wich, because there was a hubbub in the town. Knowing they would arrive late in the day, the packmen heading the previous day to Worcester had said they were unlikely to return the same day, but were now expected. Instead a message had been received that the salt heading for Worcester had not arrived. People were gathering, solemn-faced. The arrival of the undersheriff was greeted with sullen glumness. Walter Reeve, at the eye of a growing storm of disquiet, looked beleaguered.

There was not enough daylight left for a search party to have any chance of being thorough, and so it was arranged that the sheriff's men would take men out early the next day. All in all, a day that had begun in hope was ending dismally.

Chapter Twelve

Christina had avoided her lingering guest for much of the day.
When she had commented that his own manors must need his
attention, he had waved a hand airily and declared he had men
he could trust to oversee the everyday matters, and that her
need was far more important. There was something in the way
he said it, accompanying a most unsettling leer, that made her
feel sick. She had thereafter contrived to have either the steward
or a servant present all afternoon, but had developed a headache
and finally retired to her chamber, lay upon the box bed, pulled
a sheepskin over her feet, and closed her eyes. She lay in a
half-waking, half-sleeping state, time in limbo, her thoughts
jumbled, and many of them concerning the undersheriff. She
only part-registered the drawing back of the curtain, but her
eyes flew open as someone sat upon the edge of the bed. Jocelyn
was smiling down at her, smiling the smile she had learnt to
loathe on a man.

'I have brought you wine, with herbs, for I am told you
suffer with a headache, my lady.' His words were solicitous, but
he was not thinking of her comfort. 'It is said, of the weaker

sex, that foul humours arise if certain needs are not attended to. One dare not imagine how the cloistered manage. But I can offer you "comfort", my lady.'

He set the wine upon a stool by the bed, as she lay, frozen by an old but familiar dread. She wondered, hopelessly, why she should be so beset. He leant forward, his breath heavy with stale drink. As his smile became a grin, he spread his fingers and clasped her breast. She took a sharp intake of breath, which made him laugh, but suddenly it broke the evil spell. This was not something she had to put up with out of duty; he had no right. No man had the right any more. Indeed, it was an assault. Her right hand slid under the pillow, and withdrew a small but serviceable knife, which she had decided to place there the first night Jocelyn had got drunk. With her eyes upon his face she stabbed down hard through the back of the violating hand, so hard she felt it prick her bosom as it came out through the palm. She let go with a gasp. Jocelyn emitted a scream of pain, staring at the haft, then drew it out with his left hand as the blood flowed freely, and the grip changed and tightened. She saw the pain written upon his face, but more so the blind anger. He raised the knife. He was going to kill her, she could see it, and there was nothing she could do. She just stared, waiting for the icy bite of the steel, but then Jocelyn turned, unthinkingly, to the sound of a shout, and the next thing he knew he had been sent sprawling, and the knife clattering across the floor.

Hugh Bradecote had a face so grim Christina thought he might kill Jocelyn then and there, with his bare hands. He saw the blood upon her gown and his eyes narrowed.

'Did he try to kill you as you slept?'

There was incredulity in his voice, for it made no sense.

'Not as I slept, but he was about to do so when you—'

There was an angry growling noise from the floor.

'The bitch put a knife through my hand, look.'

Jocelyn got up unsteadily, moving his aching jaw, and trying to staunch the blood running down his arm as he held up the injured limb. He sounded affronted. How dare she have resisted him?

'And why, my lord,' Bradecote's voice was soft but chill, 'did she feel the need to do that?'

'I brought her wine, for her headache.'

'Indeed, and she repaid this act of charity with violence, did she? How strange.'

'My lord, he thought to—' Christina interrupted.

He silenced her with a raised finger, still gazing at Jocelyn of Shelsley.

'Tell me why, my lord.'

There was menace in the tone and Jocelyn faltered.

'It was but light-hearted. After all, she is no blushing maid, and what would a little pleasure matter to one such as her.'

Christina made a strangled noise in her throat.

'I see, so you would say that a widow is "fair game"?'

'Well,' Jocelyn avoided his eye and gave a tentative laugh, 'she should be game enough. After two husbands, and one of those Arnulf de Malfleur? What sort of woman can she—'

Bradecote knocked him down again.

'"What sort of woman", you say?' The undersheriff was not thinking as an officer of the law. In that moment the law meant nothing to him. He loomed over the cringing man, taking him by the throat and lifting him almost off his feet. 'If

179

the lady had put the knife through your black heart, I would have applauded her act, you apology for a man. A woman cannot be safe in her own bed with a cur like you sniffing about her skirts.'

He drew his own knife and put it to Jocelyn's throat.

'No, my lord, please. No more death, even him.' Christina half crawled across the bed, her hand outstretched. 'Please, I beg of you.'

There was a pause, a held breath. Jocelyn looked up into eyes so hard he thought their very glance would draw blood. Then Bradecote exhaled.

'Get out, out of this chamber, out of this manor, and if I hear that you have as much as crossed her path, I will come, and I will kill you.'

'You can't, you wouldn't . . .'

'Oh, I would, never doubt me. Out!'

With which he dragged Jocelyn to the solar door, through the hall and actually launched him half falling down the steps.

'Walkelin!' he yelled. 'Make sure the lord of Shelsley leaves immediately.'

Walkelin grinned, thinking this the end to the lord Bradecote's 'harsh words' to the lord of Shelsley.

'But it is near dark,' complained the cowed and bruised Jocelyn, crumpled ignominiously in the dirt.

'You have men-at-arms. If you are afraid, then ride fast.' Bradecote looked down at the man in total contempt. 'And if you are fortunate, you may find hospitality with the monks at Alcester, which is nearest, and has no women to tempt you.'

Bradecote turned upon his heel, and was about to go back into the hall, but stopped suddenly. There was still the matter of Jocelyn's attempt to set them upon false trails, and he was not entirely removed from their list of suspects.

'Shelsley, one thing more.'

The man looked at him with fear now, as well as loathing.

'You can be sure that I shall report your conduct in Wich, as well as here, to the lord de Beauchamp.'

'My conduct in Wich?'

'Do not play the innocent,' snarled Bradecote. 'You tried to delay the proper execution of the sheriff's business and the restoring of the King's peace.'

'I protest.'

'Shut up and listen well. You were seen, not just vaguely, but well enough to be recognised.' Here the undersheriff permitted himself a sneering smile. 'We had the description of "an old man with a white-flecked beard, and portly" pretending to string a bow, the same man who described a chestnut horse in good detail. Where did you see that horse for real, Shelsley?'

'I never . . .' Jocelyn began, and then swallowed convulsively, and shut up.

'Walkelin, take the lord of Shelsley into the stables and let Serjeant Catchpoll have words with him . . . in private.'

Walkelin grabbed the man, still scrabbling to his feet, far from gently.

'No! I will tell true.' Jocelyn of Shelsley was not a courageous man in the best of circumstances, and having had a woman drive a knife through his hand, for no good reason other than she was not prepared to let him have his way with her, then be knocked down twice and threatened with death, and pushed down a flight of steps, he was in no way able to contemplate being 'mistreated' by the sadistic-looking bastard that was Serjeant Catchpoll. 'The horse was simply one I saw at the stables in Wich, just a chestnut horse being led out by a nobody.'

'Invisible, was he?' Bradecote did not look at all appeased.

'I mean he was just a man leading a horse, neither young nor very old, thinner than me.'

'Doesn't say much,' murmured Walkelin, rather enjoying the chance to revile a member of the lordly class without fear of penalty. He shook his 'prisoner' a little and achieved a sneer that Serjeant Catchpoll, emerging to see the cause of the disruption, considered almost as good as one of his own.

'Well, you had better hope that meagre information helps us find him, and that he has no knowledge of you, because this case will end in hangings, and if the stretched necks are lordly, so be it.'

'Me? Why should he know me?' The lord of Shelsley, quivering in Walkelin's grasp, opened his eyes wider. 'You want to implicate me in these crimes? But you seek an archer.'

'We let's folk implicate themselves, much tidier,' growled Catchpoll, folding his arms and looking as if assisting them to do that was one of his pleasures in life.

'An archer has brought down the victims, but we think someone else has planned the crimes, and just at this moment a lord who has been keen to throw us off the scent, and one who has the potential to profit from the death of Corbin FitzPayne looks a good option.' Bradecote was still too angry to enjoy the deflating of the puffed-up Jocelyn of Shelsley.

'But his death was not intended,' wailed the panicking lord.

'How do you know that?' interjected Walkelin.

'I mean it cannot have been. There are all these thefts of salt, after Corbin's death.'

In truth, Bradecote still thought the death of Corbin FitzPayne a simple case of a man being in the wrong place at the wrong time, but it served his purpose not to admit this.

'That is to be proved when we bring this to conclusion. I suggest you pray hard at Alcester, and then return to your own manor and remain there. If we hear of you "wandering" it will be a good sign of guilt. Now, go.'

Jocelyn needed no encouragement, but Hugh Bradecote did not wait to watch him ride away. He turned, and went tight-lipped back into the hall, and fought to step back from the white-hot killing anger that had consumed him as he did so.

He did not knock upon the solar door but entered without hesitation. Christina sat upon the edge of the bed, her feet still bare, pressing a kerchief to the oozing cut staining the fabric of her gown at her breast. She looked up as he came in, and tried to smile, but it wavered and died on her lips.

'Is that what men will think of me?' she whispered. 'Any woman who has been Arnulf de Malfleur's is fit only to be used like a . . .' Her voice caught on a sob.

'It is not what I think of you,' he said, kneeling before her and taking her hand, and adding, 'nor any decent man.' Unconsciously he took the cloth from her grip and gently pulled down the edge of the gown just enough to reveal the wound on the soft fullness of her flesh. 'It is not deep, just a small cut, but you must have used a fair amount of force to go right through his hand.' He wiped the welling scarlet from her flesh.

She laughed unsteadily, very conscious of his touch.

'I did. I thought I did not have to suffer this, not this time.'

'You don't, not again.' He looked into her eyes, not smiling, but reassuring.

'I warned you, didn't I, that if you found Jocelyn dead it would be my fault. Well, he isn't dead, but I stabbed him. Do you want to put me in chains and present me before the Justices?'

'Self-defence was never a crime, and when I came in he was clearly on the point of . . .' Bradecote did not want to think of having arrived a minute later.

'Yes, I know. Thank you.'

'I did nothing.' They both knew that was a lie, but saying 'I saved you from death' sounded as if demanding thanks.

'You stopped him. You knocked him down, twice. I hope your knuckles are not sore, my lord.'

She smiled and touched his hand. It was the most tremulous of smiles, the most delicate of touches. He felt the intimacy, the wave of desire, and then there was an awkwardness that settled upon them. Of all times, this was not the time, when she had just defended her honour to the point of risking death; to take advantage would be wrong, even if part of him felt she wanted him to do so. He gave a twisted smile which was half grimace, and got up from his knees, brushing them down, embarrassed, avoiding her eyes.

'I should go and . . . do something.'

She blushed. She had felt it too, the wanting him to lie with her and yet being so proud of him for resisting.

'Yes, I understand. I will make myself presentable.'

He simply nodded, and turned to go.

'Thank you, my lord,' she whispered, and he felt the 'my' was suddenly personal.

The undersheriff found excuses not to go back to the hall until the time to eat. In part he needed to calm himself after a most tumultuous hour. Hugh Bradecote was not a man whose temper ruled him, but he had been killing mad for a few minutes. Had Christina not prevented him, he would almost certainly have put an end to Jocelyn, and without compunction. Even had his own feelings not been involved, the cur had thought to use a woman for his pleasure against her will, and prepared to commit murder because she had tried to defend her honour. Rape and murder were capital crimes, and it was only by the grace of God that she had been spared. Had he arrived a couple of minutes later . . . His stomach churned at the thought, which recurred in his head. And then there was that near embrace, and more. Christina FitzPayne was important to him – it sounded easier in his mind to admit only that, for how could it truly be what his gut feeling said, love, after only knowing the woman for a week? Kneeling before her, it had been so tempting to reveal his feelings, as it had been to press her back onto that bed, but the voice of sanity said it was too soon, that it was a madness upon him like a fever, and like a fever it would break. His heart told him otherwise. These two elements were in conflict, and the heart was in the ascendency. It argued with cold, unemotional sanity, in terms sanity could understand, listing those things that contributed to his feelings. He admired her spirit, though it meant she had a temper to her. He had experience of meekness in Ela, and for all there had not been arguments, she had frustrated and annoyed him almost the more for her subservience. He also pitied Christina, though she would be appalled to hear it. There was no such thing as 'fair' in life, he had been taught that early, but she had suffered through no fault of her own, and to a degree few had to face. He wanted to show her that life could have pleasure and laughter and, yes, that word, love.

At which point sanity told him he simply missed the comfort of a woman in his bed, and release to his body, and was merely attracted to an appealing face and comely figure. Desire, it said, was not love, but a mere physical thing like thirst, to which heart responded by saying that he had not felt 'desire' for any other woman in the period since Ela's death. Sanity grinned, and declared the world was full of ugly women.

When widow and undersheriff next met, it was over the evening meat, and there was a new constraint between them. It was almost as if they had parted in anger, though it was entirely the opposite that was true. They kept within themselves, cautious of showing too much, caught between fear of somehow having misread the other and a heart-lurching belief that the inner turmoil was mutual. They avoided eye contact, Christina decorously studying the trencher before her, and Bradecote covertly watching her pale hands. Their awareness of each other, of every breath, was acute, and diminished the appetite. Conversation, what little there was, ignored what had passed that afternoon in the solar, and centred upon the character of Rannulf de Lasson, and the mystery thin man. Bradecote only remembered the return of Corbin FitzPayne's horse when he broached the topic. Her first thought was to go instantly to see the beast, but he persuaded her to finish her meal. Since Christina only knew of de Lasson by distant repute, there was not much that she could contribute, beyond agreeing with Bradecote that the evidence had seemed damning, but the man on the chestnut almost certainly proved his innocence.

As she finished eating, and rose from her seat, Christina cast Hugh Bradecote one swift, sidelong glance. How was it, she wondered, that she could feel uneasy, actually because he set her at ease? Did she trust her own instincts so little? She felt that she saw right into the depths of the man, and there was nothing lurking to frighten her within, nor was it because he was in any way a shallow character. She sighed, which he interpreted as weariness.

'I understand you must be tired, my lady. It has been a . . . stressful day. If you wish to retire . . .'

'No. Please, I wish to see the horse. I am sure it is my lord's, but I would be certain.'

'As you wish, my lady.'

It all sounded so formal; it was unreal.

He offered his arm, unnecessarily but with gallantry, and she laid her hand upon it as he walked her out to the stables, the simple contact making her heart race, as it did his. The stable was in darkness, and he was loth to bring a rush light within for fear of fire, but with the door open the small amount of moonlight in the cloudless sky gave just enough to see the horse's white markings reflecting the light. She advanced, speaking softly to the animal so as not to frighten it, and it twitched its ears and nuzzled her hand.

'This is Corbin's horse. I know even in this dimness.'

She sighed and shuddered, leaning back against the solid

warmth of Hugh Bradecote. He wanted to hold her, kiss her while none would disturb them, yet somehow, with the long face of her dead husband's horse watching them, it seemed wrong. He contented himself with sliding his hand on her arm and taking her hand as she leant back, and resting his cheek against her coif. There was silence, but for the scurry of a rat and the stamping of a horse's hoof. After what seemed an age, she sighed.

'We should go in.'

'Yes.' He did not move an inch.

'It should be wrong. I am in mourning,' she whispered. 'I should not feel . . . this. I have never felt this, Holy Mary, never.'

'And I should? My son is not yet ten weeks old.' He did not phrase it as his wife not ten weeks buried, 'and my mind ought to be entirely upon my duty.'

'It is not?' She could not resist the question, though their pose gave his answer already.

'No, you know it is not. God forgive me, but I must make it so, for lives depend upon it. Until this is over . . . Christina . . .'

He used her name, and it thrilled her as much as his touch.

She sighed, and pulled away, turning towards him.

'I understand. I shall not . . . be weak, not yet.' Her voice was low, not sad but resigned.

They left the stable, decorously apart. He followed her across the courtyard and up the steps into the hall.

In the light he could see a weary sorrow on her face.

'You must be tired, truly.'

'Yes, it has been . . . a tiring day, my lord. You know, I thought I would feel pleased that Corbin's horse was home, but I just feel rather numbed by it.'

He went with her to the solar door and opened it, bowing to let her pass, and wished her a good night's rest. She thanked him with a smile, and when the door closed behind her, leant against the solid oak, took a long breath, and closed her eyes, the smile remaining.

Chapter Thirteen

Bradecote arose to a frosty morning, conscious that the day was likely to be marked by the confirmation of more deaths, and yet far from heavy-hearted, which gave him a twinge of guilt. Catchpoll's twinges were more physical, and he complained of how the cold got into his knees something wicked, nearly all the way to Wich, warming the air with his colourful language. Bradecote smiled wryly, and recommended what his father had sworn by, which was a bran poultice just the same as he used on his horses if they came up lame.

They kept to a steady trot to keep warm, and pulled their cloaks about them. Walkelin sniffed as the cold made his nose run. The ground was hard, jarring through the horses' legs, and once Bradecote's grey stumbled in a frozen cart track. Walkelin's mount, which seemed to find trotting far too much like hard work, had to be kicked in the flanks and sworn at for lagging behind and dropping to a walk at every opportunity. Walkelin's comments, about how he wished the sheriff would feed the beast to his hounds, did not even make it twitch its ears.

The sun, low upon the eastern horizon behind them, gave no

warmth, just a sparkle to the frosted leaves, and the woodland beside the road had an eerie silence to it, bar the odd scamper of a roebuck or flapping pigeon. Wich had a similar silence, but not from any slowing of the season, but rather as if the town already mourned its new dead. The glances they received were wary and glum, if not downright unfriendly.

'Cheery lot,' murmured Walkelin.

'Not surprising, after the number they have buried this month,' Catchpoll responded. 'Let's go and find more to make them miserable.'

It was a sombre company that set out from Wich upon what should be a festive holy day. The feast of St Luke was not going to be marked by any celebration, though as many as could went to the church to pray for deliverance from the affliction upon the town. The idea of something supernatural was taking greater hold, though the very solid reality of the arrows in the bodies should have dispelled it. The sheriff's men, accompanied by several of the packmen, who knew every yard of the way blindfolded, trotted off upon the road south to Worcester, a small cart with them for the load they expected to carry upon their return. The local knowledge of where would give most wayside cover aided the search, and within two hours there came a shout from the undergrowth as Walkelin, and a stocky individual who wheezed a lot, plunged into the foliage to the east of the track.

'Bodies, my lord, two of them.'

Walkelin emerged, looking a little pleased with himself, though his companion was ashen. Undersheriff and serjeant, who were casting about a little way further along, came to view where the corpses lay. There had been no attempt to rob them of clothing, indeed one still had a scrip containing a few pennies, and they appeared to have been cast into the bushes with some haste. What had alerted Walkelin was a booted foot sticking out.

'You get the feeling this was somehow interrupted, my lord?' Catchpoll scowled thoughtfully at the first corpse.

'Yes, Serjeant, but the last man who interrupted such an attack ended up in the heap of bodies.'

'Could it have been a body of men?' queried Walkelin, and received a raised eyebrow. 'Er, no joke intended, my lord.'

'And tell us, Walkelin, why this "body" of men did not ride, or indeed run, into Wich, only two miles away, shouting about the foul crime they saw committed?' Catchpoll was scathing. 'That one gets past me.'

Walkelin bit his lip, unable to come up with an answer. Bradecote knelt by the stiff corpses. Rigor mortis remained, abetted by the cold, though it was beginning to wear off. There was a ghostly rime of white upon the pale, blue-tinged faces, with the eyes that Bradecote could not but feel accused him of failure. Each had fallen to a single well-placed arrow. There was almost something clinical about it. He looked up at Catchpoll.

'This has to stop, and stop soon.'

'I know, my lord,' he spoke very quietly, lest the packmen, now huddled miserably upon the road, overheard him, 'but it is the devil of a job seeing how, from what we have, we can find our culprits. You find a corpse warm, or at least where it fell, and you can learn from them. These poor bastards can tell us little we did not know already.'

'Then let us take them back to Wich, and a decent burial. We will remove the arrows,' Bradecote murmured, closed the staring eyes with some difficulty, and stood up slowly. 'It is marginally less distressing for the bereaved.'

Their arrival back in Wich was greeted with the grim acceptance of folk expecting the worst. They brought the cart before the little church, where those most involved had remained, receiving what comfort the priest could offer. Despite the inevitability, one woman collapsed, and another turned angrily upon the shrieval officers.

'How long must we suffer this? Why should my children go fatherless because you cannot track a killer? Go on, tell me if you can.'

A voice at the rear of the group mumbled something about men only being able to track the living, and the woman snorted. Not for her the idea of a ghost.

'Fool that you are, do you think spirits would kill with weapons you can see and touch? If they were found with no mark upon them, then I would cross myself and pray, as a good Christian soul, but my man was murdered by another man, and upon the King's highway. Justice is what I seek. Justice is what I demand.'

She sounded belligerent, and if some feared her tone was dangerous to one as powerful as the undersheriff of the shire, many agreed with her. There were murmurs among the crowd.

'Mistress, we are doing everything we can, but there were no witnesses to this crime, and . . .'

'My lord? Was this upon the Worcester road, and the day before yesterday?' The voice belonged to someone hidden at the back of the crowd, by the church door. 'I may have seen something.'

The crowd parted like the Red Sea before Moses, revealing a man in tattered clothing, seated against the church wall and with a begging bowl between his knees.

The momentary elation that Bradecote had felt, plunged to his boots.

'Seen? But you are a . . .'

'Blind man. Yes, my lord, but the blind see without eyes.'

'Do you not travel with a guide, perhaps, friend?' enquired Catchpoll, catching at a thread of hope.

'Not always, though it is a help to me. But blind is not blackness, not for all. I cannot see the hand before my face as anything but a dark shape, everything is through a fog impenetrable, but with my stick and in full daylight, I can manage a little way, and I was heading here from Hussingtree, where the good folk did not wish to be generous in their alms.'

'What can you tell us then, that you saw,' Bradecote asked, '"without eyes"?'

'I was less than three miles south of Wich. I turned a bend in the road and there was something going on. I heard a man, a clumsy sort of fellow, come out of the bushes at some speed, as if chased by a boar, possibly. I was nervous, and cried out that he might know I was sightless. Being knocked over is a likely peril of one who cannot avoid things. Then there was a voice, a clear voice that shouted to hold still. I did not know whether that was to me or the other man, so I stood still. I think the other man had evil intent, for the voice, an angry voice, cried that he should be about his business and if he struck, he would be dropped, I assumed with an arrow. The noisy man was called by another.'

Catchpoll pounced upon the chance.

'Was he called by name, friend?'

'By the name Morcar. He drew away from me, and picked up something, something heavy, for he grunted as he did so, and I heard twigs and branchlets break at the roadside. Then he and the other men, for from the footfalls I would think there were three, departed with their ponies. I wondered if the man who had leapt out had been relieving himself and perhaps been surprised, and acted from instinct.' The blind beggar paused. 'It was very still for a minute or so, but I knew I was not alone. Then my rescuer came forward, and he was a quiet man, and he bade me be not disturbed, because he meant no harm to me. I asked what had happened, and he said nothing that I need worry about, and I should be on my way. Then the archer placed silver pennies in my hand and told me to pray for the souls of the dear departed, which I did in this church upon arrival and upon this holy day of St Luke. Then he left, with a blessing on his lips.'

'Archer?' Bradecote could not keep the urgency from his voice. 'How do you know he was an archer?'

'Easily, my lord. He pressed the coins into my palm. Any man knows the calluses upon an archer's drawing fingers.'

The blind man smiled.

'Can you describe this archer?'

Catchpoll ignored the looks that members of the crowd gave him.

'He was about my height, for he spoke neither down to me nor up. His voice was not of a youth nor yet an old man, but one in his prime of manhood, and he was a man of this shire, though something in the voice was odd, as if he had travelled, had heard other voices, if you understand.'

Catchpoll nodded, caught himself doing so, and then acknowledged in words.

'And this man expects to be obeyed when he commands.' The blind man chuckled. 'No doubt of that.'

'You mean like a lord?' Walkelin joined in, sounding incredulous.

'Bless you, no. I would swear he had nothing but the English for a start, and what lord would be horseless, and an archer? No, he has been where men obey, in a company of men, perhaps, and besides, his bow makes him a man I reckon as none who saw would defy.'

'You made no mention of this to anyone upon your arrival here.' Bradecote did not accuse, but was interested. 'Why was that?'

'Good, my lord, who is there to listen to the blind beggar? And besides, I thought I had avoided a beating through a kindly deed, not that there had been evil done upon the road, I swear. The archer, he sounded – except when he called out to the man, Morcar – very calm, even weary, not like a man who had been engaged upon a crime at all. There were no nerves, no edge of excitement.'

'You have aided us, my friend, and indeed the blind have seen more than the sighted.' Bradecote dismounted, and went to take the man's hand, which he shook and into which he quietly pressed coin. 'And you can tell I am no archer,' he whispered as he did so.

The blind man murmured blessing and thanks, and the undersheriff turned to find Walter Reeve at his elbow, frowning.

'You have some new piece of information for us today, Master Reeve?'

The reeve caught the irony in the tone and coloured.

'I, er . . . not as such, my lord. I just . . . no, nothing new.'

The man's worried demeanour had become permanent, decided Bradecote, and shook his head. It felt awkward, standing among people who all knew the dead, the dead they had been unable to save, and seeing the accusing eyes. The sheriff's men, seeing no use in remaining, mounted and returned on a long rein to Cookhill, where they tried to make the blind man's information the key to making an advance rather than fragments of interest. They failed, and it made all three rather morose.

Walter Reeve was indeed a worried man. He had lived, secure in his own self-worth, for years. He knew who he was, and had the pride that went with his position in the town, a position, it seemed to him, that nobody would challenge. He had the confidence of Earl Waleran, and ensured the tolls and taxes of Wich were paid in good time. He had taken what was his due for the collection, and but so little more as none might notice or begrudge. Yet in these last two weeks his world had tumbled about his ears. He was beleaguered by townsfolk who looked to him for leadership and guidance that were beyond him, and it had turned now to animosity. He felt the eyes that followed him, angry, frightened, and accusing him of incompetence, for all that he was trying so hard. He tossed and turned at night, so that his wife humphed and turned her shoulder upon him, and his dreams were tormented by a shadowy figure he only saw from the corner of his eye, but who laughed, mocking him. What was worse, the nightmare always ended the same way, with the sound of an arrow in flight and the sensation of falling.

Small wonder that he drowned his sorrows of a night in the tavern, and the ale muddled him all the more.

Despite this there was something, something whispering in a dark recess of his mind, and it disturbed him as he went about the town, vainly trying to look in control of matters. It told him he was connected with all the deaths, in a way he could not fathom. What had been borne home to him by the undersheriff was that whoever organised the attacks and killings had information on departures. Of all men in Wich, he was the man who could be guaranteed to know those, because of the toll. He had mumbled as much the night before last, when he had stumbled out of the tavern into the cold night air. It had hit him like a blow in the face, and sent him reeling, only for him to be helped upright by a friendly soul, who offered to help him home. This Good Samaritan had soothed him with soft words, and told him that his worry was an unfair burden to carry. He himself, said the calming friend, had knowledge that there was a wagon of salt heading west the day after St Luke's. At that, Walter Reeve had hiccoughed and giggled, and promptly vomited in the gutter. Upon recovery, he had disabused his companion of that error. The salt heading towards Hereford did not depart until the second day after the holy day.

'You see,' he had said sadly, slurring the words, 'it is always me who knows.'

The reeve stopped dead in the street, and a woman walking behind him, who was carrying a chicken destined for the pot, cannoned into him and cursed him in less than genteel language as she dropped the bird and had to chase after it, much to the delight of several children. They laughed openly, and encouraged the chicken to make its bid for freedom.

The man accompanying him that night had laughed, and something in that laugh now sent a shiver down the spine of Walter Reeve. He tried to think, think beyond the befuddled state in which he so often ended up in the tavern, and slowly, slowly, a horrible truth presented itself to him. He leant against the dank daub of a salt-house wall to steady himself. No, he had never seen the man who had helped him that evening, not before the attacks started. He cudgelled his brain to recall what manner of man he was, but the stranger always sat in a gloomy corner, a listener not a talker, a quiet individual who drank, thanked the host courteously, and departed. He was thin and tall, Walter remembered that much. He must tell the undersheriff. Then he shook his head. No, he had told the lord Bradecote so much that what he said carried little weight. Well, it would be different when he, the reeve of Wich, caught the man who was in part responsible for the killings, and presented him before the undersheriff for interrogation. Then his neighbours would look upon him with respect again, and Earl Waleran would send him commendation.

He wondered if the man would be around this evening. He headed to the tavern, and asked the host, as tactfully as possible, about the tall stranger in the corner. The tavern keeper frowned.

'I know who you mean, Master Reeve, but for the life of me I could not tell you aught about him. Odd, that. I would have thought if he had come to stay in Wich we would have seen him about the place during the day, upon some task.' He shrugged. 'Oh well, perhaps he will come in tonight, and you can ask him yourself where he is living.'

* * *

199

If Mistress Reeve found her husband distracted at the evening meal, it was no more than she had come to expect these last days, and she accepted his monosyllabic answers without comment. He frowned over his meal, which displeased her, since she had been particularly careful to boil the pig's trotters just as he liked, but he seemed to come out of his daze at the end, and actually complimented her upon her cooking and kissed her cheek, as he declared he was going out. She glared at him, for he did not have to say where he was going.

'Now, not that face, wife, for tonight I am going to do something that will make you proud, and my name will be upon everyone's lips on the morrow.'

With which, he kissed her cheek again and was gone, leaving her perplexed, and vaguely ill at ease.

The tavern was not a hive of convivial jollity these days, more men drowning their sorrows. Whilst those who worked in the salt houses were not directly at risk, they all felt the cloud of misery that hung over their town and trade. Voices were muted, and few looked up as the reeve entered. Those that did barely more than grunted acknowledgement. Tomorrow, thought Walter, all will be different. I shall be the hero of the hour.

He nodded to the tavern keeper, who, with a jerk of his head, indicated a table in the least lit corner of the room. Walter Reeve approached, with forced bonhomie, and feigned surprise.

'Why, it is my good friend from the other night. I give you a good evening, and would buy you ale, in thanks for your kind deed.'

Reginald eyed the reeve suspiciously.

'No need. It was hardly an act of great charity, since I was heading that way myself.'

'Ah yes,' murmured Walter, in what he hoped would sound a casual tone, 'and where might it be you are living, for you are not much known hereabouts?'

Reginald's eyes flickered, but he answered smoothly.

'I have been sent by the Brothers of Gloucester to oversee their salt houses, in these troubled times.'

'So you have been staying with Aelnoth or Samson, then?'

'With Samson, yes.'

The delay had been but a heartbeat.

'Good fellow, Samson, hard-working. The Brothers need never have concerns about his labour.'

'Oh no, I am sure that is not the case. It is more to offer support in the current, er, unpleasantness.'

'Will the Brothers be paying for the services of my lord de Malfleur's men-at-arms?'

'Perhaps.' Reginald tried to sound undecided, and took a languorous swig from his ale. 'It depends upon what service is owed to the abbey.'

'True enough.' Walter, very cleverly, he thought, did not press the point. 'Now, do let me buy you a fresh jug of best ale. I feel beholden.'

'If it means so much to you, then thank you, yes.'

Reginald wondered whether he might slip out whilst Walter fetched the replenished jug, but decided against it. After all, he was at least two steps ahead of this blundering reeve. He waited, and Walter returned, bearing his gift. He pushed his cup across the table with a murmur of thanks, and watched Walter pour himself a cup to overflowing. He nearly laughed. What did the pathetic sot think he was doing, outwitting him?

He was so sure of himself he did not actually notice that although Walter raised the cup to his lips frequently, he took very little, or that he was not nearly as inebriated as he made out. After what Walter considered a suitable interval he began to babble, suitably incoherently, about the undersheriff being led astray and the ire of the lord de Lasson. Reginald could not conceal a smirk, brief as it was. Then the reeve started to talk about the pack train for Shrewsbury, and how important it was. Reginald lapped up the information, and, instead of making his excuses, decided to linger. Walter, in an expansive gesture, knocked over the jug, sending the remaining ale to soak into the floor. Such a waste, he thought, but in a good cause. He belched, and got unsteadily to his feet.

'Come, friend, and I will walk home with you,' Walter beamed vacuously, 'and make sure you are all right.' Walter negotiated his way with some difficulty round a stool, nearly tangling his legs in it, as Reginald waited patiently. 'Come, let us go home, my Gloucester friend.'

Taking Reginald's arm, Walter headed for the door. He was thinking, and thinking fast. This man had nothing to do with the Gloucester salt houses, for Samson had been dead these five years since. He thought to take him to that end of the town, though, since his cousin lived and worked in another of the cluster of salt houses belonging to Gloucester, but had taken his wife to her mother's deathbed in an outlying village that very afternoon. The salt house would be empty, and there he could show this man he was no fool and perhaps even get information from him. They made their way, arm in arm and with Walter a little unsteady and friendly in the manner of the drunk. They were clearly not aiming for the reeve's house, and Reginald, beginning to realise they must be heading for the house of Samson, tried to make his excuses. After all, this Samson would look at him blankly, having never seen him before. They walked along a line of salt houses, Reginald becoming more vociferous, when Walter, with an amazing change of demeanour, suddenly bundled him through a door into a house in darkness. There was little light at all and Reginald was taken off guard.

'So tell me, my tall friend, who most certainly does not reside with the long-dead Samson, how long did you think it would be before you were discovered?'

Reginald, getting his bearings, replied in his normal voice. 'Why, never.'

Chapter Fourteen

The sheriff's men arrived in Wich early in the next forenoon, and headed to the reeve's house, but instead of encountering Walter Reeve, found his highly agitated wife, wringing her hands and near hysterical. Her husband had not returned home after visiting his favoured tavern, and she was already mourning him as one dead.

'Oh my lord, he said his name would be on everyone's lips and he would make me proud this day. I fear he has been foolish, and lies dead in a ditch. He has been cast down by all that has afflicted our town and last night there was something odd about him. He was not himself,' she wiped her eyes with the edge of her veil, 'not at all.'

'He went to the tavern, Mistress Reeve. But do you know if he left it?' Hugh Bradecote spoke calmly, and with gentle authority. 'And did he leave alone?'

'I went there, at first light, and got Alfsi, who keeps it, out of his bed. He said as how Walter left, drunk as so often, with the tall stranger.'

'The tall stranger?' Catchpoll glanced at Bradecote. 'I think,

Mistress, we too must see the landlord. Show us which tavern he visited, and in the meantime we will set men to search within the town. My lord?'

He looked, belatedly, to Bradecote, for confirmation of what was clearly his own decision, but the undersheriff was not concerned about how things looked, and merely nodded his confirmation.

'Whatever has happened, we will find your husband, Mistress. Walkelin, you are to gather what men you can and search every stable, outhouse and building. Serjeant Catchpoll will come with me and Mistress Reeve. Let us get going.'

They split up outside, Walkelin to knock on doors and form a search party, and the others to the tavern. The tavern keeper met them with a look of concern that made Mistress Reeve burst into tears once more, and Catchpoll suggested that she remain with the landlord's wife while the hunt continued. The men withdrew to a corner, the same one used by Walter Reeve and Reginald the night before, and spoke in hushed tones.

'Master Reeve was asking about the tall stranger in the day, wondering where he sprang from. You see he had not taken any obvious work in the town, and was rarely seen except here of an odd evening. He seemed very interested in him. Poor man had—sorry, has, been worried of late, what with the responsibility and all, but he did look quite excited yesterday.'

Catchpoll pulled at his nose, thinking.

'This tall man, when would you say he first appeared?'

'Why, must have been two to three weeks past. Courteous he was, quiet, tended to sit here out the way and drink awhile, then he would bid all a soft goodnight and leave. Few nights back, though, he left just after Master Reeve, who had taken more than he could handle again, and I gather from what I overheard last night, helped him home.'

'And did you not hear that we needed to know about any man who has only appeared here in the last few weeks?'

Catchpoll sounded exasperated, and the landlord shifted uncomfortably. There was something about Serjeant Catchpoll that made one keen not to exasperate him. Bradecote shot his serjeant a look that clearly said 'Shut up' and tried to keep the tavern keeper focussed.

'What did you overhear?'

'My lord, when Master Reeve came in, I let him know the stranger was here. He came over, right to this table, and sat down, thanking the man for his assistance in helping him home the other night. That is how I know. Master Reeve bought a jug of ale to share with him too, though I fear he drank too much. He even knocked the jug over, still half full. Mind you, I could almost swear he winked at me as he left.'

'Did you hear what they talked about?'

'I had other customers, my lord, so not really. Did catch something about Gloucester and old Samson as had a salt house of Gloucester's, but he's been dead some years.' The tavern keeper scratched his head. 'Perhaps the tall man was a relative?'

'Mmm. You say the man was tall. As tall as me?' The undersheriff was a very tall man. 'And thin?'

'Not quite of your height, my lord, and less muscled, more gangly, like a heron, I would describe him. Did not see his face clearly for he tended to stoop, like the heron fishing, you see.'

'What about hair colour, or any other things that might help us spot him?' Catchpoll was clutching at straws. 'The more you can tell us, the quicker we can find him.'

'Wore a hood, he did. Tell you what, though. Now I come to think about it, there was something odd. He had a cloak always, ordinary sort of dark cloak it was, and it hid what I caught sight of that night.'

'Which was?'

The sheriff's men spoke in unison.

'Just not what I would expect.'

'Tell us, for the sake of Heaven!' Catchpoll had to control his urge to shake the man.

'Well, he did not look the soldier type, yet he had a sword at his hip, in a good and well-used leather scabbard.'

Bradecote and Catchpoll exchanged glances, at one in thought.

'Good, you say?' Catchpoll was probing.

'Good leather, and had seen long use for it was worn and the surface a little torn. But there, perhaps he was a soldier long ago and had it from habit. Some men never forget their warrior days.'

Undersheriff and serjeant had different ideas on that. It was clear the man had no more information, so they thanked him and went outside to discuss what they had learnt.

'Our stolen horse seller and the tall man who has only been here since the trouble started seem one and the same, Catchpoll.'

'Indeed so, my lord, which does make the lord de Lasson's cry of innocence ring true. Pity, in a way, and he'll run to the Sheriff of Hereford like a rat down a hole, and make trouble. Our lord de Beauchamp will not enjoy having his ear bent by the lord Earl of Hereford, but there.' Catchpoll sighed and shook his head. 'We could do no less upon the evidence.'

'And the scabbard, as we thought, sounds very much as if it is Corbin FitzPayne's.'

'Most like with his sword still in it. Yes, cocky bastard to wear the thing, mind.'

'He would not expect it to be recognised, though. Chri— the lady FitzPayne said it was very ordinary, except for the slash in the surface of the leather.'

Bradecote turned slightly pink, and hoped Catchpoll had missed the slip. He had not, but said nothing.

'I think Walter Reeve suddenly put two and two together, about the man's arrival and the attacks, and if he has a loose tongue when ale-sodden, as many are, he could easily have given the information without knowing.'

It was at this point that a leggy youth ran up, made obeisance to Bradecote and announced, breathlessly, that the deputy serjeant had found Master Reeve and bade his superiors come right away.

'Deputy serjeant?' Catchpoll ground his teeth and muttered. 'I'll give him "deputy serjeant", with the end of my boot!'

They followed the youth, with his loping gait, which meant Catchpoll arriving at the salt house wheezing and out of breath. The youth tried to follow them in, but was told instead to guard the door, which made him feel important. The shutters had not been opened, for Walkelin wanted the public kept out, at least until his superiors arrived, and Catchpoll swore as he banged his shins upon the edge of the hollowed tree trunk that formed the 'salt ship' for storing brine. The expletives were colourful.

'Give us some light before Serjeant Catchpoll does himself a major injury, Walkelin.' Bradecote chuckled, though the laughter died on his lips as a rear shutter was opened enough to see what was in the chamber. 'God have mercy!' He crossed himself devoutly.

Walter Reeve lay with head and chest in a lead salt pan, bent forward from a kneeling position. The vat was little more than three feet long and quite shallow, but it did not take much water to drown a man. The contents of the salt pan were not, however, salty water and scum. It had been reduced so that it appeared a good way through the process and was a white slurry. Catchpoll ran a finger through it.

'Still slightly warm, my lord,' he commented in a non-committal tone, and then placed his hand on the back of Walter Reeve's neck. 'Unlike Walter here.'

'The salt houses are in use all the time, so . . . who's house is this, and where is he, and the others who work here?'

'It was a holy day, my lord, perhaps they took the day from labour?' Walkelin offered up his idea, diffidently.

'But if they did they would be here to work today, so why are they not here?'

'Besides,' added Catchpoll, 'I would be surprised if the salt was still as warm to the touch after more than a day, and why leave a boiling part way through? And do you catch the smell?'

Bradecote sniffed. They used urine in the making of the salt but there was another smell, slightly sweet, very faint, a kitchen sort of smell. He frowned.

'Shall we lift the body, my lord?' Walkelin interrupted his thought.

'Yes. No, wait. Let us learn whatever there is from him as he lies, first. Open the shutter more, there are no onlookers there as yet.'

Walkelin did as he was bid, but it did not make the scene easier on the eye. There was something grotesque about the position of the body, bowing to the salt.

'What does he tell you, then, young Walkelin?' asked Catchpoll.

'Why nothing, Serjeant, because he's dea . . . ow!'

The cuff around the ears was unexpected on Walkelin's part, and stung.

'Bran for brains! And you calling yourself "deputy serjeant", indeed!' That clearly rankled, and Walkelin winced.

'I had to think of something a bit official to call myself, to get the lad to obey at the run, Serjeant. Sorry, Serjeant.'

'You should have called yourself "Idiot Not Yet Fit To Call Himself Serjeant's Apprentice", and that's a fact. How often have I told you, the dead can tell us all sorts of things? And you have observed well enough upon the road. Have the fumes got to you?'

'No, Serjeant.'

'Then tell me what you see.'

'Er . . . he must have been overpowered, because the arms are not in the salt or at the sides of the pan. A man who could, would brace his arms to prevent him being forced into the water. We should check the body for wounds in case he was stabbed first, or his neck broken.'

'Sound thoughts, those, but we can go further.' Catchpoll looked sagely at his protégé, and was conscious that the undersheriff was expecting to learn also. 'The arms are not in the attitude of struggle, as you saw, but the right arm, look at it. It lies to his side, but also still with the palm facing back and resting on his arse. That tells me what happened was, this.'

In a flash, Catchpoll grabbed Walkelin by his right arm, twisting it and ducking underneath to end up behind him and with the young man on tiptoe and his arm up his back. Catchpoll knocked the back of his knees, and as he went down, grabbed a handful of flame-coloured hair and pushed his head forward. It was very swift, and most uncomfortable.

'Easy when you know how,' murmured Catchpoll, not even breathing more quickly. 'And for all he was no warrior, at least in looks, our killer knew that move.'

'Impressive, and well, er, illustrated, Serjeant.' Bradecote smiled wryly. 'Anything else?'

'I think we can lift the body now, my lord,' declared Catchpoll, rather enjoying himself. The enjoyment ended when they lifted the stiff remains of Walter Reeve from the vat. The position of the body, bent at knees and waist, looked even less natural laid upon the ground, but it was the face that repelled.

The eyes were white opaque like the old blind, but bizarrely flat and distorted where the salt had drawn the moisture from them. The nose was filled and rimed with the crystals, and the skin of the face unlike any that even Catchpoll had seen. The skin was peeled and blistered in places from the residual heat when he had been thrust into the thick salty paste, and the salt had dried and crusted the rest of the surface. The faint kitchen smell had been flesh, slightly cooked. It was Walter Reeve in such a way as his wife would be hard-pressed to recognise him. Walkelin turned away and retched into a wicker basket.

'Dear God in Heaven,' whispered Bradecote, and crossed himself again, instinctively. His gorge threatened to rise like Walkelin's but he fought it. 'What a death.'

Catchpoll's mouth was clamped into a thin slash among the stubble and when he opened his mouth he swore, low and long.

'Not good, not good at all. The salt was half ready as I see it, certainly hot, from the effect on the skin, that and the salt itself. I reckon as he sort of drowned and suffocated at the same time, though the first is in a way a version of the second, but what the poor bastard was drawing in was not water but hot salt. Nasty. This lanky-heron man will dance at the rope's end, I swear to God.'

There was a commotion outside, an altercation between the youth 'on guard' and another man. Bradecote sent Walkelin, wiping his sleeve across his mouth, and glad to get the chance of a gulp of fresh air, to see what was toward. He was almost bowled over, not just by a man, but two strapping teenaged lads, and a woman with a younger girl at her skirts. Before he could stop them they were inside, shouting incoherently, until their eyes adjusted to the dim light. There was a moment of horrified silence and then the woman screamed, screamed as if her lungs would burst.

'For Christ's sake, get the woman and child out of here!' yelled Catchpoll, angrily, and the man half turned and pushed both woman and girl back out the door.

'You look after your mother,' the man whispered hoarsely to the lads, and jerked his head at the doorway. They needed no second command. He shut the door behind them, and turned, his face a greenish tinge, even in the gloomy light.

'Who are you?' asked Bradecote, baldly.

'Oswald, Oswald Tuckett, and this is my house.' The man's voice was choked as he took in more of the scene and he fought to keep himself from retching.

'Yours, you say.'

'Well, it is a salt house of the Gloucester monks, but I live here, and work it with my sons.'

Bradecote and Catchpoll exchanged glances. Gloucester was what the landlord had overheard.

'Was this once the salt house worked by Samson?' queried Catchpoll.

'Samson? No, that was three houses along, and is run by Thomas now. What has happened? Some accident?'

'Accident?' Catchpoll snorted. 'Have you ever seen a man drown in a hot salt pan in an "accident"?'

'Well, no.' The man swallowed and glanced at the body, then winced. 'He might have been drunk and done so.'

'You mean he wandered in here, unchallenged, and just collapsed into the fresh boiling?' Disbelief rang in Catchpoll's voice. 'Why should the town reeve do—'

'That's Walter? Oh my God, it is!'

Oswald began to shake.

'Ah, so you recognise him. Can you explain his presence here, dead in your salt pan?'

The serjeant's tone was near casual now, as if he were but mildly interested.

'He is – he was – my cousin. Sweet Heaven, and I saw him but yesterday.'

'No doubt.' Catchpoll kept up the pressure.

'What do you mean?' Oswald was on the defensive, suspicious.

'The salt is made every day, even, it seems, on holy days, since the contents of the pan are still warm.' Bradecote joined in, keeping the salt-maker off balance. 'So why were the family not here overnight? Had you sent them elsewhere?'

Oswald blinked and stared at one then the other.

'Who are you?' he asked, belatedly.

'We,' announced Serjeant Catchpoll, in his most impressive tone, 'are the sheriff's men, and this,' he indicated Hugh

Bradecote with apparent pride, 'is the lord Undersheriff of the shire. I am surprised you have not seen us about Wich this last week or more.'

'No, I . . . My daughter had a spotted fever and we kept within doors as much as possible until a day or two back,' he made a rough obeisance to Bradecote, and added, 'my lord.'

'And yesterday?' Bradecote accepted that the reason sounded 'right', but was not going to accept it blindly.

'We had a boiling in the afternoon, though took the morning as a holy day and went to church and did not fire the pans until mid afternoon, it must have been. Then, as the light failed, word came that my wife's mother was dying. She broke her leg last week and it sent her downhill fast. She lives in a village just outside Wich, and I would not send my Emma there in the dark, so we all went. It was right we should.'

'What about the boilings?'

'They were doing well, but it would be madness to leave the fires unattended. We raked out three, but that one,' he nodded at the one from which they had taken Walter Reeve, 'was at the point we would have built it up. You see we boil, but not too fierce, the lead being soft. So we let that one die of itself. It was down to a red glow and we reckoned it safe and contained in the stone of the oven there. It would have been out by mid evening.'

'You remained at this deathbed all evening?' Bradecote did not doubt the reply he would receive. 'And there are those who can vouch you did not return until now?'

'Oh yes, my lord. The wife's brother, and an aunt.' Oswald nodded vigorously. 'My wife's mother died about the middle of the night.'

Catchpoll scratched his grizzled chin.

'So when did you see your cousin Walter?'

'As we were leaving. I told him where we were off to, and he offered sympathy to the wife.'

'How did he seem to you?' Bradecote adopted Catchpoll's casual tone. 'When you parted.'

'Quite bright, sort of sparrow-chirpy, you might say, my lord. Might have just been that he was off to the alehouse, of course.'

'So he knew you would be away all night?'

Oswald looked at Catchpoll.

'Of course, I told him so.'

'And did he have anybody with him, or say he was meeting anyone?'

'No, he was alone.'

'Fair enough,' Catchpoll sniffed, and looked to his superior, who shook his head. There was no reason to think Oswald Tuckett had anything to do with the killing. 'We will need your house a little longer, until we can return the body to the widow. Best you keep the family out the way an hour more.'

'Aye, I will take them to the church,' he shuddered, 'and will ask the priest to come and sprinkle holy water upon my pans.'

Dismissed, he left swiftly.

'So, Catchpoll, do you read what happened the same way I do?'

'Depends, my lord, upon what you say.'

'I surmise,' and here Bradecote leant his head to one side and forced himself to look at the remains of Walter Reeve, 'that Walter thought he could capture the tall stranger, and maybe

215

even get him to tell what he knew before he brought him to us. He wanted to be the man of the moment.'

'He achieved that,' Catchpoll noted, with a macabre grin, 'but not in the way he expected.'

'No. He thought he was cleverer than his opponent, and he was not. He found the man in the tavern, bought him ale to lull him, perhaps even get him a little drunk, and pretended he was in his normal state.' Bradecote smiled at Catchpoll. 'Ah yes, I did take note of the tipped-over jug. He wanted the man to "help" him home again, but he brought him here, not sure what he said to do so, and once inside declared himself to the tall man, who decided he was too dangerous to live, and so killed him. How's that?'

'You want me to clap, my lord?' Catchpoll grinned, which took away the chance of his words being seen as insubordinate sarcasm.

'No, your agreement will suffice, you wily old bastard.'

'Then you have it, my lord.' Catchpoll took the epithet as a compliment. 'Trouble is,' and he pulled an earlobe thoughtfully, 'I do not see our killer being likely to hang around Wich for a while. We can make known his description, but he would be a fool to return, and if he got his information from the reeve, unbeknownst to the man, well, his source has, er, dried up in more ways than one.'

'Your sense of humour, Catchpoll, is twisted.'

'Indeed, my lord. Better laugh than throw up your last meal like Walkelin there.' His face grew serious again. 'Best we force the body into a semblance of repose, and cover the face, my lord, not that it will be easy, but we cannot take him to his widow like that.' There was no humour now, ghoulish or otherwise.

'Er, how do we, um . . .' Walkelin looked at the contorted frame, 'achieve that?'

'By force, if necessary, lad.'

It was, and Walkelin had recourse to the wicker basket a second time.

Chapter Fifteen

The ash tree had once been a fine specimen, but its very height had marked it for destruction, and a bolt of lightning had riven it in two. The part that fell had been taken, bit by bit, though it was a good mile from Ombersley, and there were those who shook their heads over taking the result of a lightning strike into their homes. Lightning was the work of Heaven, and if Heaven had judged the tree, they said, it must have been possessed, and woe betide any that used the condemned branches as firewood. Bad luck was sure to follow. Despite this, it was now only the surviving trunk, bearing the deep white scar and dead portion of upper branches, that remained, and in the dimming light those pale fingers pointing skyward had a spectral appearance.

The Archer was not concerned. He waited patiently, in the undergrowth opposite, at one with the softly rustling woods. Not for him wild superstition, though he might have thought arrow shafts from such a tree had a special quality when hunting. That was something unconscious, passed from his father when he was but a small boy, and nothing, he would have told himself, to do with elves, spirits or celestial judgement. Like Catchpoll, the

Archer had seen enough deaths, been the instrument of them often enough too, not to worry about those who had ceased to draw breath. He prayed for those he knew and to whom he had been close, and left the rest to be prayed for by their own kin. He did not think they walked in the night, nor called upon the wind. And yet, though he tried to keep them shrouded, he did have his 'ghosts', the images that surfaced occasionally and sent a shudder through his soul; the look of surprise, and accusation, the frozen bewilderment of the moment of death, as his lord half spun round to face the man whose sword had slashed hard enough to slice even the backbone; his father crawling towards him, calling his name, raising a bloody face made blank by the empty, gory sockets; a soldier given up to the bloodlust of battle, striking through an imploring woman and the squalling babe in her arms. Those did not stay 'dead and buried', and no priest would ever exorcise them, but he knew most fighting men had them, and they accepted their existence as they did old wounds that ached when the weather grew damp.

The sound of the horse's hoof beats brought him from his abstraction. It was a time of day when it was unlikely to be any but the Messenger, and today, he thought, the Messenger had trouble, for the horse was walking lame. Well, he could sleep out, if he had the skill as the Archer had, or he could find shelter in some villager's dwelling. It would mean he arrived unhappy, and the Archer, who had an intuitive dislike for the man, smiled to himself. He greeted the tall figure with a very cheerful 'Good even, Master Messenger', and Reginald, who was in a filthy mood, grunted in return.

'How long has your beast been lame?'

'These three miles since, may it die a death!' Reginald jumped slightly, despite knowing the man would be somewhere about, but the voice sounded disembodied.

'Have a care to his feet, and you should need less care to your own, Master Messenger, but three miles is not far to walk upon a brisk evening.'

The Archer doubted the other man looked after his horse with any care.

'If I wanted advice on horseflesh, or on walking, I would not seek it here,' replied Reginald, with acerbity.

He was tired, his boots pinched, and, as the Archer had foreseen, he would be asking shelter in some stinking hovel, plagued with noisy children and livestock. It was not a prospect that thrilled him.

'Let us get on with this and I shall be away,' he declared.

'By all means. I wonder, by the way, how long this is to continue. I am at a loss to see why anyone should want so much salt, or so many lives ended.'

'You are not paid to wonder, Archer, just to loose your arrows straight. And best for you that you just stick to the thing you're paid to do, for my lord is not one to cross.'

'Then throw down the coin and tell me the next task.'

'The carts heading for the Benedictines at Shrewsbury leave tomorrow. Strike just south of Kidderminster, where there is a ford. They will be there in the mid afternoon. No survivors.'

'Throw the scrip and turn around.'

Reginald did as he was told. He heard the slight sound of the coins in the bag. Then, oddly, he heard the bag fall upon the ground, and the chink of silver once more.

'No survivors. You know, I grow weary of this. I have taken the silver for south of Wich, but leave you to find another way

220

of ensuring your "no survivors". Your lord can pay another or perhaps send you.'

Reginald turned, swiftly, but faced nothing.

'You cannot. My lord has paid—'

'For work done, Master Messenger. I choose to take no more work.'

Reginald lost his temper, for he was frightened. His lord did not take kindly to failure.

'You do so at your peril, Archer, for none cross Baldwin de Malfleur and live to old age.'

There was a silence, but not the silence of Reginald standing alone upon the track, he knew that. He smiled. So the Archer could be scared.

'I thought that would wipe the smile from your face, Archer. You have heard of Bal—'

'I know Baldwin de Malfleur.'

Reginald almost jumped. The tone of the voice had changed. There was no laughter in it, which was as he expected, but it was a tone as cold as the grave.

'And now I know why "no survivors". It would be his way. But I thought him long dead, drowned.'

'Why no. His vessel foundered on his return from the Holy Land, but he survived and later came home to inherit his brother's lands after the lord Arnulf died before Lincoln.'

'Tell me, how did Arnulf de Malfleur die?'

'A bad death, from the bloody flux.'

'That is good. Ah yes, that is indeed very good.'

Reginald shivered. To rejoice in such a death for any man was a foul thing.

'Master Messenger, you have spent these last weeks bringing

221

messages to me. Now, I have one for you to deliver from me, to Baldwin de Malfleur.'

'You send one to him?' Reginald made a spluttering sound, which the Archer ignored.

'Tell him he is going to die, very soon, and all the priests in the shire cannot shrive him of the sins upon his black soul.'

'But why, Archer?' Reginald could not contain his curiosity. 'Why should you want him dead?'

There was no answer. He and his lame horse were alone upon the trackway.

Wich had been in uproar from the moment that it was known that Walter Reeve was dead. Rumours spread about what had happened to him, some more unlikely than others, but all dwelt upon the fact that it had been a gruesome end that had sent Mistress Tuckett a shrieking wreck and left her husband sick to his stomach. It had been one thing when the killings had been of Wich men but not within the town. Now every citizen felt threatened, feared who or what might be around every corner. The populace had, after the initial panic, withdrawn into their homes like snails into their shells. Bradecote had tried to make an announcement to as many as possible that they were to report any sightings of a tall, thin man, with receding hair, or a chestnut horse with a lightning blaze down its face. He wondered how many had taken it in. There were already mutterings about 'curses' and 'devils' and Catchpoll sucked his teeth.

They left in the afternoon, since the idea that the murderer would be ambling around Wich when the body was likely to be discovered was far from likely. Deprived of the town reeve as their point of contact, they arranged to meet with the tavern keeper next morning, having put it out that any information should be passed to him. The man himself received this news with paling cheek, regarding it as being a probable death sentence. They did explain that if anything were said of use it would quite possibly be in the tavern and without intent. Privately, and in some relief, he thought his alehouse would most likely be deserted, and any drinkers who came to him that evening would almost certainly choose to go home in pairs.

'Trouble is,' declared Catchpoll, morosely, as they rode back to Cookhill, 'since they are starting to understand that Walter Reeve was killed because he knew something, they are all going about trying their damnedest to know nothing.'

'Just when we might be getting somewhere, they will act like a flock of sheep, all bleating and running around in circles together.' Bradecote sighed.

'Should we go to de Malfleur, my lord? We have the excuse of his cart, or one that might be his.' Walkelin wanted to do something that might be productive.

'But when we get there Walkelin, we have nothing to use as leverage. At least with de Lasson we had the presence of the stolen cart. And I do not think that being thought suspect would worry de Malfleur a jot. He would relish it, in fact. I can just see him laughing in our faces, for we have no evidence whatsoever.' Bradecote was not hopeful.

'If he is connected, then the man upon the chestnut may have returned to him.' Walkelin was dogged.

'True enough, young Walkelin, but as the lord Bradecote says, us riding in all official just to tell him his cart might have been found, and asking after our chestnut-horsed murderer, will make him a very happy bastard. It may also mean that if Walter Reeve's murderer does go back to Rushock, de Malfleur will dispense with him, permanently, and we needs him alive.'

Catchpoll was able to think several steps ahead.

'Sorry, Serjeant.' Walkelin looked dejected.

'No, it was a fair enough thought, and if we could spare you to keep a covert watch upon de Malfleur's manor . . . Might we yet be reduced to that, my lord?'

'We might, Catchpoll. We might. Let us see what the morrow brings first.'

He was wondering if he dare let Christina know that they were, admittedly in desperation, now looking at de Malfleur as a serious suspect. He was not sure whether she would applaud, berate him for not doing so from the beginning, or turn inward and silent from the memories it gave her. She would have to know about the death of the reeve of Wich, and he knew that would be a cloud over their evening.

As it was, he managed to avoid all mention of de Malfleur, and she took the news of the latest murder better than he had expected. She had met Walter Reeve at various times, but did not know the man as a personality. Bradecote obviously did not give her details of the manner of the man's death, but she showed interest in the killer being that same man who had sold Corbin's horse and who wore his scabbard, and possibly his sword.

'It is odd, but I bear a grudge against him for that, though he did not fire the arrow. It is a foolish thing, for sense says that whether one man or another took those things when Corbin's soul had departed the body is immaterial, and yet it angers me. Would it make him complicit in the crime? Would he, will he, hang for Corbin also, when you catch him?'

'You have confidence that we will? Just at this moment I wonder, though it has been a second bad day, and I am weary. I keep blaming myself for the fact that Walter Reeve felt he had to prove this alone and not bring the information to me first. I had been so dismissive, because of all the false and foolish leads.'

She looked at him, touched by his guilt, his humanity. No man she had ever encountered would have felt that.

'Guilt can be a dangerous thing, my lord. It can feed upon itself, make a minor failing into a major sin, turn one from going forward and leave one wallowing in a regretted past. I speak as one who knows it well, but if you let the guilt do that it will hinder you in your search for justice for Master Reeve, and that is your duty, to him and to the law.'

She spoke gently, but her words had weight. They sat in the hall, though she would have as happily had him in her solar, but he did not trust himself where none might enter without a knock. His fingers twisted the cup of hot wine upon the table, and at which he had been staring, but then he turned to look at her, fully, a half smile on his face.

'You are the voice of wisdom, my lady. Every undersheriff should have you at his elbow.'

'There are many undersheriffs, my lord. I think,' she paused, and fought the instinct to lower her gaze, 'I would be best at the elbow of but one.'

There, she had said it, made her position clear, brazenly, boldly. How much more forward could a woman be and keep even the vestige of honour? Her eyes searched his for his response, and what she found made her heart thump. He took his hand from the cup and reached for hers, holding it so the thumb stroked slowly across the back of her hand. The skin was smooth and soft. The hand was halfway to his lips when he suddenly disengaged, hearing a servant enter to clear the remnants of the meal. She hurriedly moved her hand, which appeared frozen in space, in an airy gesture accompanying a vacuous and general remark in a voice that mocked itself. They contained themselves while the wench remained, but upon her departure, gave themselves up to embarrassed laughter, though it joined rather than divided them. They were certain of each other, except when they doubted themselves, so keen to be right that they feared they must be wrong, and the words 'too soon' hung in the air, though their instincts clamoured otherwise. It made them the most timorous and tentative of lovers, but every word and silence, every touch and almost touch, was redolent of love. There was just the hesitation to give in to its dictates.

Bradecote knew his own mind, knew also that if he gave in to physical passion, he would be swept away by it, and that however much she desired that also, she would regret it, feel that very guilt she had mentioned. He wanted a future with her in which there was no guilt about anything that had happened before. He wanted her to walk into his arms unfettered by her past, and if he lay with her, in Corbin FitzPayne's bed, and within a month of his killing, she would know guilt. Therefore he held himself in check, which had, at first, confused her.

Men took what they wanted, she knew that, and she knew, with every fibre now, that he wanted her, her body as well as her heart. That the two were contained in the same thought was a thing of wonder, and when first it hit her, she was cast into self-doubt by his contained response. She feared she was inventing what she wanted him to feel, but with every meeting these last few days she grew in faith, and in amazement at his consideration and self-control. Self-control and a man; she shook her head at the unlikely combination, but it made her love him the more, and she dared to think that word now.

After the laughter came the silence, companionable yet strained by what was not said, by what did not take place. Bradecote finished his wine, self-consciously, knowing she watched him. As he set down the cup and was about to rise, she spoke.

'My lord, might I ask to come with you, to Wich, tomorrow? I am bound within all this, yet have perforce sat at the edges of it. I would like to stand instead in the middle, when the end unfolds.'

A voice in his head told him it was unwise. Endings were not tidy, usually frantic and messy, and he would spare her that. Alternatively, she would see just how much they were casting about in desperation. Well, if she saw him as less the hero, at least she would see truth.

'I would not recommend it, my lady, for I fear you will have a day of boredom, and my pride will be pricked, for you will see how inept and frustratingly unsuccessful I can be, hunting for even a described man. There is no indication as yet that we are "at the end" at all. We advance by steps only. You may lose faith in me completely.'

The accompanying smile gave the lie to the last part.

'I shall bear that in mind, my lord, but sometimes we do not know which is the last step that brings us to our goal,' she replied, twinkling through the mock seriousness. 'Take my men-at-arms with you, too. If they are given both horse and rider's description they are more eyes to seek, and employment will do them good rather than gloomy idleness here.' She sighed. 'I doubt not they would like to feel involved in finding their lord's murderer.'

Bradecote rubbed his eyes with one hand. He was not sure they would be any real help, but it would clearly please her.

'But you need your rest, my lord, and I will leave you to it.'

She stood up, and he did so with her, and would have taken her arm to the door as before, but she set her hand lightly upon his and shook her head, smiling.

'Sleep well, my lord.'

On impulse, she stood upon tiptoe and brushed his cheek with her lips, then hurried to the solar door without looking back at him. He stood, still as an effigy, with a smile upon his face.

Chapter Sixteen

Riding with Christina beside him felt good, thought Bradecote, as they made their way to Wich in the crisp cold of the morning. He had helped her up into the saddle, looked up into the face framed in the fur-lined hood, and seen a smile that warmed the chill of an October day as if it had been midsummer. Catchpoll would have hung back, but Christina was determined that her presence should not interfere with their routine, and also a little self-conscious lest she show her burgeoning feelings before the serjeant. The undersheriff therefore had Catchpoll to his left and Christina, largely content to listen, to his right. Walkelin followed behind with the Cookhill men, combining listening to his superiors, imagining the men at his back were under his command, and attempting to get his misbegotten mount to keep up.

'My lord, I do not wish to be in your way, though I would like to hear of any developments. I thought perhaps I might visit Mistress Reeve this morning. I am not so foolish as not to know it will do her great credit with her neighbours and kindred if she receives a long visit from a "lady", though I do not know the poor woman.'

'That sounds a good idea. I was a little concerned, since we will be heading for the tavern, which is no place for a lady, under any circumstance.'

'And if you should hear anything from those who come with condolences, my lady . . .' Catchpoll looked past his superior.

'Oh yes, Serjeant Catchpoll, I know, I shall immediately send word to you, if you are not all merry as mayflies in the alehouse.'

She dimpled, and laughed as all three proclaimed their sobriety. Underneath, however, Catchpoll was doing some serious thinking, and was coming to the unpalatable conclusion that their chances of actually finding Walter Reeve's killer, even though they knew what the man looked like, were slim. It would be beyond hope to think he would amble into Wich for all to raise a hue and cry after, though with luck he did not know that his horse would be recognised, so that perhaps he might be spotted upon the roads.

'My lord, the man who killed the reeve was seen riding out to the north from Wich.'

'Yes, but that was several days since, Catchpoll.'

'If, and I admit it is a long shot, he went from killing Walter Reeve to giving directions to the Archer, then there are three chances out of four he was not heading straight up the north road after the killing.'

'But he could have passed through or round, yesterday,' announced Walkelin, with depressing accuracy.

'Through would have been very risky, but round, yes, perhaps, if he saw the Archer in the morning. However, if he was to meet the man last night, it is possible he will strike north today. The main road is swiftest, so if he avoids the town itself, he will want to join it as soon as he can. If you have no other reason to keep us in Wich, I would like to carry on through and spend the forenoon, at least, out on the north road, a couple of miles outside of the town. If he cut round he would be certain to have rejoined the road by then.'

'It is worth the attempt, Catchpoll.' The undersheriff nodded. 'Yes, you take Walkelin and the men, and go on and see what you can find out, even if it is that travellers heading south have already seen the horse going north. Of course, if he did meet the Archer again, another attack is planned, and we do not know where.' He grimaced.

Christina was biting her lip, unsure whether to ask what might be a foolish question, but then took a deep breath and posed it anyway.

'Do you think this man hides in the woods?'

'The tall, thin stranger? Possibly, but with his horse too, I somehow think not, my lady.' Bradecote looking enquiringly at her. 'You have a thought?'

'Only that if he had been learning of the salt departures by listening at the tavern, he would be leaving late in the evening perhaps, and must therefore have had somewhere to stay in Wich, even if it was just a stable where he kept his horse. The packmen know horses. They would recall if the horse was in the town, more than the man.'

'The lady has a point, my lord. The horse might be a better trail to seek than the rider.' Catchpoll nodded approvingly.

'Then after checking whether any information has come in to the tavern keeper, I will take my lady FitzPayne's advice, and go to the stables where the packmen keep their ponies.'

* * *

Reginald, son of Robert, was not a happy man. The night had been as unpleasant as he had feared, and the fawning hospitality of the cottar and his family had made his ill humour even worse. He liked to be treated as important, but there were limits to how much grovelling he could take. He needed to get back to de Malfleur, but his horse had a bruised heel and would be useless for several days. Reluctantly, he would have to go into Wich and hire a horse of some kind. Keeping to his character as the down-on-his-luck knight should work easily enough, and since he had always kept hooded and cloaked when eavesdropping, there was little likelihood of anyone recognising him if he held his nerve and was suitably autocratic. He took a cap edged with coney fur and set it upon his head at a debonair angle, and led his horse into Wich, an hour before noon, giving the impression of a man uncaring about whether he was seen, and was thus ignored.

Christina had done as she intended, and gone directly to the reeve's house. The widow was attended by an assortment of women come to commiserate, give advice, or simply be at the hub of gossip. The arrival of the lady FitzPayne caused quite a flutter, Mistress Reeve going so far as to get up from her bed, upon which she had been reclining whilst reciting her woe, and order a girl to fetch refreshment for her illustrious guest. Christina felt rather overwhelmed. Mistress Reeve, or as she already styled herself, the Widow Reeve, was certainly in a state of shock, and the enormity of her loss, in terms of how her life would be hereafter, had not struck her. She was distressed, but had sought escape from thinking about the whole thing by throwing herself into the outward signs of mourning, by 'playing the widow'. It struck

Christina that being able to come to terms with her loss in private had been a lot easier and better, for how might this dame feel when finally alone and ignored as life moved on? What words of comfort she gave sounded hollow in her own ears, but she knew the value of snobbery. The reeve's widow would preen herself at a later date if she could claim that 'my lady FitzPayne had said to me how similar our situations had become', though it was a patent lie on Christina's part. She found there was a limit, however, on how long she could keep up the pretence that she herself was in deep mourning, when inside she felt renewed and excited. She felt a little guilty, not for the lies she told the widow, but for how fast Corbin had become merely part of her past, and that even her anger and determination to have justice for her husband had become secondary to being with Hugh Bradecote, and seeing his task fulfilled. She therefore made her excuses a little earlier than she had intended and decided to go in search of the undersheriff.

She was thinking ahead, anticipating what she might say, certainly not thinking about a chestnut horse, or a man she recognised of old. She was not sure of her direction, but thought she recalled a stable at the western end of the town and headed that way. She had just recognised her destination when she stopped with a gasp as she saw, coming towards her, one of Arnulf de Malfleur's retainers leading a horse as described by Hugh Bradecote. Reginald, she remembered his name, seemed to have prospered, for he wore a hat that, until close inspection, looked quite lordly. Then she saw the scabbard, Corbin's scabbard. For his part, Reginald did not see the lady until she screamed 'murderer'. He looked in horror towards her, a snarl of anger contorting his face. A lad with a pitchfork emerged from the stable, and Reginald drew steel, but was overwhelmed by two hefty men, one wielding a sack of grain, and the other a bridle used like a flail.

Bosom heaving, Christina approached as he struggled between them.

'Murderer,' she repeated, and slapped him hard across the face. 'My husband's horse you sold, my husband's sword you wear, and you killed the reeve of Wich.'

Reginald said nothing, but the lad with the pitchfork pressed the tines so tight against his back that he felt them prick his skin. The other townsmen growled.

'Bind him, and keep him close held until the undersheriff gets here. Send about the town to find him.' The lady had the power of command, and another lad was sent running off. As he did so she called after him. 'And tell him I am for Rushock.'

She looked at Reginald, and he had never seen a woman as grim. Men pinioned him, and she stepped close, lifting Corbin FitzPayne's sword from the dirt where it lay. Then she stepped back. For a moment Reginald thought she would run him through with it, then her expression changed.

'I will sully this honourable blade with worse blood than yours,' she whispered, 'and I want to see you hang at a rope's end.' She pressed the point to his cheek, and he flinched. She pushed, and the tip pierced the softness. He gurgled, and she laughed, hysterically. The men holding Reginald gazed at her with concern, but she withdrew the blade to leave his cheek streaming blood.

'Remove the sword belt.' She looked at the lad with the

pitchfork. He was not going to disobey this frightening lady. She took it, sheathed the sword with a gentle hiss as it slid into its home, and turned upon her heel.

The undersheriff had been first to the very stable where Christina later saw the man he sought, but learnt nothing. After a fruitless hour he had almost given up, when success favoured him, out towards the Feckenham road on the eastern boundary.

'Nice bit of horseflesh, that chestnut,' remarked the stable owner, ruminatively.

'Did you not hear we were looking for such a beast?'

'No, my lord, can't say as I did, but I had the toothache these two days past, and wasn't really listening to gossip.'

Bradecote contained his impatience.

'The man who stabled this horse with you, what did he look like?'

'Why a tallish fellow, thin, slightly stooping walk to him. Paid well, he did.'

'And did he sleep in the stable also?'

'Him? No fear. He took lodging with old Avice. Deaf she is, deaf as a post, but a tidy soul, and glad of the pennies. He wasn't here all the time, mind. He said his lord sent him hither and yon, and Wich was sort of in the centre of things, but her being deaf he didn't disturb if he came in late.'

Bradecote groaned inwardly. If only this had been brought to light earlier.

'When was he here last?'

'Oh, he left yesterday, early. He'll be surprised to hear all the news when he comes next.'

No, the man had no inkling at all that he had anything of

use to pass on. Bradecote wondered if the reeve's killer had gone direct to the Archer in the morning. They must surely meet by place and time, and hopefully that meeting had been later in the day or any chance Catchpoll had upon the north road was gone.

It was nearly noon when Bradecote made his way back to the tavern, to be met with the news that Serjeant Catchpoll and 'the lad' had come back 'a while back', but had gone to the stables on the Leominster road, because someone was 'looking for you'. Confused, but keen to find out what was going on, Bradecote set off at a run.

He arrived, a little breathless, to find Walkelin standing outside the stables, looking alert and official. His expression was wooden. The men-at-arms stood about, idle.

'What is going on?'

'The man who sold the horse and killed the reeve is inside, my lord. Serjeant Catchpoll is, er, having words with him.'

There was something in Walkelin's manner which indicated that whatever was going on might not be just verbal.

'I had best go in, Walkelin. Where did you find him, by the way?'

'We didn't, my lord. He was taken here.'

Bradecote did not like confessions gained by force, but the knowledge of the manner of Walter Reeve's death made him less concerned than usual. He went in, closing the door behind him, and his eyes adjusted to the dimness which smelt of hay and horse, and now, a measure of fear.

Catchpoll was breathing a little hard. Reginald stood, his hands bound and high above his head, the rope thrown over a beam and tied off. He stood almost upon tiptoe to prevent his arms pulling from their sockets, his face was strained, and there was blood on his mouth.

'My lord, we have him, but he's playing mute.'

'We cannot simply beat—'

'My lord, he was recognised by the lady FitzPayne, who had him held and sent for you.'

'Well, we had no doubts as to his identity, not with that . . .' He paused, as the implications of Catchpoll's statement hit him. Christina had found him?

'Then where is she?'

A stab of panic ran through Hugh Bradecote.

'That my lord, I am trying to find out. The cloth-eared fools here cannot recall where, but she said she was going somewhere. This is no time for niceties.'

'No, it isn't.' Bradecote's face was grim. He approached the tired and aching Reginald. 'My serjeant has an "active" way of asking questions. I usually prefer simple words. Now I will ask in very simple words. Where did the lady FitzPayne go?'

Reginald started to smile, which was unwise, since it changed to an exhalation of pain as the undersheriff hit him square in the solar plexus. He tried to double up but lifting his knees wrenched his arms from their sockets. Catchpoll raised an eyebrow, but looked approving. He had not thought the lord Bradecote capable of a move like that, not with him being so 'squeamish' about obtaining confessions.

Reginald focussed on the undersheriff's face, which told more than he would have wished. It said to Reginald that this really mattered to the man, and though he knew it would cost him more pain, the knowledge that he could see the sheriff's officer at a disadvantage a bit longer gave him resolution. At the back of his mind was also the reception that the erstwhile lady of Rushock would get from Baldwin de Malfleur. He remembered her from the days when she was mistress of the hall, knew the way his old lord had treated her, and recalled the vicarious pleasure it had given him. Be she never so well born, a woman was just a woman to be used. Knowing the lord Baldwin, he recognised that the undersheriff had more cause to look worried than he could possibly know. He kept his mouth shut.

'I asked you a question,' Bradecote spoke quietly, 'but you do not answer. Unwise.'

Reginald braced himself as well as he could for the blow, but was so winded by the force, he felt for a moment as if he would never breathe again. This man would kill him if he had to, no doubt, and he had yet a delay.

'Home,' wheezed Reginald, which was a sort of truth.

'To Cookhill?'

Bradecote could not see why she would have ridden back there, not come to him.

Reginald nodded, so that the false truth became a complete lie. At heart, he knew his chances of escaping the noose, or a plain lynching, were slim. He had no love for Baldwin de Malfleur, would not give his life for him, but there was something to be said for knowing the law would arrive too late. Over the years, the de Malfleur love of twisting the knife had spread to the minion.

'You lie. She would have come to me.' Then suddenly he thought what her departure meant. If she had gone somewhere it must be somewhere she knew, and the chestnut horse had been seen heading north. It fitted; he wished it did not, but it did. 'Oh my God, she's gone to Rushock.'

He heard the slight hiss from Reginald.

'Catchpoll, this,' in his frustration and fear he kicked viciously at Reginald's legs so that they gave way and the man cried out at the pain in his arms, 'comes with us. Walkelin!' the yell reverberated through the stable and a pony kicked out in surprise.

Walkelin poked his head around the door.

'Yes, my lord?'

'Our horses, and fast.'

'Yes, my lord.'

The face disappeared and they could hear the sound of running.

'How much of a lead has she got on us, Catchpoll?'

'Lot less than an hour, as I reckon, my lord. If we ride swift, and she does not, we might yet overtake her. But we have but six men, my lord, and de Malfleur has men-at-arms to spare.'

'How many would die for him?'

'Matters not, my lord, if he offers good coin to whoever puts us out the way.'

It was true. Bradecote tried to think straight.

'I only ask about numbers because I will be alongside you, my lord.'

'We bluff, Catchpoll. We bluff, and we pray.'

They could hear the sound of horses.

'Cut him down and bring him with us, on the swiftest pony you can see here, and give him into Walkelin's charge.'

Without looking at Reginald, Bradecote strode to the door and gave Walkelin his orders.

'I don't care if you flog your beast to death to get some speed out of it, Walkelin.' He swung himself up into his saddle. 'We have to reach Rushock fast. The lady FitzPayne's life depends upon it.'

Walkelin nodded, tight-lipped. After a minute, which seemed an age, Catchpoll emerged from the stable with Reginald, wrists bound and roped upon a serviceable dun pony.

'This beast might delay us, my lord.'

'I know, but . . .' Bradecote, his horse on the fret as it sensed his agitation, looked at the prisoner, and spoke with a calm deliberation.

'If she has come to harm, I swear upon oath, I will kill you so slowly, Hell will seem a respite.'

Chapter Seventeen

It was impulse, a white-hot wave of outrage and anger, which sent Christina FitzPayne on the road to Rushock, to a place she had thought never to have to enter again. It was as she had said, ever since his name was first mentioned: it came back to de Malfleur, and nobody had taken her seriously, even Hugh Bradecote. It was as though her life would never be her own and untainted while the canker of the de Malfleur influence remained, and she wanted to excise it, and do so herself. She had told the undersheriff if she found whoever killed Corbin before him, there would not be enough fit to string up afterwards. In the turmoil of what had followed these last ten days – sweet Heaven was it only that long? – she had forgotten her oath. Seeing Reginald with Corbin's sword, dishonouring it by his wearing of it, that had returned. She knew Bradecote needed Reginald so that he might find the Archer, or she would have drawn that sword and hacked at him with it, piece by piece, with the unflinching cruelty of a woman goaded beyond measure. The knowledge that the whole series of evil events stemmed from Baldwin de Malfleur filled her with the white-hot anger of vengeance as only one who had suffered long years at de Malfleur's hands, as she had, could know. That she had Corbin's sword hanging from the saddle did not mean she felt 'armed', and she wondered what she would do when she encountered Baldwin, for how she would get close to him had not entered her train of thought. All she knew was that he had been responsible for Corbin's death, for the little scrap that would have been Corbin's heir and had ended in blood, for all these wicked deaths, and she was going to kill him, preferably not quickly. It was vicious, vindictive and visceral, and she took her horse at a pace to which it was scarcely accustomed, urging it to a speed that astounded a pedlar who had to leap from her path. That a lady should travel so fast, and one unattended, made him wonder what lay ahead of him, and so he took his ease for a while and ate a heel of cheese, so that he did not simply walk into whatever had caused the lady's flight.

The distance should have given her time to come to her senses, even as she was forced to lessen the pace a while to let her horse get second wind, but it rather stoked her wrath. It was Nemesis herself upon a sweat-flecked horse that galloped into the bailey at Rushock and skittered to a halt. The men-at-arms lounging between their duties did not think of the lady as a risk, merely some overheated and overwrought woman come upon an urgent errand. That she should come to de Malfleur at all was a surprise, but they shrugged, and simply pointed to the hall when she demanded to know the whereabouts of their lord. They did not watch her dismount, nor saw the sword concealed in the folds of her skirts.

She trembled, so fired with anger, and at the same time filled with a gut-loosening panic at entering the hall where once she had been mistress. Her ghosts crowded in upon her, ghosts of misuse and cruel torment, of babes lost to death and, in some ways worse, to the evil of their sire's blood, of misery so profound that she had prayed in the little chapel where Arnulf never went, that God would be merciful and strike her dead, for death was preferable to her existence. As the door of the hall creaked open at her pushing, she felt as besmirched as in that old life, tainted, degraded, but this must be done. Her courage rose once more.

Baldwin de Malfleur had been hawking, not with any great success, and had returned home morose and inclined to find fault with everything and everyone. In truth, he was bored. Even the salt thefts were starting to bore him, for they did not give him any scope for action himself. He wondered whether returning to the Continent might be more exciting, for there were feuding lords aplenty and strife in Normandy and Anjou that would give scope for intrigue and devilry. England, even with the claim and counterclaim of King and Empress, seemed dull and flat.

He had yelled for more wine, and was expecting a harassed and suitably frightened serving girl. What entered was a Fury, almost spitting her words at him.

'Murderer. Foul, scheming, evil . . . bastard!' screamed Christina FitzPayne, leaving all ladylike language behind.

Baldwin de Malfleur raised an eyebrow, and smiled. This was going to enliven a boring day.

'The fair Christina, with words of salutation upon her pretty lips, oh, and a sword in her hand. How charming of you to call, and so unexpected too.' He did not see it as a great risk.

His calm enraged her the more. She made a growling noise in her throat, and her free hand clenched into a fist.

'If I had known you were coming I would have laid on entertainment, jongleurs, perhaps, or a player upon a pipe.'

'Why?' she cried.

'To keep you amused, of course, unless you thought I might supply you with more private "amusement". Widowhood has its drawbacks, hasn't it?' He could not resist feeding her incandescence. 'And I am sure I could oblige.' The smile was so lecherous she felt sick.

Her eyes widened in outrage.

'Why the killings? It makes no sense.'

'Oh, does it have to do so? I did not realise. You see, you think like so many people, don't you? You think "why?", whereas I think "why not?"'

'But . . .'

'Arnulf, of so blessed memory, had a reputation for, shall we say, bluntness? Everyone says "You are Arnulf de Malfleur's brother", not "you are Baldwin de Malfleur". Now, I could simply rampage around as he did, effective, but really not very clever. He did rampage rather a lot, didn't he? However, I am the more subtle member of the family. My men have been escorting salt carts this last week, profiting me just enough to keep them in my employ, and giving me the delight of being called "the noble lord de Malfleur who saves the salt". I just love the irony, do not you? And even if I am found out, and depart this very dank and dismal shire, I shall be remembered as far more the devil than lumbering Arnulf.'

'You will not depart this shire, but life itself. I shall kill you.'

The words came out through gritted teeth, but he only laughed.

'Indeed, my lady. With what? Your bare hands or that heavy sword? I never thought you a dame who liked a man's weapon.' The leer returned. 'That is no use to you. Will you kick and scratch me to death? Or rather lash me with that tongue of yours? I could give it better employment.'

He was mocking her, but she was struck by the realisation that lunging at him, prepared as he was, would achieve nothing, and it made her growl in frustration.

'Oh dear, was fiery vengeance so strong it forgot so much as a weapon you can handle? Here, this is' – he drew a dagger from his belt and tossed it to her, close enough so she jumped lest it strike her – 'something that might help.'

He had created a dilemma. Did she abandon the sword and take up the dagger alone, ignore it or take it up with one hand and keep the sword in the other? He knew what he had done, and grinned.

She dropped the heavy blade and picked up the dagger, swiftly, wondering if she could throw it with any force and accuracy. Tackling a man prepared was likely to prove a failure. Hot tears of frustration salted her cheeks, and suddenly she snapped. It did not matter that she might fail – would fail – she just wanted to kill him. She launched herself with a high-pitched snarl, but he stood with remarkable speed and grabbed her wrist as she struck downward.

'You know someone should have taught you, my dear, that the downward blow is always easy to parry, and if you want to use a knife effectively,' he twisted her wrist so that the knife fell to the floor, 'you should always use it to strike upwards.'

He bent to pick it up with his free hand. He had not bothered to grab her left hand, since he controlled her quite effectively by the threat to break her arm. What he had not reckoned upon was her bringing her knee up, sharply, into his face as he bent down.

He grunted in pain and fell back, bleeding from the nose, but was not deterred from picking up the knife. He stood, and wiped his sleeve across his face. He stared at the blood with some surprise, then to her horror, smiled at her. It was not a pleasant smile.

'Oh, so you can fight dirty, after all. Perhaps that was unwise, though, for, you see, I am still here, still have the knife, and you have nowhere to run.'

She backed away instinctively, but found herself against a trestle table. He grinned in a vulpine way, and snatched her left hand, pulling her close and twisting the arm, this time up her back. She felt his breath on her cheek and tried to turn it away.

'Oh no, fair Christina, you did that once before, long ago, but this time there is none to tell.'

He held the blade to her cheek so that she had to look back at him or feel its edge. He bent and kissed her, without lust but simply to hurt her. His hand behind her grabbed at the veil and pulled, tearing the fine fabric and revealing her dark, plaited hair. She squirmed, but could do nothing, pressed against the table so that the knee she had used previously to good effect, was rendered useless. He set the knife aside beyond her reach. After all, his strength alone would do his work now. Then he reached round with his now empty hand to grasp her wrist and free his left to loosen the plait. It was all part of a slow violation of her dignity.

'You are an added bonus, Christina. I had not thought you would be part of this.'

'You are a loathsome cur,' she whispered.

'No doubt. I do not find the appellation offensive. Indeed, it might be said to be a compliment. I wonder how I will compare to Arnulf? He was a "hungry" dog as I recall.'

The tremor that ran through her, pleased him, fired him. She felt sick and wondered if she could provoke him enough to end it with the knife before the nightmare became a reality.

'Once I could not have you, and you cost me years of exile, for which you will pay over these next sweet hours. But now, I take what I want, as I want, use you until you are no longer worth the having, and then, if you are lucky, I will kill you.' His voice was soft, and the more chilling for it.

She castigated herself for a fool. How could she think that happiness could be hers, that she had a future with a man who respected her, who would show her love, when her destiny was bound to this place, this blood. There was no future, there was only dishonour and the release of death. She closed her eyes and took in one long last gasp of free, untainted air.

Then there came the sounds of shouting outside, and de Malfleur stiffened.

'Our "liaison" may have to wait, my dear,' he whispered, and propelled her from the hall, into the passage, and thence into the yard.

Undersheriff and serjeant rode in at the gallop, marginally ahead of their men, and made a good impression of arriving

247

with many followers, even though they numbered but half a dozen and were outnumbered two to one. Catchpoll yelled to unseen support to 'remain without' to prevent anyone leaving, and called upon the men at the rear to catch up. It was a good act, and bought them time.

Bradecote and Catchpoll yanked their bridles round to get their mounts to a sudden halt, and, circling, demanded, in the King's name, to see the lord de Malfleur. A man-at-arms reacted instinctively to command and simply pointed to the hall, even as the Cookhill men fanned out at Walkelin's command to block the gateway for real. Before the sheriff's officers could cross the bailey, de Malfleur emerged from the hall with Christina before him, his knife now pricking the skin just below her ear.

'Ah, the ever delightful Serjeant Catchpoll and the oh-so-worthy undersheriff. Were you looking for me?' He glanced down at Christina. 'You did not say I would be receiving more guests, my lady.'

'Let the lady FitzPayne go free, de Malfleur.'

'Oh, do be sensible, Bradecote. Why should I do that? I rather think she is my pass out of here. You see, you are going to get off your horses and stand very still right where you are now, and if you draw your swords or step towards me I shall slit the lady's pretty white throat, from ear to ear. Pity, for that was only to be the very last part of our charming tryst, and I was so looking forward to it, all of it.'

He made to mime the action and at the end just nicked the skin so that she let out a small cry and blood dribbled down the side of her pale neck. He was watching Bradecote closely to see his reaction. It was all that he had hoped. So the undersheriff was the stupidly noble sort and had an eye to the lady, did he? That was all the more to his advantage. The sheriff's men dismounted as ordered, slowly, Walkelin half raising a hand so that the Cookhill men-at-arms remained still mounted. Unless de Malfleur specified it, they were better upon horseback, even at a distance. In fact de Malfleur seemed to disregard them, focussing on the lord Bradecote's discomfort. De Malfleur continued, still sounding calm.

'You wouldn't want that now, would you, Bradecote? Is the lady to your taste? Would you like to have her? Perhaps I have already?' He rested his cheek next to hers and grinned. A muscle twitched in Bradecote's cheek. De Malfleur was enjoying himself, the adrenalin coursing through him. The loosened hair was just enough of a tease to put that doubt in the undersheriff's mind.

Christina tried to reassure him with her eyes, but only succeeded in looking as if she pleaded for rescue.

'What I have not yet found out, having been engaged in "other activities" since dear Christina's arrival,' he leered provocatively, and heard Bradecote grind his teeth, 'is why you have all eventually come to my door. I am merely curious.'

'Your man killed the reeve of Wich.'

'Did he? I wonder why. Not that the reason interests me. So you have taken the erstwhile efficient Reginald, have you? You may hang him, if you like. I do not mind, though I admit I would have hoped he could keep his mouth shut and prevent this untimely intrusion.'

'He did not need to speak, for lady FitzPayne recognised him with her husband's sword at his belt.'

'Ah, he was not worthy to have that, clearly. I can see why that might upset you, my dear.' He glanced down. 'So that was why you had the sword. It makes a little sense.' He looked back at Bradecote. 'Though if my man has taken this, er, reprehensible course, it cannot be proved that I knew of it.'

He did not care whether it could be proved or not. He already had his plan of escape forming in his head. The cold steel of the knife pricked to keep Christina silent.

'The man, Reginald, did not come up with this alone, for your men,' Bradecote was drawing a bow at a venture here, 'were used, and he has not sold the salt, so he would not have money to buy the services of the Archer.'

'Very interesting, but mere speculation. You know, I think I preferred Fulk de Crespignac as undersheriff. He did not meddle where he was not needed.'

'We also have the testimony of the man himself,' growled Catchpoll.

De Malfleur was a cool one, he would give him that, thought Catchpoll, though he saw him as the sort who did things for the sheer excitement. Such men could be unpredictable, seeing just how far they could go, prepared to stake everything.

Walkelin had taken in the situation at a glance and made a big decision when they had first arrived, sending Reginald and a man-at-arms immediately back, outside the gatehouse. It received the briefest recognition from Serjeant Catchpoll. As Walkelin correctly saw it, there was a stand-off and Reginald would be something de Malfleur would want out of the way, permanently. He had caught sight of him for certain, and that was enough. The situation was finely balanced. De Malfleur's men, taken off guard, might be twice in number, but were not leaping to their lord's defence. They seemed to stand back from the proceedings, watchful, prepared to act only if commanded or threatened. The men from Cookhill looked uncertain, seeing their lady with a knife at her throat and blood oozing down to the neck of her gown. De Malfleur's smile became a little more fixed, but he had confidence that he would still make his escape, and in style. It would add to the notoriety he would leave behind. He would still be the bigger legend than Arnulf.

Hugh Bradecote was trying desperately to keep up the appearance of total calm, though his insides were churning and his mouth was dry. He did not want to look Christina in the eye, for fear that de Malfleur would see the unspoken connection between them even more. The bastard seemed to have an inkling, but that might have been pure guesswork, hoping it would hit home if true. The more he knew she meant to him the greater the risk to her life. Yet he wanted to look at her to tell her, as little as he felt it, that all would be well, and that he would save her, somehow. The blood on her pale skin taunted him with his impotence.

Catchpoll sensed the desperation in the man beside him. Bradecote was doing well in the circumstances, for it must be hard to keep the outer shell of calm with the woman you had uppermost in your thoughts at the point of a blade wielded by a man perfectly happy to use it. Most men used a hostage simply as a shield. De Malfleur did so also because he enjoyed the power of life . . . and death. The serjeant watched him as a cat did a mouse, assessing the next move from the tiniest hint. Years of people watching had taught the wily Catchpoll nearly all the signs, and de Malfleur was giving off bad ones. He had little hope that it would work, but he tried using the paternal voice of calm reason.

'Give yourself up quiet, like. There is nowhere to go, nowhere to hide.'

Why the man should give himself up to the noose, he had no idea, but sometimes it just worked.

De Malfleur laughed openly.

'Of course there is somewhere to go, there always is. The world is very large, and this piddling shire very small, though it is all the world you may ever see, Serjeant.'

Bradecote made a decision.

'Let her go, de Malfleur, and you may leave unharmed.'

'Forgive me if I doubt that. You look a pathetically honest soul, but trusting you with my life seems, shall we say, rather dangerous. No, far safer to take the lady with me. So you will provide me with a horse, yours from preference, since you do at least seem a good judge of horseflesh, and I shall depart, with any men who choose to follow me.' He glanced over the men-at-arms, all watching to see how this would end. 'The lady comes with me to ensure you comply, and you have not the time to dither. Just remember, my knife will slip at the first drawing of a blade.' He grinned, looking at Bradecote's impotent rage. 'Oh, it is very frustrating for you, no doubt, since you would love to play the hero, but truly, there is nothing you can do, Bradecote, nothing anyone can do.'

'Except a good man with a bow,' a new voice rang out, and from an unexpected place.

Nobody had seen the Archer slip in through the postern gate, even in a bailey of men. He had travelled across country since the previous evening, undeterred by the darkness, stopping only to doze for an hour or so to rejuvenate his tired body. He had broken his fast with an elderly couple, who had shared their oat broth and been left speechless when their guest had disappeared silently, but having left a scrip heavy with silver, spilt across his stool. The Archer wanted nothing of de Malfleur's except his blood, and that he had sworn an oath to have.

Chapter Eighteen

A single moment of pure fear crossed Baldwin de Malfleur's face, but then the customary assurance reasserted itself.

'Ah, the Archer. Perhaps I should have guessed you would find out in the end. You had a nasty habit of that, didn't you? And yet, it was so worth the risk, just to imagine you, you who would want me dead, killing at my behest.' All pretence of innocence was cast aside. 'It has such a glorious irony to it, and has given me much pleasure.' He smiled, a long, feline, and ever so slightly bored, smile.

'I thought you drowned off the Levantine coast, or I would have found you four years ago.' The Archer's voice, noted the bound Reginald, with a certain satisfaction, had lost its customary poise. 'You murdered Ivo of Clent, a fair and Christian lord, foully and under the cloak of battle. I neither know nor care why. For that alone, before all deeds here, you owe a death.'

'Why? Well, I think it was because I could. He was so "caring" and keen to be virtuous, so irksomely noble, it was a relief as well as a pleasure. He kept on about it being "A Duty

To God", and refusing to take what was available. Virtue is vastly overrated.' Baldwin spoke with total confidence again, and mockery in his voice. He saw one of his own men had taken up a bow and nocked an arrow. 'The undersheriff here reminds me of him.' He sneered. 'And by the way, this lady, whose throat I shall slit anyway, was once my brother's wife. You happened to kill her second husband on the Feckenham road, for which I thank you most genuinely. I think she liked brother Arnulf as little as did your thieving father, but she may have liked the one who claimed her thereafter.'

Baldwin was enjoying this now, liking the reactions he was getting from the sheriff's man and duped bowman, but saw the Archer tense, and spoke swiftly.

'Ah no, Archer, much as you might like to do so, you will not save her, and kill me, because you have a choice, a choice in which there is actually . . . no choice to be made. You see, there is a man of mine with an arrow nocked and aimed at you. If you loose at me, you will be dead as I fall, assuming you do not hit this fairer target.'

He moved Christina's body to cover himself a little better, and his smile broadened. He was not afraid. His man-at-arms was dead meat of course, but that was a mere incidental. The Archer would save himself, for what man would not, unless he was a fool or—

The thought stopped as the arrow entered through the orbit and pierced his brain. The knife pressing into Christina's neck pricked and then fell from the dead hand as Baldwin de Malfleur crumpled silently to the ground. As a death it was swift and far better than most of those present thought he deserved.

The man-at-arms was taken aback for a moment, during

which time the Archer had nocked a second arrow, but he recovered in time to loose first. The shot was mortal but not clean, striking the Archer not as he intended, straight through the heart, but just above, a few fingers' breadth below the collarbone. The force of the impact made the Archer stagger back, as if hit with a sack of flour. The look of vague surprise was replaced by one that, Catchpoll later remarked, seemed more like affront. The Archer took a breath that scarce seemed to work as the blood filled his lung, steadied himself and, to the man-at-arms' indescribable horror, took aim.

'Not worthy . . . to call yourself . . . archer,' murmured the Archer, and sent his own steel-tipped ash unerringly to its target. Then, with a sigh, he sank to his knees.

Christina had not moved, though de Malfleur had fallen behind her. She stood as still as a carved saint in a church niche, her eyes still wide with horror, and a thin trail of blood from below her ear trickling to stain the neck of her gown. Bradecote ran forward as she began to sway, and caught her before she fell, clasping her so tightly to him she could barely breathe. He rested his cheek against hers, and his voice, murmuring in her ear, shook.

'It is all over, all over. You are safe. Oh dear God, I thought I had lost you, Christina, and I could do nothing to aid you. What madness made you come alone, what madness?'

The anger of relief seized him, and for a moment he could have shaken her, but then it passed. He buried his face in her loosened hair and felt her trembling.

Catchpoll went to the Archer, now so bowed his forehead would have touched the ground had the protruding arrow not prevented it. He helped him more upright. The eyes, already losing lustre, caught sight of Christina. Struggling as he was to breathe, the Archer tried to call her.

'Lady, no malice . . . to you or yours. Forgive me.'

She raised her head and looked at him, then moved to approach, Bradecote's arm still around her waist, supporting her. She leant down slightly, her pale hand, with the long, delicate fingers, extended in a benediction.

'For life that was lost, a life has been saved, and we share a past at de Malfleur hands. I forgive you, Aelward the Archer.'

Her voice was low and soft, yet he heard her words and half smiled. His grip upon his bow, which he had still in his hand, tightened.

'Aelward the Archer,' he repeated, as if remembering something long forgotten, and kissed the tensioned yew, feeling the slight vibration within it. A bow strung, he thought, muzzily, was a live thing, a true and faithful companion. His bow had kept faith with him to the end. 'I struck true,' he whispered, and the breath was bubbled with blood.

'You struck true, Archer, no shame to your craft,' said Catchpoll softly, with understanding, as Aelward died.

Christina blinked, tears running down her face, and she knew not whether they were for Corbin and the lost baby, herself, or the crumpled form before her.

'I was right to forgive him? Not disloyal to my lord? I had sworn vengeance, but . . .' She was suddenly uncertain, confused. 'There was no hate, was there, and . . . he killed de Malfleur.'

Bradecote was lost for words, and it was Catchpoll who found them.

'You did right, my lady. Your lord was a fair man, a man who would understand. All that are born come to death one way or another. It is as it is, and there is something to be said for a quick end against a lingering one. I think he would have forgiven this man.'

She took a long stuttering breath, as all that was bottled up within her found release in an anguished cry, and her hands covered her face. Her frame shook with wracking sobs. Bradecote wrapped his arms about her, buried his head once more in her tresses and, overwhelmed by the relief of her survival, made no attempt to quieten her. This much he had learnt from being married; there were times when a woman needed to weep. His body supported, comforted, demanded nothing, offered everything.

Catchpoll, conscious that this was a private moment in very public view, turned to Walkelin, who had led Reginald in on the end of a rope like a hound.

'That one we can hang,' declared the serjeant, with a mixture of relief and relish. It had already occurred to him that William de Beauchamp would not be best pleased to find the instigator and prime instrument of the killings had evaded the noose by death. Justice had not just to be done, as it had been, but be seen to be done.

'I killed no man upon the King's highway,' whimpered Reginald. 'I only did as my lord instructed, told the Archer where to be, paid the man. I can name the men who took and hid the salt, I can—'

'Yes, and they will hang also, make a pretty show of it in Wich when the Justices come, but even if you were not there getting your hands dirty, ferret-face, you are up to your neck,

258

which will be stretched, for this. And since you will swing for the murder of Walter, the reeve of Wich, whom you assuredly killed, you might as well swing for the rest.' Catchpoll had warmed to his theme. 'You'll get a better crowd for a start.'

'Tie this miserable animal to a post, and make sure he cannot climb on a horse and trot off, for it would be a pity not to have a good hanging out of this,' he addressed Walkelin, 'while we set about sorting out this rabble, but get the names of the men who thieved quickly, lest they try and silence him. Guard him, and if he plays games . . .' Catchpoll turned and looked about him at the de Malfleur men. With the exception of the single man-at-arms who had taken up a bow, presumably thinking he would receive largesse for saving his lord, all the rest had simply watched and waited. Whatever else he had inspired, de Malfleur had not inspired loyalty in any other than the previously taciturn Reginald.

The undersheriff still stood by Aelward's body, the lady he claimed within his hold, oblivious of everything now except her.

'It shames me, that I could do nothing, that I was powerless, Christina, but if I had stepped but one pace forward . . .' he whispered.

'I understand, my lord.' Her voice was unsteady and tearful but she looked up at him and her eyes looked trustingly into his. 'This is . . . real, not a nightmare and a dream?'

'Is standing thus the nightmare, lady?' He smiled tenderly at her, knowing the answer, and the colour returned to her cheeks. 'You would have me let you go?'

'No, you know this is the dream, it must be a dream. I . . .' she frowned, trying to find the words she wanted, '. . . I never wanted, never felt, never knew I could want . . . Never let me go.'

She was floundering, and he took pity on her confusion, bending his head to stop the words with his mouth. As once before, he felt her respond.

'When you first kissed me,' he murmured as he broke away to breathe, 'my bold Christina, you did not mean it.'

'Not when it began, but then,' her arm slid around his neck and her voice became the merest sighing breath, 'I meant it. For the first time in my entire life, I meant it.'

He kissed her again, and her fingers were in his hair, drawing him deeper. It was dangerous, exciting, and this was, his voice of reason told him, neither the time nor the place. He ignored it. He kissed her cheek, her neck, and tasted the iron of blood.

'I had almost forgotten, you bleed a little, but it is not severe.'

He let her go for a moment, and, dragging out the hem of his undershirt, used strong teeth and fingers to tear off a strip to make both pad and bandage.

'My lord, your shirt!'

'You may stitch me another. It is a wifely task.'

He pressed the pad gently over the wound.

'You mean . . . ?'

'Of course. You think I would hold you as I have, if I did not want you as my wife?' He laughed, a little unsteadily. 'With Serjeant Catchpoll probably watching us too?'

'My lord, oh Hugh, you do not object that I am twice a widow, have borne children?'

'No.' He smiled, winding the bandage about her neck. 'Very fetching. Christina. You said you had never felt as you do when

I kiss you. You have never loved before. I would have you if you had, but that this should be new to you . . . means it is special. And I had a wife, remember, have a baby son. Ela was a good woman, a loving wife, God rest her soul, and I was fond of her, but, Heaven forgive me, never loved her, never burnt for her, as I do for you.'

'You do? You . . . burn?'

'I do.' His arm slipped about her waist once more. 'Let us hope the lord de Beauchamp, who is my overlord as well as superior, does not simply count the bodies that were buried before we got to the bottom of this, and gives his support to our union. It is my only concern.'

Behind him, Catchpoll gave what he considered to be a discreet cough but actually sounded like a beast of burden about to expire. Bradecote rather self-consciously let go his hold upon the lady, who yet leant slightly against him, and turned.

'My lord, we have secured the three men identified by the weasel Reginald. We bring both the other bodies also?' Catchpoll had little doubt of the answer but it was a way of bringing his superior back to the matter in hand.

Bradecote looked down at the body of Aelward the Archer.

'It is a pity if we have to take him. De Malfleur I will happily parade before half the shire, and I am sure they will all cheer. The widows in Wich will have little sympathy for the Archer, and who is to blame them. Yet I am glad we did not have to hang him,' muttered Bradecote, his face suddenly solemn.

'No, my lord, he deserved and got a better justice than that. I've been serjeanting a good many years, and once or twice only have I come upon a killer like him. Murderer almost seems the wrong word, if you understands me. He did not do it from greed, nor malice, nor lust for the flesh or power. He did it because he was an archer, and the best, and he was there to follow his craft.' Catchpoll shook his head. 'Odd, isn't it. He would surrender his life to get the justice for his lord, and to save the lady FitzPayne here, hand his coin to a beggar, but drop nine men in their tracks for no more reason than that was what he was paid to do. Had he not come here at this hour, I doubt we would ever have found him, truth to tell. He would have gone to some other shire and been employed as his father was perhaps.'

'Can that not be what happened?' Christina touched Bradecote's arm. 'Would it not be possible to say that de Malfleur was taken by an arrow from Serjeant Catchpoll or your man Walkelin?'

'I am afraid there are too many who witnessed it, my lady.' Catchpoll sounded regretful.

'Serjeant Catchpoll is right.' Bradecote laid his hand upon hers. 'There is no help for it. And if we do not show he was flesh and blood, then we will have tales of ghostly archers along the Salt Roads and responsible for every loss, accidental or otherwise, for generations.'

'Then I will say what happened here, that he saved me, that he had justice for Ivo of Clent, that he . . .'

Bradecote was shaking his head, and she frowned. He did not want her to see what might happen in Wich. If the townsfolk were vindictive, the corpse might not receive good treatment. He had seen women spit upon bodies, and worse. She, who had forgiven, would be hurt by it.

'You cannot forbid me, my lord.'

Her expression was mulish, yet he still found her enchanting.

'No, but I would suggest most strongly that you stay where I will take you, in the church, until I come to take you home to Cookhill. You can pray for Aelward's soul, which will do him more good than declaiming over his body. We will tell everything that happened, so that the good of his end is known also. I do not command, for I have not that right, not yet, my lady,' and his eyes glittered in a way that sent an excited shiver down her spine, 'but please do as I say. I request.'

'And I can refuse you nothing,' she whispered, very, very softly.

One of the de Malfleur men, a household servant from his unwarlike demeanour and cowed expression, appeared and diffidently enquired as to what would happen.

'My lord, I ask because we are lordless, and because the men-at-arms are most likely to drink all the ale in the manor, and steal what is worth the stealing in its confines, be it livestock, goods from the hall or the maidservants from the kitchen.' He looked to lady FitzPayne and then the undersheriff. 'Whatever they had to put up with as servants, my lord, they have not been at risk from a drunken rabble of men who have nobody to control them.'

The man put it as delicately as he could, though he knew that the lady must, from her own experiences at the manor, have a good idea of his meaning. Bradecote frowned. The men they had brought from Cookhill, and he gave silent thanks for Catchpoll's good sense in getting him to bring them, would give them enough to get their prisoners safely back to Wich, but he would not care to leave a small number here, especially since they were the average sort of men, not the naturally belligerent type that de Malfleur encouraged.

'We will decide in the morning,' he announced, 'for we should not reach Wich in daylight anyway if we departed now.' He turned to his serjeant. 'Catchpoll, the men-at-arms are to be kept in their chamber, and with guards upon the door, in watches.'

'My lord,' Christina's voice was brittle, 'I would rather sleep in the hogescote with the swine than in that hall again.'

'I hope that will not be necessary.' He smiled but knew she was perfectly serious. 'Would you concede to take your rest in the buttery? The household servants could remain in the great hall, where they would feel more secure, and we could bed down in the passage between the two well enough.' He coloured. 'I mean Catchpoll and myself in the passage . . . not . . . and you in the buttery.' He floundered, and Catchpoll hid a smirk. 'I mean that you need not enter either the great hall or solar again and will sleep protected.'

She nodded, biting her lip, and her fingers, still upon his arm, squeezed it in thanks.

'The corpses, my lord? Should they go in the chapel here?' Catchpoll sought a command.

'Not de Malfleur,' declared Christina, her voice hard and firm again. 'He never used it in life, not other than as a place to sin.' She recalled the stolen kisses that had earned his exile. 'And it would be unfair to place Aelward next to him. Let the Archer have the chapel to himself.'

It meant little in reality, thought Bradecote, but it would give his lady ease.

'The bodies can go upon trestles, for I do not wish to present them rat-bitten in Wich, the Archer as my lady dictates, and de Malfleur,' he looked at the corpse with the one eye wide in surprise, and the other arrow-filled, 'anywhere under cover, an outbuilding will do.' He spoke then again to the servant. 'Have the household cook prepare a meal.'

'Yes, my lord.' The relief in the man's voice was audible. 'Straightaway, my lord.' He was glad to have simple authority to obey.

Catchpoll disappeared to make arrangements for guards and duties, and set Walkelin to secure Reginald and the other prisoners, though not close enough that they could show their reaction to him having placed their necks in the noose.

'You understand?' whispered Christina, looking up into Bradecote's face. 'I couldn't . . .'

'No, I understand, and I do not want you to have to revisit the past. I want it cast into the fire and forgotten, and for your life to start from now.'

She sighed. He did understand, miraculous as it seemed, and a great burden of misery and guilt and fear sloughed from her.

She would not even eat within the great hall, and so Hugh Bradecote took his meal with her in the unusual surroundings of the buttery. Neither, it had to be said, cared a jot, or could afterwards say what they had eaten. It was enough to be quiet and alone together. He was conscious of not wanting to act the lover in this place or in such circumstances, though he knew neither Catchpoll nor Walkelin would spread word of their intimate meal, and so they talked, of small things, not all private; of favoured dishes; of childhood memories; of baby Gilbert. He saw her eyes soften in the candlelight when he told her of his son's imperious demands for food, and how the baby had both wet nurse and nursemaid wrapped around his tiny, pudgy finger.

'They are so strong in grip, baby fingers,' he said, wonderingly. 'I could lift him from his cradle with his fingers gripping mine, and would have done so had I not been scolded like a five-year-old by his nurse. And in my own solar!'

She laughed, and their hands touched, finger to finger, and entwined.

'You will love him?' He did not really pose it as a question.

'As his mother, and not just because I have no child to love, and he no mother, but because he is your son, because . . .' The words struck her as inadequate to convey her feelings, and yet momentous. 'Oh, am I mad? Can such feelings spring so fast from such sorrowful beginnings, from the anger, from the pain?'

'How can I judge,' he whispered, smiling, 'if you do not tell me which feelings?'

She coloured, and lowered her eyes.

'They are so strange and new and . . . overwhelming.'

'Tell me.'

'When I lost Corbin's baby, and him, I felt cold inside, almost as dead as them. And yet here I am, so alive and . . . You said you burnt, burnt for me. I have only burnt with anger, with loathing, only been consumed by fear and hate until now, until you, Hugh Bradecote, and suddenly I understand that it is indeed possible to burn with . . . love.' She made a strange half-giggling, half-sobbing sound. 'I have found love.'

Then his self-control wavered, and he drew her from her seat, pulled her into his lap and held her, her head resting over his heart, until the candle guttered, and her slow breathing told him she slept deeply, exhausted by events and emotions. He laid her gently upon the pile of sacks and blankets, which was the best they could make her for a bed, and rolled himself in a single blanket across the doorway that none might enter. She slept, as he had promised, protected, and safe, in a place where she had never known safety.

The night had been clear, and the sliver of moon had overseen a sharp frost. Bradecote woke with chilled feet, but a warm glow within, and stretched in his aching physical discomfort, sighing. This he instantly regretted, as the cold rushed in through the gaps he created in his blanket. The smile, however, remained. He tried to concentrate upon what had to be done that day, taking into account the reaction of the people in Wich. Keeping them from meting out their own justice might be the most difficult part.

He heard Catchpoll mumbling discontentedly, as his older, stiffer joints objected to moving, and then scratch himself. Reluctantly, he rose, and poked his head around the door into the hall, where the servants slept, perhaps, he thought, in some relief at the loss of a master such as Baldwin de Malfleur. A serving wench, her cap askew upon her head, raised herself and looked blearily at him. He beckoned, and she came to curtsey clumsily before him. He bade her fetch water, should the lady FitzPayne wish to wash her face, and to bring bread, cheese and small beer for them to break their fast.

He went out into the yard, catching his breath upon the cold, and then blowing into his cupped hands and stamping his feet to improve the circulation. His exhalations hung as dragon-breath clouds in the air. He checked that the guard upon watch had not succumbed to sleep, and was pleased to find the man alert. Corbin FitzPayne had kept sound men, who could be trusted. He was thankful for it, since even if he won de Beauchamp's support for the match, he suspected that he would be leaving Christina on her own at Cookhill some time at least.

An hour later, Bradecote addressed the inhabitants of the manor. The men-at-arms looked surly, the servants worried.

'This manor is held no more by any of the name de Malfleur. Until such time as its lordship is decided, it shall be held by the lord Sheriff as the King's Officer in this shire. Those who work upon this manor shall continue in their labour, and the steward shall—'

'My lord, the steward departed when all was bustle yesterday, him being guilty as he thought, as the lord's man.' The man who had come forward the previous evening, spoke up. 'Small loss he is, but still . . .'

'Name yourself.'

'Me, my lord? I am Will, son of Eadfrid.'

'Then since you took enough charge last evening, you will act as steward, at least until such time as a new lord takes his place here.'

'But what of the men-at-arms, my lord?'

Bradecote looked at them. They had a disconsolate look

now, but he remembered them in Wich, cocksure bullies who sent fear through peaceable men. He did not think many were local in origin, in fact he would guess most were the scum that Baldwin had attracted on his journey home to his inheritance.

'To those of you who are prepared to remain and work upon this manor over the winter, and deal justly, I say stay, but if you want to continue as you did, then quit this shire, for if you break the peace, assuredly I will break you.' His voice was magisterial, and there was a general shuffling of feet. 'And do not think yourselves far enough away from Worcester that your deeds will go unknown. There was money paid to guard salt loads. Steward, give each man who departs ten days' payment in coin, and there is the cord cut. Do not return. For those that stay, there is the chance of employ in the future and security for the winter months, with food for your bellies and a hearth to warm yourselves by. It is your decision. Make it now.'

Catchpoll watched approvingly. The undersheriff had a good way with plain words, he would grant him that, not just in dealings with the fancier sort of folk. The group parted, with the majority seeking to find adventure elsewhere, but a fair few, with roots in the manor, or an eye to a local girl, prepared to wait and see who would take the lordship.

A few minutes later, the three sheriff's men, Christina FitzPayne and the Cookhill men, trotted out of Rushock, with three bound prisoners and a small one-horse cart, upon which the covered corpses of Baldwin de Malfleur and his true nemesis lay side by side.

Christina did not look back, but instead at Hugh Bradecote. 'I shall never enter those gates again, my lord, in person or in thought. I am free of it at last. It has no hold upon me now.' And she smiled, exultant.

Chapter Nineteen

They entered Wich at a walk so that everyone saw them, and on a loose rein so that it was clear there was no longer any reason for haste. Catchpoll and Walkelin brought up the rear, and the men-at-arms were arrayed on either side of the bound men and the cart. It made a statement. Bradecote was caught between relief that he could show that they had been successful and that the townsfolk could sleep at ease in their beds, and concern lest they vent their anger upon the prisoners or the dead. He had men, but not enough to prevent a crowd taking action, if only they realised their power, and he was concerned for Christina. He glanced at her profile, the nose with the merest hint of being retroussé, the curve of her lips, the lock of dark hair escaped from her coif, all framed by the fur of her hood. It was the same beautiful Christina, and yet oh so different, for there was a joy to her now, and the veil of shadow that had clung to her was lifted once and for all. He had her heart, he knew that, and it thrilled him, but her hand was not guaranteed. Cookhill was held of de Beauchamp, and as Corbin had been his vassal, the lord Sheriff of Worcestershire could influence, and in these troubled times, effectively decide, the widow's fate. The King, even should he hear of it, had greater things upon his mind than the fate of a woman with a dower share of a minor manor or two and not held direct from the Crown. No, if William de Beauchamp gave his permission, they could be wed as soon as it was decent to do so. The pity of it was the size of the 'if'.

The cry of a woman, calling down curses upon the prisoners, brought him back, sharply, to the present. He heard Catchpoll's monotone warning to the men-at-arms to keep a tight formation. He looked about him at the faces watching them.

'My lady,' he spoke softly, and did not look at Christina, 'I would be happier if you went directly to the church. This is no place for you.'

'You think I might be frightened . . . after yesterday I hardly think—'

'I cannot guarantee your safety if the inhabitants of Wich decide to try and take the prisoners and hang them out of hand, before we can lock them away safely. I should perhaps have skirted round and taken the men directly to Worcester to await trial there, but these folk need to know for certain that the culprits are caught, and this is where they should eventually face justice.'

'Will they not just wait until you go, and take their vengeance then? There is no reeve to organise the watching and guarding of them.'

'True enough, but once they have seen they need not fear any more, I will get the prisoners to the castle in Worcester. They can be returned after standing trial when the Justices come.' He did not mention the fate of the corpses. It would be quite likely they would be strung up anyway, so that all might see, and he did not give much for their chances of a decent burial. 'Please, go on ahead to the priest. I will collect you from the church when I have spoken to the crowd.'

She nodded, and urged her horse into a trot. He watched her, and one worry at least was removed. By the time he halted his men in the open space near the church, Christina had disappeared inside. The townspeople gathered round, a hum of antipathy circling about the undersheriff's party. He knew he had to impose his authority before things escalated.

'Good people of Wich,' he proclaimed, 'the men responsible for the attacks upon the salt have been taken. I bring them here that you might see for yourselves. Behind it all was Baldwin de Malfleur, the lord of Rushock. I bring you his body, and that of Aelward the Archer, who was employed by him to ensure none survived the attacks. De Malfleur did not want the salt. He wanted to create fear, and he did so. The Archer killed him for an act of treachery in the Holy Land, and surrendered his own life to save that of the lady FitzPayne. The man Reginald, who killed Walter Reeve, we took yesterday, in Wich, and he will face trial for that crime and for the salt thefts.

'I bring you these, both the alive and the dead, so that you shall know there was nothing of ghosts about the events, that the archer was a mere man, and that, beyond your normal caution upon the roads, you need have no more fear to be about your business.'

'Leave them here, and we will show them justice.'

It was a woman's voice, hard and shrill, and a murmur of approval went around the crowd. Catchpoll growled at the men-at-arms, who looked edgy.

'No, though I understand your feelings. The law must be

followed, and these men must stand trial before the Justices in Eyre. If you took it all into your own hands upon this occasion, there would be no protection for any of you, in the future, if falsely or mistakenly accused.'

'But they are clearly guilty.'

'So might you seem, to others, friend. I doubt not their guilt, but they were not caught in the act and so must await trial, not receive summary execution. If and when the Justices say they are guilty, you will see them hang. I am Hugh Bradecote, undersheriff of this shire, and I say this before you all.'

Bradecote spoke with the confidence of one who would be obeyed, imposing his will. There was mumbling, and shuffling of feet, and those who looked as if they might voice a challenge he looked straight in the eye until they faltered and dropped their gaze.

Walkelin looked to Serjeant Catchpoll, who had a half smile upon his grizzled visage, and relaxed. If the serjeant was unconcerned, he could afford to be also.

'Serjeant Catchpoll, you keep a guard upon the cart, though any who wish to see proof of what I have said may look upon it. Walkelin, the prisoners are under close guard and are not to be harmed, understood?'

'Yes, my lord.'

Catchpoll dismounted and jerked his head at a man-at-arms to do likewise. They stood at the tail of the cart. Nobody moved for a minute or so, it was like a tableau, then a woman edged forward from the crowd, and went to peer at the bodies. In an odd combination of gestures, she crossed herself and then spat upon the ground. Bradecote took a silent breath of relief, and dismounted. He walked slowly and deliberately across to the church, knowing he was watched, and opened the creaking door.

The atmosphere within was cool and calm. Christina was on her kneels at the chancel step, and he stood for a moment, unwilling to disturb her prayers. She had much for which to offer orisons. She must have heard him, however, because after a minute or so she crossed herself, rose, genuflected and turned to come down the nave towards him.

'Is all well, my lord?'

The question was posed with a smile, since he would not otherwise have entered so quietly.

'Indeed, my lady, all is well. I must . . . we must . . . Christina . . .' He stepped forward and took her hands. 'I must continue on to Worcester, but you should take your men home, home to Cookhill. We must part, for now.'

Her fingers gripped his, but she smiled up at him.

'I do understand. I shall do as you bid, my lord, for it will be good practice, will it not, for the obedience due of a wife.' Her voice faltered. 'It will be permitted, by the lord Sheriff?'

'I think so; I hope so. I cannot be certain, my love,' and he saw her bite her lip at the appellation, 'for William de Beauchamp is a tempersome man. He might take some persuading.'

'But you will be persuasive, my lord, yes?'

'For certain, as persuasive as a man can be who has taken ten days to solve crimes that have claimed far too many lives.' He pulled a wry face.

'You were as swift as it was possible to be, with the lack of information.' She coloured. 'I am sorry.'

'Do not be, for your aid far exceeded any hindrance.'

He smiled at her, and saw the answering smile in her eyes, and felt the pressure of her fingers increase. Despite their location, he lifted her chin to kiss her softly, but halted as the door creaked.

'My lord,' Walkelin popped his head around the door, 'I think you should come. The lord Sheriff is here.'

Bradecote squeezed Christina's hand and went out into the wind, which whipped his cloak about him. William de Beauchamp was arriving with a show of force, the full panoply of shrieval authority. He wanted Wich to know this was his shire, and events such as had rocked the town these last few weeks would not be tolerated. As he drew close it could be seen that his features were set in an uncompromising severity. Bradecote hoped that the news he could present to him might at least soften his expression in private. Serjeant Catchpoll, who was still standing with the guard over the corpses, abandoned his post and came forward. Bradecote heard the door creak behind him, and knew that Christina was there. He took a deep breath, and strode forward with an air of calm confidence.

De Beauchamp glared down at him, and the eyes narrowed. So he had made an end to it had he? Well, about time too. If Bradecote thought he was about to be showered with praise before the populace, he had another thing coming. They had to know William de Beauchamp was a hard man to please, and not one to cross. He let the silence continue for perhaps half a minute.

'So, my lord Bradecote, it seems you have achieved your goal, at least while there are still good people of Wich left standing. Tell me,' and his eyes gave the signal that it should be in a way fit for public consumption, 'what and how this has been achieved, at last.'

Catchpoll spared the undersheriff a grimace. If the lord de Beauchamp was in one of these moods, he would need a lot to please him.

'My lord, we have taken into custody all those connected with the murders of your vassal, the lord Corbin FitzPayne, the packmen and drivers, and the thefts of salt upon the King's highway, including the man who killed the reeve of this town.'

He saw the surprise cross de Beauchamp's face.

'The reeve is dead also?'

'Yes, my lord. Unfortunately, he believed he could apprehend one of the culprits on his own, and did not bring his information to the law, for which error he paid with his life, though he did it for the benefit of his town.'

It was like presenting the facts as a mummery, thought Bradecote. What he had just said was designed to remind the people that going to the sheriff's officers was less dangerous than going it alone, and to give the reeve's widow some pride. If her husband had been a fool, at least pretend it was solely for his town.

William de Beauchamp raised an eyebrow, but said nothing. He then looked to the cart.

'You appear to have pre-empted the noose in some cases.'

'My lord Sheriff, the two bodies you see are those of the man who planned these crimes, and arranged for their carrying out . . . Baldwin de Malfleur of Rushock, and of Aelward the Archer, who was the instrument of the actual killings.'

'De Malfleur, by the Rood it is.' The sheriff peered a little closer. 'Small loss, I would say. He appears to have an arrow in his eye. And the other body has the addition of an ash shaft sticking out of it. Was there an unexpected shower of judgemental arrows, Bradecote, or a falling-out of thieves?'

'Not the former and not quite the latter, my lord. We discovered the identity of the man behind the crimes and went to Rushock but de Malfleur was holding lady FitzPayne as a hostage, as a shield. Aelward the Archer arrived independently. He had discovered he was doing the bidding of the man who had foully murdered his lord, Ivo of Clent, in the Holy Land. De Malfleur admitted it freely. De Malfleur had a man ready to kill the Archer, but Aelward chose to save the life of lady FitzPayne and sacrifice his own.'

De Beauchamp did not enquire, at this point, how the lady FitzPayne came to be a hostage. He saw her advance and stand beside his undersheriff, and he thought he noticed their fingers touch, surreptitiously.

'It is as the lord Undersheriff says, my lord. I would not stand here now, were it not for Aelward the Archer. He killed innocent men, but his last act was to strike down the guilty.'

'My lady. My condolences. Corbin FitzPayne was a good man, and a loyal one.'

She made obeisance.

'Thank you, my lord.'

He dismounted, handed his horse over to a man-at-arms, and turned back to the question of culprits.

'So who have we to put before the Justices for hanging?' He was no longer speaking for public ears.

Bradecote managed not to smile at the assumption the Justices were just there to confirm the guilt of those brought before them. The sheriff was of Catchpoll's mind. If they were not guilty, they would not be caught and brought before the Justices.

'We have the three men who stole the salt and were complicit. They also stole FitzPayne's horse and belongings. There is also the man who organised the attacks and liaised with the Archer. This man is held solely responsible for the murder, and a gruesome one at that, of the reeve of Wich.'

'He'll hang, whether it was gruesome or not, though you can tell me about the details later.' The sheriff lowered his voice. 'But you are saying the man who actually killed all who fell in the attacks, and the man who planned the whole thing, are already beyond justice.'

'Beyond hanging, yes, my lord, but they are dead, which is just, and God will judge them also.'

'As he will judge us all, Bradecote,' murmured de Beauchamp, wryly, 'but that was not really my point.'

'My lord, all of Wich knows that everyone involved with these deaths is either dead or for the rope. They will get over their disappointment at not seeing two of them struggling at a noose's end soon enough.' Catchpoll, the pragmatist, interjected.

He was quite right. There was relief that there would be no more killings for the salt men to shake their heads and mourn. William de Beauchamp had not yet finished.

'Earl Waleran will need to find a new reeve, and by the way, I had word from the Sheriff of Hereford that you had been poaching upon his ground, and harassing a lord of his shire.'

'My lord,' expostulated Bradecote, 'we did so only because there was direct evidence that we had to investigate immediately. Had we found cause to wish the lord de Lasson taken into charge, we would, of course have contacted Miles of Gloucester.'

'Of course you would,' agreed the sheriff, eyes dancing. 'I take it de Lasson was not entertained by your treating him as the suspect in a murder?'

'My lord,' Serjeant Catchpoll knew that de Beauchamp had no real liking for the man, and grinned, 'he was outraged and then mightily concerned.'

'Oh good,' murmured the sheriff, whose missive from the Sheriff of Herefordshire had made complaint in formal terms, but had no real substance. Miles of Gloucester knew that in the heat of the chase, a sheriff's man might cross boundaries. 'So now this matter is closed, and we can all go home. I wish you had solved this earlier, for it would have spared me a journey, and there are how many innocent corpses rotting in the ground?'

'My lord!' Bradecote glanced at Christina and then back at his superior.

'Ah, my apologies, my lady. That was in poor taste.' De Beauchamp made a growling sort of apologetic sound in his throat. 'How many dead, though?'

'Nine, including the reeve, my lord.'

'Hmmmm. Am I expected to show pleasure at this?'

'We worked with what we could find, my lord, which was not much, initially. We were indeed hampered by the lord Jocelyn of Shelsley, who thought it amusing to provide false trails for us.'

'Him? Man's a worm!' declared the sheriff. 'Though he holds of me. His father was the better man.'

'He is also guilty of attempted rape and attempted murder.'

'Is he? Never knew he had it in him. You live and learn. Is he to be taken for these offences?'

'In the circumstances, my lord, it would be better not.' Bradecote did not wish to give details and embarrass the lady at his side, but she did not so much as blush.

'My lord Sheriff, I had to defend my honour with a knife.' She spoke with haughty outrage.

Christina was not impressed by the sheriff's attitude, but at the discovery of the 'victim', de Beauchamp changed his tune. He had assumed some peasant had been less than willing. Whilst he did not approve, he would not have taken any action in law, unless pressed, but this altered matters.

'Ah, you do not want to accuse him, my lady, in public?'

'No, my lord, but I would ask that if my husband's brother is not living, and cannot claim the manor of Cookhill and the other honours held by my husband, that he, a cousin, should not benefit.'

'A cousin? Ah, I see. No, my lady, I would not have Cookhill held by such as him.'

De Beauchamp saw her relief, and the brief glance as she looked up at Bradecote and smiled.

'My lord Sheriff,' Bradecote looked a little flustered. 'I would ask that you might give your permission for the lady FitzPayne . . . That I might . . . when the mourning period is over . . .'

The sheriff schooled his features into solemnity.

'You would wish to take the lady to wife, eh? Well, I will think upon it. We will discuss the matter further when you come upon your service at All Souls.'

It was not a refusal, thought Bradecote, which was perhaps

the best he could have hoped for after the reaction to the death toll, and only a short time to wait.

As an afterthought, de Beauchamp asked the lady herself if she was content to entertain the idea, not that he doubted her response. She blushed and dimpled.

'Then I shall return to Worcester. You are with me, I take it, Catchpoll?'

'Yes, my lord.'

'Are you returning through Worcester, Bradecote?'

He did not expect a positive answer.

'My lord, I will return to Bradecote, and my son, but would prefer to do so having escorted the lady FitzPayne back to Cookhill.'

'Yes, I do not suppose her men-at-arms are enough protection.' The sheriff grinned. He had seen Walkelin in charge of the Cookhill men as he arrived. 'Off you go, then, and mind, you have not as yet got my approval, remember.'

Undersheriff and widow both coloured, but she laid her hand upon Hugh Bradecote's arm and dipped in obeisance to de Beauchamp. Bradecote bowed to the sheriff, nodded at Catchpoll, led her back to her horse, and threw her up into the saddle.

Catchpoll watched as Bradecote left, head held high, leading the Cookhill men, and with Christina FitzPayne at his side.

'You will not say no, will you, my lord?'

'You getting love-soft in your old age, Catchpoll?'

'Me, my lord? No, but I would prefer to work with a man who didn't have his heart in his boots, and hated your guts.'

'Oh, I would not worry, you old dog. I will let him stew till his service is ended. He can have her come Candlemas, and if

FitzPayne's brother does not return, he can have Cookhill also.'

'I think he would be content with the soft armful.'

'Aye, but I would be best served with a good vassal holding Cookhill. Now, let us get home before the stench of this salt town ruins my appetite.'

Author's Note

In order to make it easy for readers to follow Bradecote and Catchpoll about Worcestershire, I have generally used modern place names, but in the case of Droitwich, the centre of this tale, I have used the old form as was used in the Domesday Book and into the twelfth century, and have it as Wich. In Old English 'wic' was a word meaning a place, or town, but was frequently applied to one which was an artisanal or trade centre. The name Droitwich did not exist until the fourteenth century.

Salt was a vital commodity, and the brine pits, where the brine was of a very high salinity, had made the place a centre for its production since the Roman occupation. It was very much a single-trade town, and the salt was supplied to as far afield as seventy miles away.

ALSO BY SARAH HAWKSWOOD

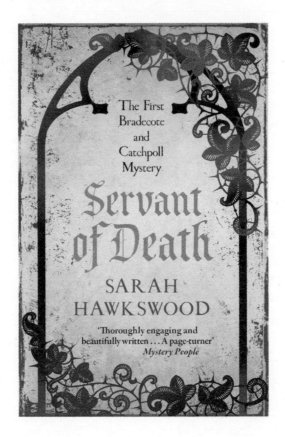

The First
Bradecote
and
Catchpoll
Mystery

Servant of Death

SARAH HAWKSWOOD

'Thoroughly engaging and
beautifully written ... A page-turner'
Mystery People

June, 1143. The much-feared and hated Eudo – the Lord Bishop
of Winchester's clerk – is bludgeoned to death in Pershore
Abbey and laid before the altar like a penitent. A despicable
man he may have been, but who had reason to kill him?

As the walls of the Abbey close in on the suspects, Serjeant
Catchpoll and his new, unwanted superior, Undersheriff
Hugh Bradecote must find the answer before the killer strikes
again . . .

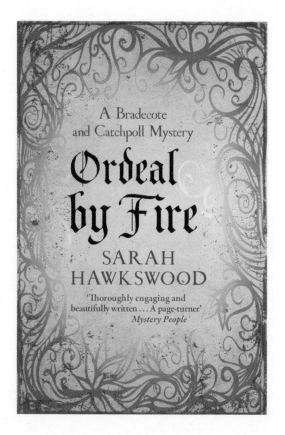

A Bradecote
and Catchpoll Mystery

Ordeal by Fire

SARAH HAWKSWOOD

'Thoroughly engaging and
beautifully written ... A page-turner'
Mystery People

September 1143. Serjeant Catchpoll hopes a fire at a Worcester silversmith's is just an accident, but when a charred corpse is discovered following a second fire, he has no choice but to call in the undersheriff. Hugh Bradecote may be new to the job compared to his wily colleague, but his analytical eye is soon hard at work.

With further fires and a hooded figure stalking the streets, the duo must piece together the arsonist's vengeful motive.